An Affair of Egypt

Other Five Star Titles
by Barrington King:

The Way Upcountry
A New World Won
All Through the Night

An Affair of Egypt

Barrington King

Five Star • Waterville, Maine

First Edition
First Printing: January 2004

Set in 11 pt. Plantin by Al Chase.

Printed in the United States on permanent paper.

Library of Congress Cataloging-in-Publication Data

King, Barrington.
    An affair of Egypt : a novel / by Barrington King.—1st ed.
      p. cm.
    "Five Star first edition titles"—T.p. verso.
    ISBN 1-59414-099-5 (hc : alk. paper)
    1. Egypt—History—1919–1952—Fiction.
  2. Suez Canal (Egypt)—Fiction.   3. Americans—Egypt—
Fiction.   4. Conspiracies—Fiction.   5. Birthfathers—
Fiction.   6. Journalists—Fiction.   I. Title.
PS3561.I4728A68 2004
813'.54—dc22   2003063101

For Sarah, remembering Cairo days and Egyptian nights

Part One

THE LAND BENEATH THE STAIRS

Chapter One

Alex Fraser had always understood that Americans never much cared about foreign parts, or about history, which pretty much came down to the same thing, because foreign parts and history both meant Europe, which is what Americans had escaped from. There were exceptions, of course, not only the rich of Boston and New York and Philadelphia, and later Chicago, who sent their daughters abroad in an exchange of money for titles and social prestige. There were others, who had different kinds of connections—often over several generations—with foreign parts, but these in lands where skins were dark. They were missionaries or brokers of the agricultural produce on which early America's economy was based, particularly tobacco and cotton. His family's game had always been cotton, and Egypt their destiny.

His grandfather had been a colonel in the Confederate army and, after the war, had taken up an offer to join a military mission to help train the Egyptian army. The British occupation of Egypt put an end to that, but he had stayed on to broker Egyptian cotton, the long-staple kind that was almost identical to the Sea Island cotton that had been, from the beginning, the family's stock in trade. He had a son in Egypt, the mother being a Southern belle he had brought with him as a bride to Cairo. Their son became a cotton broker in turn, came back to America, to his appropriately named hometown of Thebes, Georgia, to reestablish his roots and get a college education, married a second cousin from another cotton family and, like his father, took her back to Egypt with him. There Alexander Fraser III, named for his grandfather, was born and there his mother died in one of the plagues that periodically sweep through Egypt as they have done since Biblical days.

His father had brought little Alexander back to Georgia at such an early age that he had only the vaguest memories of the land of his birth, but vivid, full-color ones, with pyramids and palm trees and sunsets. Then, at age six, his father too had died, and he had moved into the huge old house of his maternal grandmother and lived there until he went off to the University of Virginia, majored in journalism, and eventually went to Washington as correspondent for the *Atlanta Journal*.

Sometimes change in the course of your life is due to a conscious decision you have made, often impetuously. That is how his life was given a new and very different direction one early June evening of 1939, at the River Bend Country Club. He had come back from Washington for a few weeks, something of a minor celebrity, having dropped the III from his name and shortened his Christian one to Alex, a reporter with his own byline for a major Southern newspaper, who even attended President Roosevelt's press conferences, the equivalent in Thebes society of supping with the devil. The reason that he had come back was the settlement of his grandmother's estate, which left him the big house and various cousins her money. He supposed that his grandmother had hoped he would settle down in Thebes with his beautiful and rich almost-fiancée, the sole heir of another cotton family. The "almost" was because he had, for a couple of years, avoided one way or another the engagement announcement of this family-arranged marriage.

When he had taken possession of his grandmother's house, almost the first thing he did was search out the key to the long dark closet under the stairs, and begin again the investigation that had been interrupted so many years before. He cut the cord binding his mother's letters, with cancelled stamps all showing the Sphinx in various colors and, sitting on a worn Oriental rug, began to read. It was only with the third letter that he realized that the "My Darling" letters to his mother were not from his father but from another man.

That same afternoon he received a telegram informing him that the position of foreign correspondent for a newspaper consortium was his if he wanted it, with the choice of either Rome or Cairo. And although the revelation of his mother's letters and the offer of a job in Cairo could be seen as fate, nevertheless the decision was his to make, and from it flowed everything that happened subsequently.

The evening at the River Bend Country Club was one of those periodic dinner dances, this one black tie, and he had become so absorbed with the matter of Egypt that he found there was not time to go to the Davenports' home where another couple was to pick them up. He called Nancy and said that he would take a taxi to the club and meet her there. And then he shaved, put on his tuxedo, the telegram that he had received in the inside breast pocket, and called a cab.

By the time he got to the club the dancing had already begun, and he spotted Nancy across the room, dimly lit by turning colored lights. She was dancing with someone he didn't know, and for a few moments he watched her smooth motions on the floor, in a form-fitting, low-cut dress, pale blue and sequined. The sooner the better, he told himself, crossed the room and broke in.

"What's wrong?" she said.

"Why do you think something's wrong?" and he felt her body go tense beneath his hand. It was a beautiful body that he had seen for the first time the week before in a tourist cabin a number of miles from Thebes, where she had decreed they go because, she said, it was silly to wait any longer to go to bed together, but her parents mustn't know.

"Why do I think something's wrong? Because as your future wife, I must be sensitive to your every mood, my darling."

He said nothing but danced Nancy out onto the terrace, let her go, but continued to hold her hand. They both stood looking at the moonlit river winding below them.

"Nancy, I can't do it," he said.

"Do what?" she said, letting go of his hand.

"Marry you."

She jumped as though he had touched her with a live electric wire. "You had better be kidding."

"I'm not."

She turned toward him. "Would you care to tell me why?"

"I can't live in Thebes."

"Alex, please don't do this to me. I can live in Washington, at least for a few years, if we eventually come back here."

"I've been offered a job as foreign correspondent in Cairo, Egypt, and I'm going to take it. You don't want to go there. It's better that we face the fact now that it won't work, that we belong to different worlds, before the engagement is announced."

"How gallant of you. Goddamn you! And after you already got me into bed."

"Which, as I recall, was at your initiative."

"Yes, knowing that we were going to be married!"

"Nancy, this isn't the nineteenth century. You're just as marriageable as before, and you can do a lot better than me."

"Well, there at least," she said in an icy voice, "you are probably right. I was never very keen on this, you know."

This was what he had hoped for, that she would find a way of not losing face, of not being humiliated.

"I know, but your parents . . . Call me anything you want to them and anyone else, by the way, and I won't deny it."

"No, I won't do that. It would be beneath me. So, why don't you just go off to Egypt and screw up your life like your parents and grandparents before you."

And then Nancy Davenport strode back into the crowded room, and he suspected he would never see her again. He walked the three miles back to town along River Road and mused on how he had got himself to where he was, how the moonlit river had somehow transformed into the barely remembered Nile, how he had just done something despicable—and didn't care . . .

When he was eight years old he got up the courage to penetrate the long dark closet under the stairs at his grandmother's house, which he understood, without it ever being quite said, was off-limits to him, and brought out into the light of an autumn afternoon objects from Egypt that had belonged to his mother. His grandmother was away at some club meeting, and the maid who was supposed to keep an eye on him was napping at the kitchen table. He knew the things were there, because he had heard them spoken of, sitting on the floor playing with lead soldiers, while the adults talked, assuming that small children didn't hear and, if they did, didn't understand what was being said. In later years he thought, don't they remember hearing their own parents and uncles and aunts converse and taking it all in?

The objects that he brought out were so miraculously unlike anything in his everyday world, that they could have been from another planet, another solar system in the blackness of outer space. There were heavy strings of glazed beads joined with clasps of gold, and amber ones, and an ivory fan with a view of the pyramids painted on it, a wooden drink stirrer from the Semiramis Hotel, a worn silver coin with the profile of a curly-headed man on it, with the horns of a goat. There was a tiny inlaid box containing some crystals that smelled like perfume, except stronger and stranger, and little blue ceramic figures covered in hieroglyphs that he later learned were called *shabtis*.

There was also a packet of letters tied with cord and the knot sealed with red wax impressed with an image of flowers, and on the top letter there was a cancelled stamp showing the Sphinx. These objects were wrapped in stained linen, and he fancied that they were the wrappings off mummies. There were other objects wrapped in linen, but he was not able to see them, because he heard his grandmother's car coming up the drive, and he scurried to rewrap what he had seen and get it back into the closet before his grandmother came up the front steps and into the house.

That was his first encounter with what he had heard referred to by his elders as "that Egyptian business" or by his uncle as *"l'affaire d'Egypte."* Both sides of the family were in the cotton trade, and his mother's brother traveled to France from time to time on business and scattered French phrases about when he wished to impress.

To himself he referred to his venture into the things of Egypt as the "affair of the closet." He must have been found out, because a few days later a locksmith arrived and cut a round hole in the closet door, leaving on the floor curls of blond wood, set a brass lock in the hole, and sealed the closet as securely as the packet of letters or the tomb of a Pharaoh. From that time on he got it into his child's head that he was being stalked by something dark from ancient Egypt, but of course this feeling faded with the years until it vanished. Or so he thought.

When he got back to the house from the country club he made a phone call to the sender of the telegram—night being a good time to get hold of newspaper people—and told him that he would take the job and that he preferred Cairo to Rome. Then he called the station and reserved a seat on the early morning train to Washington. Before going to bed he went back to the closet, found an old suitcase and put all of his mother's Egyptian things into it.

The seat next to his on the train to Washington was empty, and he put the suitcase with his mother's things on it. It had been a suitcase of hers, of scuffed pebbly leather, with hotel stickers on it from Lisbon and Rome, Alexandria and Cairo, and one from the Winter Palace Hotel in Luxor in Upper Egypt, the hotel to which all of the letters to his mother had been addressed. Then it occurred to him that his father had probably never seen the objects from the closet, perhaps did not even know of their existence. How had they come to rest in his grandmother's house?

As he opened the suitcase he thought that it was like opening a Pharaonic tomb filled with objects that told a story but the key to which had been lost. He picked up a blue-glazed *shabti* covered in hieroglyphs that meant nothing to him. They too would tell a story to someone who had the key. Next he picked up a quarto-sized accounts book bound in half-leather. But what it contained was a daybook, a kind of travel diary, with payments and expenses noted, of an American officer in Egypt, obviously his grandfather, Alexander Fraser II, one-time colonel, CSA.

Flipping through the pages filled in a neat nineteenth-century hand, it seemed that his grandfather had been mainly concerned with supervising the building of lighthouses and that his work had taken him to remote places far up the Nile, on the Red Sea and into the Western desert, a vast change from the battlefields of the Civil War.

At the back of the book were a number of pages of neat pen-and-ink drawings of lighthouses, or designs for lighthouses, and maps showing where these were to be placed along the Red Sea and Mediterranean coasts of Egypt. He remembered that his grandfather had studied military engineering at West Point, but he could not have imagined to what strange ends this would lead him. In the margins of the book there were some notes added in pencil, including a complaint on his work being inordinately delayed by his inability to get the Fresnel lighthouse lenses from France through Egyptian customs, even with what he thought were quite substantial bribes. Another marginal note was more general, even philosophical, musing on the probability that where the lighthouses were to be placed was related to the strategic defense of Egypt and the newly built Suez Canal. About which, nothing had apparently been said to his grandfather by the French and British advisers to the Khedive of Egypt who had asked him to undertake these engineering works.

Then at random Alex took items out of the suitcase: programs from the Cairo Opera; a clipping from the *Egyptian Gazette*, with a photograph of his mother, elegantly dressed at a garden party; a small leather jewel case lined in satin containing the gold ring with the stone that had been impressed on the wax sealing the packet of letters. This returned him to the letters, not just passionate but unreservedly sensual. All the letters had been mailed from Cairo and were written on stationery of the Gezira Sporting Club there. Above the name of the club, embossed in green on the flap of the envelope there was inked in "B.P. 123." The letters were unsigned. He refrained from reading any more of them, feeling something that was between embarrassment and shame, but he knew that eventually he would return to them.

From time to time, as he rummaged through the contents of the suitcase, he would look up for a while and study the landscape of Georgia and, after lunch in the dining car, the Carolinas and Virginia. The towns and farms they passed seemed so ordinary. Did the lives of the people who inhabited those houses harbor secrets, or were most of these lives as nondescript as the houses in which they were passed? Certainly adultery in Egypt would be beyond their ken.

Chapter Two

He took a cab from Union Station to his apartment building on F Street, went through his mail and then called his paper to give two weeks' notice. The managing editor expressed regret but wished him luck in his new job. His ego was a bit bruised by not being offered a higher salary to stay with the *Journal*, but probably someone was at hand eager to take his place. Then he called the office of the American Newspaper Consortium and made an appointment for the next day with its foreign editor, Arvid Dahlsted, who had first approached him about going overseas for the ANC.

It was a fine day in early October and he walked down Pennsylvania Avenue, where the trees along the sidewalk were beginning to turn color and the streetcars clanged down the center of the street, past the White House, where the guard at the gate nodded familiarly to him, past the Treasury, to the National Press Club building where the ANC had its offices. The receptionist announced him and Arvid Dahlsted opened a frosted glass door and stuck his head out.

"Alexander Fraser, come on in."

"They call me Alex," he said as he followed Dahlsted into his office. "I only use Alexander in my byline. I like to think it makes me sound older and wiser than I am."

"Yeah, it sounds like someone you ought to know."

In the office the Venetian blinds were drawn, and the only light came from a gooddisk gooseonecked desk lamp. Three teletypes clattered away in one corner of the room.

"Have a seat, Alex."

Dahlsted installed himself behind his desk and picked up a cigar he had been smoking, relit it. He was a Swede from Minnesota, but he had remade himself in the image of H. L. Mencken. He parted his red hair in the middle and wore suspenders and striped shirts with white collars and cuffs.

"Cairo, is it? Well, I won't have any trouble filling Rome. There's a long waiting list. I see from your application you were born in Cairo of American parents."

"Yes."

"You didn't choose Cairo for some sentimental reason, did you? Because your contract will specify that we can move you at any time."

"I left Cairo when I was three. It means nothing to me. Oh, I suppose I'll look for traces of my family when I get there."

"You may have chosen well. We're filling Rome only because the present incumbent has taken to the bottle—a hazard of the profession, as you well know. But Cairo is a brand-new position, based on a hunch of mine. You don't believe all this bullshit about 'peace in our time,' do you?"

The Munich Accords had been signed in the fall of 1938, and it now looked as if England and France had been euchred once again by Hitler.

"No, I think there's going to be war in Europe."

"And soon. The way I figure it, Chamberlain has given Hitler a free hand in Eastern Europe in exchange for leaving the precious British Empire alone. The French don't like it, but they're too weak politically to break ranks with the Brits. Hitler has gobbled up Czechoslovakia and now it looks like it's going to be Poland's turn. But in the end the British and French will have to fight, only then Germany will be a lot stronger. I'm positioning ANC to be ready for war. The readers of the newspapers that we service don't give a damn about what happens overseas, as long as their lives aren't affected. But when they see war coming and maybe America getting drawn into it, they'll be thirsty for news, and I figure the Mideast is going to be a hot spot."

"I agree."

"Cairo is the best place to put a man. When war comes Hitler will go after the Suez Canal, to cut the British and French off from their colonies in the East. Mussolini won't be able to do it alone."

"I agree."

"But that's in the future. For now your job will be to burrow in, get the contacts and access that you will need when war comes. Report anything that's major, like a change in the Egyptian government, particularly if it brings clashes with the British in Egypt, any aggressive moves by the Italians in Libya, and, of course, the finding of some new Pharaoh's tomb. That's about all our readers will absorb for now. If I want something more I'll let you know case by case."

"Sounds reasonable to me."

"Good. Although you'll be our Mideast correspondent, we don't have the money for you to go flitting all over the Eastern Mediterranean, though you'll need to get to know Palestine. The Jews and the Arabs are already at each other's throats, and both sides are making terrorist attacks on the British. You can take the train to Palestine from Cairo. What else you want to know?"

"Competition?"

"Not much. The Brits take Egypt seriously, for obvious reasons. Reuters, the London *Times*, the *Telegraph*. They will wonder why you're there, and assume you are a U.S. government spy on the side. Let them. It'll make what you trade them for what they know more valuable, so you'll be able to give out less in exchange. The French are more interested in Syria, and the Agence France Presse man is in Beirut. The *New York Times* and the American wire services favor Jerusalem, or Istanbul, if the correspondents could have their way. They have stringers in Cairo, but that will change quick if the situation heats up. Else?"

"Office and office help?"

"You'll have to find an office for yourself, within the budget for that. Miss Burrows has the numbers. You really won't need office help at this point, but we want you to look professional. You should have someone to answer the phone, make appointments. We have a stringer in Cairo now, a woman, a Copt woman. You know about Copts?"

"Christian Egyptians, descendants of the ancient Egyptians."

"Right. The Moslems don't much like them, and they don't much like the Moslems, but the Moslems need them. They're the bookkeepers, stenographers, foreign language correspondents, things the Moslems don't much want to learn. There are some wealthy influential Copts you'll want to get to know. Nadia, our stringer, belongs to one of those families, but I guess she's been cut off without a cent by her parents. She will be glad to take the job of office assistant. We pay her by the piece now, and we use damned few stories from Cairo. Whatever you pay her will be better than what she makes now.

"Nadia knows the Cairo game, and it's complicated. Melting pot, crossroads of the Mideast, all that. The city's almost a quarter foreign. Lots of Brits, of course, and French, many of them with the Canal Company. But there are also thousands of Italians, Greeks, Sephardic Jews who call Egypt home, Maltese and assorted Levantine types."

"You seem to know a lot about Cairo."

"I was there for a few months in '35, when I was covering Mussolini's invasion of Ethiopia. Loved it. Oh, that reminds me, there is one thing I will pay for, and that's membership in the Gezira Sporting Club. On an island in the Nile, six hundred acres of sybaritic luxury floating in a sea of abject poverty. Race course, golf, polo, the works. It'll save you a lot of legwork. Snooty British club, with a quota, a small one, for Egyptians, but anyone influential belongs. When you make your call on the American minister, see if you can't get him to contact the club secretary. It will take that to get you in. What else?"

"I've got the picture, I think."

"Good. We'll talk again before you go. I'll send you to Miss Burrows now for the financial stuff. Tell her I said to book you on the Pan-American flying boat to Lisbon—you'll like it—and from there by the British Imperial Airways flying boat to Alexandria. Was the salary I offered you okay?"

"For now. If war comes, I'll want more."

"Yes, I know newspaper men. Then the shoe will be on the other foot."

As he walked over to the office that he shared with two other correspondents of out-of-town newspapers, he thought that he had handled the interview about right. If you don't know a great deal about a subject, the less you say the better. When he got to the office Max was there, typing away.

"You had a phone call a while ago. I put the name and number on your desk."

The name meant nothing to him. He sat down and dialed the number, and the phone was picked up instantly.

"Christopher Weston?"

"Yes. Is this Alex Fraser?"

"Yes."

"I hear you're going out to Cairo, and so am I. I'm with the State Department, and I'll be attached to the American legation there. I thought you might like to have lunch."

"Sure."

"How about tomorrow?"

"Fine."

"Twelve-thirty at the Press Club building okay?"

"Yes. I'll be down at the entrance."

"Great. Then I'll see you tomorrow."

He put down the phone. He was puzzled as to how Christopher Weston had known he was going to Cairo. He had accepted the assignment only two days before and had told no one but the man he would be working for and the ANC office manager. Weston had also known that he was called Alex.

Now he had to deal with Dorothy. It would not be as unpleasant as telling Nancy he was leaving her life, but still he did not look forward to it. Dorothy never spoke of love and was certainly not interested in marriage. She came from an unconventional family and led an unconventional life in Washington. She was an artist and made ends meet by working in an art gallery. They had been going together for about a year. She enjoyed life and liked good things but had little money. He took her to the best restaurants and night spots, and on weekends to the country. She would spend the night at his place every week or so. It was not exactly an exchange, but she knew what men wanted and she wanted it too. He would miss her.

Christopher Weston arrived at exactly twelve-thirty and they recognized each other right away. Weston was about his age, dark-haired and handsome, in casual clothes, but tailor-made and expensive. He suggested they walk over to the Occidental for lunch.

After they had ordered, he waited for Weston to start the conversation. He expected the young State Department man to explain how he knew about his Cairo assignment, but instead Weston asked whether this would be his first time in Egypt.

"I was born there."

The timing of Weston's reaction was just a bit off, leaving the impression that he already knew this.

"Oh. Parents missionaries?"

"No, my father was a cotton broker. But I don't remember much of anything about Egypt. My mother died there when I was three and my father brought me home. There was a slump in the Egyptian cotton market, and he would probably have come home anyway."

"The market for Egyptian cotton is good right now, but the Egyptians have pretty much squeezed out foreign brokers, sell it themselves. It's made a lot of the big landowners immensely rich. They're all pashas now and make their deals at the Mohammed Ali Club."

"You have obviously been in Egypt."

"I was at Port Said for two years, as vice-consul, and then I was lucky enough to be sent to the School of Oriental Languages in Paris to learn Arabic. A year's not enough, I can tell you. Now I'm going back to Cairo as special assistant to the minister. I hope we can keep in close touch when we get there. I'll be responsible at the legation for public relations and the press, among other things."

"Sounds good."

Still Chris Weston gave no hint how he knew Alex was going to Cairo, and Alex had the feeling that if he really wanted to find out how, it would be better not to ask directly. He was beginning to size up Weston, and he seemed completely self-assured, able to parry any unwanted questions, but there was something he could not quite pin down. He read money and family background in Weston, but those didn't lead to Port Said.

"How was Port Said?" he said.

"Boring. If I hadn't been able to go to Cairo once a week, to pick up the diplomatic pouch, I would have gone nuts. Port Said's only claim to fame is as the dirty postcard capital of the world. Every sailor knows this, and they always buy some as their ship waits to enter the canal. The other thing they buy is booze, and then they get into fights and end up in jail, and the American vice-consul has to get them out. I spent more time at the jail than at the consulate. The other odd fact about Port Said is that the great passion among those who have the money, and the leisure, is bridge."

"Cards, you mean?"

"Contract bridge, to which my boss, the consul, was completely addicted. His family gave some money to the first Roosevelt campaign, and what better reward could they claim than to have him sent as far away as possible, and Port Said is pretty far. He could play bridge for twenty-four hours on end, with *suffragis* bringing sandwiches and drinks at appropriate intervals. That left all the work to me, but that is thankfully a closed chapter in my life."

Alex listened carefully, but Weston steered the conversation along without ever touching anything serious and solid, like a boatman poling a fragile craft over rocks just beneath the surface of the water. He turned to journalism and the Roosevelt press conferences that Alex had attended, and at last came back to Cairo.

"I'm taking off for Egypt in a couple of days," he said. "Anything I can do to grease the skids for you—two weeks, didn't you say?"

"Actually, there is. Could you put the minister in mind of

supporting my membership in the Gezira Club?"

"Consider it done."

The next night he took Dorothy out to dinner at the most expensive restaurant he knew, and broke the news to her, over after-dinner cognac, that he was leaving Washington.

"This assignment, for how long?" she said, in an overly casual way.

"My contract doesn't allow me home leave until I've been in Egypt for eighteen months."

"Eighteen months. By then I'll have another fellow, I suppose. I'm not good at waiting." She reached across the table and put her hand on his. "No regrets though. We had a good time, didn't we?"

He wished she didn't look so sad. She wasn't beautiful, but she did the best with the looks she had, and this evening she was particularly attractive in the candlelight.

"Well, what shall we do now?" he said.

"Go to your place."

Dorothy always made love with enthusiasm, but that night it was with an abandon that approached desperation. In the middle of the night he was awakened by a strange sound, and realized it was Dorothy crying. It was like a cold hand upon him. She had never spoken of love, and now he began to understand why. She finally went to sleep, but he did not. He had thought taking leave of Dorothy would be easier than taking leave of Nancy Davenport, but it wasn't. It was much, much worse.

In the morning they had breakfast together, as they always did when she stayed over. There was silence between them, and then she got up, dressed for work.

"I hate good-byes, Alex," she said, then leaned over and kissed him on the forehead. "I'm going now. Don't call me."

He started to speak, but she put her hand over his mouth. "Go with God," she said and went through the door.

For a long time he sat at the kitchen table and looked out over the desolate landscape that he had made for himself. He had deeply hurt two women, made it almost impossible to go back to live in the home of his ancestors, had thrown away a promising career for some romantic dream of an Egypt where passions were long spent, and he an intruder on the past. He had no close friends and no nearer relatives than some cousins in distant places. This was what freedom meant. He was free to follow, alone, whatever course he chose. No wonder people clung to their roots, to family and friends, to a warm hearth on our small planet hurtling through a cold and indifferent universe.

Chapter Three

What you expect and what you get are, famously, two different things. He left for Egypt weighed down with guilt over his treatment of two women who had cared for him in different ways, and uneasy over his mother's love affair that he had unintentionally discovered in a packet of letters in a closet beneath the stairs. The Roman poet Horace said that by going to far places in hope of changing ourselves all we change is our skies, but he was not sure that was really true.

On the Pan-American flying boat across the Atlantic a change *had* come over him. The plane was indeed a flying boat, a huge construction of wood and canvas that creaked and rolled like a ship; luxurious in its appointments, meals and service, and even with curtained sleeping bunks like a Pullman car. By the time they touched down on the water at the Azores for refueling, he had read the other nine letters to his mother on Gezira Club stationery that made up the rest of the dozen in the packet, and in letter seven, by the date of the postmark, he came across a reference to "our child."

Rather than devastating him those two words gave him release, even justification, for the folly of having given up everything he had known for a romantic dream of Egypt. By not knowing who his father was, he was released from the burden of family and society in Thebes, Georgia. He could be anybody. This put his Egyptian adventure—and that's how he now saw it—in a very different light, and made his recent view of himself as a naked soul in a cold and indifferent universe seem a bit adolescent. It also put his mother's Egyptian affair in an entirely new perspective. From the letters it was clear she had been deeply in love with whoever his real father was, and that trumped everything on the table. And then he thought of Chris Weston and his boss in Port Said who played bridge around the clock, and he laughed. At age twenty-eight he still had plenty of time to look on life as a game of cards rather than as a tragic drama.

He had his first glimpse of Egypt shortly after dawn, as the Imperial Airways flying boat made its descent to Alexandria. There was nothing but emptiness from the blue Mediterranean to the horizon, nothing but sand, pink in the early morning light. Then the conglomeration of Alexandria came into view and the Nile delta, green and lush, and between the delta and the desert there was no gradation. The sand simply ended and the lushness began, palm trees and orange groves, green fields and reedy marshes.

At the Imperial Airways dock there was a man standing at the bottom of the gangplank, in a crumpled linen suit, holding a sign with Alex's name on it. He wore dark glasses, and his black hair was wavy and pomaded, his mustache turned up at the ends.

"I'm Alex Fraser," he said.

"Victor, from Middle Eastern Travel. Your office asked that I accompany you to the train station." He took his watch, which was attached to his lapel by a gold chain, out of his breast pocket. "We have just enough time to make the early train. Here is your ticket. There will be someone to meet you at the Cairo station. Do you have baggage checks?"

He handed over the checks for his three valises, including the one that had belonged to his mother, containing everything that he thought worth bringing with him into his new life. Victor snapped his fingers and a dark-skinned man in a nightshirt-like garment, that he had already learned was called a *galabiya,* came running up. Victor said a few abrupt words to him in Arabic and handed him the checks.

"We can wait in the taxi while the wog finds the bags."

As they walked to the waiting cab, Victor said, "Your first time in Egypt?"

"First time."

"Life's not bad for Europeans here if you have some money. I don't normally do this kind of work. I'm waiting for an appointment to the Ottoman Bank."

"I see."

Having made the point that working at a travel agency was beneath him, Victor had nothing more to say. When they got to the taxi he climbed into the front seat with the driver and began reading a Greek newspaper. It was the first of many small lessons Alex would learn in the weeks and months ahead, in the subtle game of social distinctions based on race, religion, position and wealth, that obsessed this cosmopolitan society. He had taken an instant dislike to Victor, not so much for his spoken denigration of the work that he was being paid to do, but for his unspoken contempt for the baggage porter as some kind of subhuman. He soon found that everybody played this same game of social status except the Egyptian peasant, the *fellah,* who had nobody to look down on.

The Alexandria that they drove through was such an exotic mix of sights and sounds and smells that his senses were stunned and he could get no clear picture of what life in Egypt was like. There were plenty of cars choking the narrow streets, but far more carts and wagons drawn by donkeys and horses and camels. The uproar from car horns, the curses of cart drivers, street vendors calling their wares or banging cymbals to get attention, was deafening.

The air was thick with dust and the scent of manure, of oranges piled in pyramids, and powdered spices, brown and red, green and yellow, in sacks outside the spice merchants' shops. There were a few Europeans in the streets in Panama hats, fat and prosperous Egyptians with red tarbooshes on their heads, and scrawny laborers and cart drivers in skullcaps or turbans or bareheaded. It all passed in a blur. Then he was in a first-class compartment of the Alexandria-Cairo train moving out of the station.

He shared the compartment with a tall middle-aged Englishman who could have been called, he supposed, distinguished in appearance. His cream linen suit was uncrumpled, his shirt tailor-made, tie of heavy silk in some school colors, a decoration in the lapel of his jacket. He was deeply tanned and his gray hair and mustache were carefully barbered. A folded copy of the London *Times* lay on the seat and a leather Gladstone bag beside his feet.

The Englishman studied him for a time, as though he wondered whether it was worth starting a conversation. Finally he said, "You're American, aren't you?"

"Yes."

"My sister married an American. Divorced now, but that's how I can usually tell."

He spoke as a bird-watcher might about identifying a species, and Alex was mildly annoyed.

"You're here on business, I suppose."

"I'm a foreign correspondent."

"Which paper?"

"The American Newspaper Consortium."

"Don't know it."

"A group of smaller American papers that pool together to

31

keep correspondents abroad. I'll be stationed in Cairo."

"That's where I live. I didn't know there were any American correspondents there."

"I'll be the first."

"What's up?"

"Up?"

"What's gotten your country interested in this part of the world?"

"Hitler is beginning to get our attention."

"Wouldn't have thought America had quite woken up yet. There'll be war, of course. Munich just bought a little time."

He regarded Alex silently for a minute and then drew a wallet out of his jacket and held out a business card. Alex handed him one of his, and read Drummond's out loud.

"Arthur Drummond, Director, Navigational Security, *Compagnie Universelle du Canal Maritime de Suez.*

"Navigational security?"

"Not as romantic as it may sound. Means basically that I look out for ships getting through the canal without accident or incident. That lowers the insurance rates, and that's what my masters care about."

"And what does that involve?"

"Making sure that the navigational aids, lights and radio beacons and such, are working properly, along the canal and in the Mediterranean and Red Sea approaches. I'm also supposed to watch out for 'hostile elements,' which means mostly Islamic fanatics—Moslem Brotherhood and such—who might take a fancy to sinking a ship to block the canal, that kind of thing."

"Might I ask you how you got into this line of work?"

"My family's been in this part of the world for three generations. My grandfather started out as a ship chandler after the Crimean War, and my father expanded the business into supplying navigational devices to ports and steamship companies. So, you might say I came into my line of work quite naturally."

"Except for dealing with 'hostile elements.' "

"Even that. If you are dealing with agencies of government in this part of the world you have to know all about dispensing baksheesh. You know what that is?"

"A gratuity for favors rendered, on a higher level a bribe."

"Exactly. That will usually buy you information on whoever may be out there plotting against you."

"And then?"

"You pay off the right people, bring the Egyptian authorities down on them, which usually comes to the same thing."

"But if that doesn't work?"

"You resort to other methods. The company directors don't much care what these are, as long as they get the desired results."

Alex didn't quite know what to say to that matter-of-fact remark, and he looked out the window at the passing agricultural scene.

"It's incredibly green and fertile."

"Gift of the Nile, as they say. Every year the flood brings a new deposit of topsoil from upriver. You could put a stick in the ground and it would grow. Never cared much for farming though. Ties you down."

The conversation became more general and eventually petered out, and Drummond picked up his newspaper. He figured Drummond had told him as much as he had because he wanted him to know he could be useful to a newly arrived American and, with war approaching, it could be useful to him to be on good terms with an American correspondent. This was confirmed as the train was pulling into Cairo station.

"I say, we should have lunch some day soon, Fraser."

"Delighted," Alex said.

Drummond took Alex's card from his pocket and looked at it. "I'll give you a call."

He had expected to be met at the station by someone from Middle Eastern Travel, but instead his office assistant was there. She must have been given his compartment number, because she was standing on the platform opposite when he stepped down.

"Nadia Simatha," she said and held out her hand.

She was tall but slim and small-boned, with dark eyes and red-brown hair and lovely skin of a color that he could never quite put a name to but, depending on the light, it reminded him of old gold, blond tobacco, honey, roses or apricots.

"And this is Hassan," she said, gesturing to a giant black man with tribal scars on his cheeks, "the office messenger, general handyman and guard."

"Sir!" Hassan boomed out, coming to attention. He had apparently once been in the army.

"Hassan will bring your bags. We can go on to the car."

Waiting at the curb was an old Packard convertible in mint condition, midnight-blue, with its white canvas top up.

"Don't tell me this is the office car."

She laughed. "No, nor mine. It belongs to friends. It's a big car, and I didn't know how much luggage you might have."

A uniformed driver opened the door for them and Hassan arrived with his bags, carrying them as easily as if they were three pillows, put them in the trunk and got in the front seat with the driver. And then they pulled away, out into the heat and dust of Cairo and traffic and noise surpassing even that of Alexandria.

"Well, this is Cairo," she said.

"It will take some getting used to."

"It will come quicker than you imagine, and then you'll either love it or hate it."

"I plan on loving it."

"Good," she said. "In that case you will."

"Are you having any luck in finding an office?"

"I have an office for you, on Gezira."

"The island in the Nile."

"Yes. It's quiet and pleasant there, and it's a prestigious address, and that's important here. I also took the liberty of buying some office furniture on the used market. It was very cheap, but nice, so there's a good bit of money left over from what was advanced for furnishing."

He was very impressed with Nadia Simatha. He would soon learn that she was always as calm, quiet and unhurried as she was on meeting him. In her place he would have been nervous and trying to please. He would also soon learn that anything you asked her to do was done as you wanted and often with something added that you had not thought to ask for.

"I'm sorry I took away your job, but I hope you will stay on with me in the new capacity."

"I wasn't sure, but now that I have met you I will stay on."

"You don't know anything about me yet."

"I know," she said, and looked at him with those calm dark eyes. It was a look he would get to know well.

"I'm very pleased," he said. "The pay's not much."

"I'll be frank with you. I don't need the money, but I do need a job."

Then Arvid Dahlsted's comment that her parents had cut her off without a sou wasn't quite the whole story. He looked at her hands. There was no ring, but he judged that she was in

35

her late twenties. It was one thing he had forgotten to ask Dahlsted.

"Are you married?"

"I was, but I am legally separated from my husband. I knew from the beginning that the marriage would not work, but my parents arranged it and I had to go through with it. When it became clear that it would never work, I simply told my parents I was leaving my husband. That's why I have to have a job with a reputable organization. I must maintain my independence."

He had learned something else about Nadia. That she could—or so it seemed—be astonishingly frank about what she felt and thought.

They had crossed a bridge and were now on the island of Gezira, and it was quiet and pleasant. The streets were lined with jacaranda and flame trees. The houses were large and surrounded by tall hedges, with lush green lawns where crested hoopoe birds—Nadia told him their name—bobbed up and down like mechanical toys. There were also a few modern office buildings, and they pulled up in front of one of these.

The lobby was cool and marbled, and there was a modern elevator to the top floor but one. The office already had his name and title in gold leaf on the frosted glass of the door, and there was a view in one direction of downtown Cairo and in the other of green fields, on one of which a polo match was going on.

"The Gezira Club," she said. "Oh, and I have this for you."

She picked up a paper from a desk and handed it to him. It was an application for membership in the Gezira Club. It was all filled out, with the signatures of his sponsors, the American minister to Egypt and the president of the American University of Cairo. At the bottom of the form there was a rubber stamp and the word "approved" and the signature of the club secretary.

"How did you do that?"

"I know people," she said.

"Do you know an Arthur Drummond, who was on the train with me? He is in charge of 'navigational security' for the Suez Canal Company."

"Yes. I saw him get off the train. It is said that he also works for British intelligence."

"Doing what?"

"Well, he would have access to all kinds of things, wouldn't he?"

"I heard that you knew things."

She laughed, and she was suddenly not just good-looking but beautiful. She was wearing a dress of undyed linen and a necklace of several strands of beads that looked as though they had come from an ancient tomb. He thought of his mother's things from under the stairs, and the pieces of undyed linen from a dress in which they were wrapped, and how as a child he had imagined that it was the same linen in which mummies were wrapped, and he wondered whether Dahlsted had told her that he was born in Egypt.

"I'm almost afraid to ask if you've found me a place to live."

"I have right of refusal on the apartment directly above, as a clause in the lease on this one. I didn't take it outright, since where you live is more personal than where you work, isn't it? Would you like to see it now?"

"Of course."

She led him into a small room lined with storage shelves that gave off an odor like the crystals in the inlaid box under the stairs of his grandmother's house.

"What's that smell?"

"Sandalwood," Nadia said.

A metal staircase wound up to the floor above, at the top of which she unlocked a door leading into an apartment that seemed to be identical to the one below in size and shape, but it had a terrace and was furnished in a rather gaudy Middle Eastern style.

"The former tenant left his furniture. You can buy it for next to nothing."

"I'll take it," he said.

"Then you want the apartment."

"I sure do."

"You haven't seen everything," and she opened a door into an enormous pink marble bathroom with a sunken tub and two large blue mirrors.

"Pretty awful, isn't it?"

"I'll get used to it."

"The owner of the building is Lebanese," she said, as if that explained sandalwood, and pink sunken tubs and blue mirrors.

They went back into the living room and then into a bedroom with a large bed in pseudo-Pharaonic style and more mirrors.

"Lebanese," she said again. "Your girlfriends will like this apartment."

"Girlfriends?"

"You're not married and you're not homosexual, so I imagine you will have girlfriends."

"How do you know I'm neither?"

"I know."

"We've just met, and I don't know anything about you except what you've told me."

"But then your country is two hundred years old and mine is five thousand," she said in a teasing way.

She looked into his eyes and he sensed that what her remark and her look were meant to do was to tell him that if there were girlfriends, there wasn't the remotest possibility that she would ever be one of them.

She turned away and opened glass doors onto the terrace, and they went out and looked down on the polo match.

"I'll have pots of flowers brought," she said, "and then it will be quite pretty. There's a tiny kitchen and a little stove that runs on bottled gas. Do you cook?"

"As a matter of fact, I do. In the part of the South that I come from, men cook. It's a kind of French thing."

"Then if you don't need a cook, Hassan can keep your place tidy, and you won't require other servants."

"This is perfect, you know. I'm very grateful to you."

"It won't be perfect, nothing is. Tomorrow is Sunday. What would you like to do?"

"Certainly not take up any of your time. Can I use the Gezira Club right away?"

"Yes, I've paid your dues. Your membership card is on your desk in the office."

"Thanks," he said. He was sorry that she had created an emotional distance between them, because at that moment what he most wanted to do was take her in his arms and kiss her full on the mouth.

"Then I think I might just relax tomorrow," he said, "at *my* club, if there's a pool."

"There is. I'm glad you like your *garçonnière*. How do you say that in English?"

"Bachelor digs, the Brits would say. It's not in the American vocabulary."

"Anyway, your girlfriends *will* like it. Which reminds me, there is a woman you should meet, American, rather French-

39

Canadian. Her name is Catherine Molyneux."

"The photographer."

"Yes."

"I know her by reputation. What's she doing here?"

"She came down from Paris to Egypt to do a fashion spread for *Vogue* and has stayed on to do some work for the Egyptian tourist office. She is very well-connected in the magazine and newspaper world and has a temporary membership in the Gezira Club through the tourist office. Would you like me to give her a call?"

"You really do know people, don't you?"

"Do I take that to mean yes?"

Chapter Four

After his bags had been brought up to what was now his home in Cairo, Nadia and Hassan left and he was alone. It was very quiet in the office, and the street noises were only a faint murmur far below. He should have felt elation at having an office and furnished apartment waiting for him and, best of all, an office assistant who was, it seemed, a dream come true.

His recently dismissed feeling that he was a naked soul in a cold and indifferent universe, didn't seem entirely out of place in the empty office with the sun going down over an ancient city. The idea that you are not alone, he said to himself, and that there is an infinity of time, is a youthful illusion.

On these contradictions, he decided to forget it all and go out into the growing twilight. He walked beneath the eucalyptus trees, along the canal that separates Gezira from the Giza side of the Nile and the pyramids, where it was already dark. There were houseboats tied up along the island's retaining wall, and one of these was a restaurant where tables were being laid for dinner. He walked across the gangplank and into a bar constructed of bamboo, sat down on a stool and ordered an *arak,* because he had never had one. It was milky in appearance and tasted of licorice, and he didn't much like it. He was offered a small table beside the railing on the river side, took it and ordered a lamb dish that was recommended. Sitting there he realized that his real problem was simply that he was lonely.

As he ate his dinner, almost alone on the dining deck, various craft floated downstream, and it was peaceful and quiet. Then something very curious happened. A luxurious motor launch—it must have been about sixty feet long—slowly passed, moving upriver, its powerful engine softly chugging. On its deck was the midnight-blue Packard with the white canvas top that had picked him up at the railway station, with big steel and glass headlights and white-sidewall tires. He thought it looked like a Pharaoh's sarcophagus being taken away on a funeral barge to some place of burial in a royal tomb.

Back at his apartment, he found that he was too tired to unpack, and took out only a pair of pajamas and shaving things. He was not surprised to find fresh linen on the bed. The phone rang. It was Nadia.

"Everything all right?"

"Yes, fine."

"I've spoken with Catherine Molyneux. She would like you to have lunch with her tomorrow. There's a buffet on Sundays around the club pool."

"Thanks, again, for everything," he said, but did not mention the apparition of the Packard being taken solemnly up the Nile.

The entrance to the main club building was through a marble rotunda, a writing room, according to discreet signs, to one side, a reading room to the other. Around the walls of the rotunda teletypes clattered away, as in Arvid Dahlsted's office, with the latest news, but also stock prices from London, Paris and New York. As the yellow paper rolled off the machines, it was gathered up and hung in long strips on the wall.

He ventured into the reading room, its walls lined with encyclopedias, atlases and other reference works, the main newspapers of the Western world attached to wooden rods and hung on a rack, and deep old leather chairs scattered about in which newspapers and books could be perused. The room was silent and empty.

He crossed over to the writing room, with its desks and green baize tables. An elderly Egyptian, wearing pince-nez, looked up from what he was writing with a broad-nibbed pen that he dipped into an old-fashioned inkwell. He could have been a high functionary of Ptolemaic Egypt, disturbed by some plebeian intruder. As he retreated from the writing room under the disapproving stare of the old Egyptian aristocrat, he saw in a mahogany tray beside the door club stationery, sheets and envelopes of heavy rag paper embossed in green, that had not changed in thirty years. Perhaps this was the room in which his mother's lover had written those dozen letters to her in Luxor.

Straight ahead from the rotunda was a vaulted corridor shimmering with light from the pool beyond. He looked at his watch. It was just noon. He had asked Nadia how he would know Catherine Molyneux, and she had replied in her usual cryptic way that he would know.

He paused at the entrance to the pool area and surveyed the scene. The pool was oval, and around it were arranged chaises longues. Most of them were occupied by men and women of varying skin colors in bathing suits. Beyond the pool was a bar and, under a striped awning, a long table being loaded with food. Waiters in red tarbooshes and cummerbunds moved about, their starched white gowns bearing a cursive green monogram, "GSC."

A blond young woman in a navy blue bathing suit removed the dark glasses she was wearing and looked at her wristwatch. It was Catherine Molyneux, but the reason he knew this was that he had seen her picture several times in magazines. She was considered beautiful, but now she looked older and drawn. She sat up and gazed out over the palm trees and playing fields, and it seemed to him as if she were seeing something in the distance that made her sad. He walked over to where she sat. His shadow fell on her and she looked up.

"Alex Fraser?"

"Yes. I recognized you from photographs."

"My glamour days," she said with a self-deprecating smile. "No more . . . I saved you a place."

She pushed a pile of fashion magazines off the chaise longue next to hers. "Would you like a swim before lunch?"

"Not particularly." He had intended to swim, and when he checked in at the club office he had been assigned a locker where he had put his bathing suit and a towel, but it no longer seemed interesting.

"Then why don't you put up the umbrella and sit down?"

He put up the big beach umbrella, and it cast a pool of shadow over them both. With the glare gone he could see that she was indeed beautiful, but not perhaps drawn and sad so much as just tired. There were blue shadows under her eyes and a tightness to the corners of her mouth, as though she were under some strain.

"I very much wanted to meet you," she said, and smiled broadly. "I have an ulterior motive."

"Oh."

"You're brand-new here."

"Yesterday."

"Are you planning to travel some in Egypt, the get acquainted thing that you can charge to the home office?"

"I am. In fact, ANC wants me to do just that. They made it clear that they aren't waiting impatiently for copy from me."

44

"I was wondering whether you might care to team up?"

"In what way?"

"There's some interest in my photographing 'the un-known Egypt,' but there's no way a single woman can travel to out-of-the-way places here. The tourist office was aghast at the idea. But if I traveled with a man . . ."

"I would be delighted." He couldn't think of a single reason against her proposal, so why not respond instantly and enthusiastically?

"I'm not propositioning you, by the way. I would have been very reluctant to bring up my idea, but Nadia said you were a gentleman and I could feel safe with you."

He laughed. "I wouldn't have necessarily characterized myself that way, but if Nadia said that, it must be so. She seems to know everything."

A bell was rung and people began to get up, moving toward the buffet table, the men putting on loose shirts, the women caftans, as did Catherine, a filmy saffron-colored one.

The buffet was enormous, exotic and visually a work of art. There were large bowls of swirled appetizers, mauve and pink and green, yogurt sprinkled with mint leaves, stacks of flat bread, pyramids of tiny okra, mounds of eggplant, stuffed vine leaves, tiny meatballs, silver trays of rice pilaf, tabouli, legs of lamb being sliced by a dark-skinned man wearing a white apron and toque, desserts of all kinds, cakes and bak-lava and pomegranate seeds and rose petals floating in syrup.

"The food here is gorgeous," Catherine said, "and now I don't mind, having lost twenty-five pounds."

That accounted for the drawn, tired look, of course, and he said, "How long have you been here?"

"Three months, and how many more depends . . ."

They went with loaded plates to a table for two under the

trees. A waiter came with wine and mineral water.

"This is the good life," he said, "or is this just the way things are here?"

"Both," she said. "Listen, if you are going to travel around with me in Egypt now and then, there's something I need to tell you. I've been through some bad times, in Spain, during the civil war."

"I saw some of your pictures."

"It was exhausting, terrifying, and I saw things that I couldn't believe."

"Bad?"

"I couldn't, if I tried, make up things as bad as what I saw. In the end I thought I was going crazy. When I got back to Paris, so did my doctor. He said I needed six months away somewhere quiet, where the pressure was off, doing nothing, or he couldn't take responsibility for what happened to me. It scared the hell out of me, and on my doctor's advice I chose Egypt. But, of course, I can't just not work. That would drive me crazy, too. So, if I'm sometimes a little strange, you'll understand?"

"Of course, but you're going to be fine."

"Maybe," she said.

He was glad that he had accepted her proposal to travel together before she had told him what she just had, which might have left her suspecting that he had accepted because he felt sorry for her.

"There's something else," she said.

"I'm prepared for anything," he said, though he wasn't.

"What travel I've been able to do outside of Cairo has been with a small group that goes out on weekends—sometimes for longer—to visit archaeological sites and such. There were eight of us, but we've lost one, and I was wondering if you might be interested in joining our group?

Actually, Nadia asked me to bring this up with you, she's one of us, but not to let you know it was her idea. But I have let you know, haven't I?"

"Yes, you have. Why did Nadia not want me to know that it was her idea?"

"She thought you might think she was trying to suck up to her new boss."

"I already know Nadia better than that. Yes, I think I would be interested in going out with your group, but how did you lose one of your members?"

"Drowned in the Red Sea on one of our trips."

The next morning as he was preparing to shave, regarding his ghostly image in the blue mirror, the doorbell rang. It was Hassan with a basket of groceries.

"I fix your breakfast, *effendi*," and he passed through the main room and into the kitchen.

By the time he had finished shaving, breakfast was laid out on the kitchen table, scrambled eggs, toast, jam and thick Turkish coffee.

"Coffee okay, *effendi?*"

"The coffee's fine."

"*Mazbout,* means just right sugar."

"Yes, it's just right."

Hassan shifted from one foot to the other, as Alex soon learned he did before launching into a sentence in English.

"Miss Nadia say she wait for you in office."

"Why don't you go now, Hassan, and tell Miss Nadia I'll be down in a few minutes. I'll clean up the breakfast things."

"As you wish, *effendi.*"

Alex went out the front door and down to the office by the elevator, sensing that the circular iron staircase from the storage room was considered by Nadia to be a private thing.

He found Nadia on the telephone, exuding a charm to someone on the other end of the line that was quite unlike the quiet, private person she had so far showed him. But then, he thought, Cairo is not Georgia, and I have a lot to learn.

She put down the phone and looked up at him, and the quietness returned to her face.

"Good morning," she said.

"Good morning."

"May I call you Alex?"

"You'd better."

"Well, Alex, I've already done a lot of things toward your first weeks here, but I just realized that I've been presuming. You will have your own style and want to put its imprint on your work."

"Let me worry about that, Nadia. I'm easy in my skin, and you just do what you think is the right thing. You'll have no instructions from me, no limits put on how you operate."

Before the words were out of his mouth, he knew that he had said just the right thing. She gave him a look that said a great deal, and all of it was good. It was exactly what she had wanted to hear.

"What I have done is made appointments for you with the people who I think will be the most important for you to meet first."

She handed him a typed list of names with her handwritten notes on times and places and such. He went down the list.

"The American minister and the president of American University, Cairo. Yes, besides other reasons, I need to thank them for sponsoring my membership in the club."

"How was it?"

"You mean, how was Catherine Molyneux?"

"Well, that too."

"She's been through some bad times, I gather."

"Did she tell you that she had to be hospitalized for two weeks after she arrived in Cairo?"

"No." He decided not to venture farther down that path for the moment. "Two British colonels?"

"One is regular police, the other Special Branch. King Farouk is more comfortable with the British in charge of security for now, for several reasons. They'll be spying on you, so you'd just as well let them know that you know."

"The heads of the Egyptian, Italian and Greek Chambers of Commerce."

"The Egyptian can unlock the doors to pashadom, the Italian and Greek will be flattered and can provide you with more malicious gossip than you can ever possibly use, but some of it will be useful."

"A department store owner?"

"Jewish. His brother is the Grand Rabbi of Egypt. They'll appreciate the attention, and it will send a message that America is not indifferent to the fate of the Jews in Egypt."

He looked down the rest of the list.

"No government ministers?"

"Stage two. After the politicians understand that you are well plugged in, they'll be seeking you out. If you are too eager with them, they'll just suppose they can put you in their pocket, as a chip to use against their opponents."

"Not the British ambassador, who pretty much runs Egypt, doesn't he?"

"Let's see how long it takes him to invite you to something."

"Then there is the group of eight less one."

"Catherine has spoken to you?"

"And she has already phoned you to tell you she has, hasn't she?"

"Yes."

49

He wanted Nadia to know that though he was giving her carte blanche to manage his affairs, he wasn't to be taken for granted.

"Would you like to meet them?"

"Sure. When?"

"Tonight?"

"You're in charge of my social schedule."

"Actually, they want to meet you."

"Look me over?"

"Something like that."

"I won't be blackballed, will I?"

"No," she said with a nervous laugh. "The group doesn't operate that way."

He was intrigued, curious to know who, beside Nadia, Catherine and himself—if he was accepted—rounded out this group of amateur explorers. What he dimly began to perceive that day was that he was about to embark on a stranger journey than he could have imagined.

Chapter Five

If you first see a place that is new and strange by night, this first view forever colors the way you think of it, even if later the place becomes so familiar to you that it seems quite ordinary by daylight. This is what happened to Alex that night, as Nadia and he made their way to the house that had been the Essabi family home in Cairo for 300 years. They had taken a taxi to the nearest *midan,* a little square with an ancient mosque, dying palm trees and a coffeehouse where men smoked *nargileh* water pipes and played dominoes, or trictrac, as it is called in the Middle East, as they had no doubt been doing in this *midan* for at least 300 years.

From there they proceeded by foot, as the street was too narrow for cars, but there were gas lamps. Nadia said that this was because the rich old families that had ancestral homes in the quarter saw to it. The street ended at the front gate of a tall narrow house, its windows covered with the wooden latticework that is called *mushrabiya,* behind which lights flickered on three floors. But the music that floated on the evening air was not a medieval Arab strain, but Django Reinhardt and Le Club Hot de Jazz playing "Sweet Georgia Brown."

A Nubian servant with tribal marks like those of Hassan, and holding a lamp, opened the door and led them up narrow stairs to the top floor, where a long room was lit only by a chandelier of glass cups in which wicks burned in oil. The floor was covered in overlapping Oriental rugs, and five people sat on cushions in a circle around a *nargileh,* the mouthpiece of which had been passed by a man to Catherine Molyneux.

"Hashish," Nadia said. "It's harmless enough."

The hashish smokers got to their feet, and one of the men lifted the arm off the windup phonograph that had been playing "Sweet Georgia Brown." And then the two men and two women that he did not know came forward and shook his hand in what he thought was a curiously formal way. Their names were Nicole Leigh, slight and wiry, with a short feathered haircut, and a grip like that of a man; Artemesia Chakerian, dark-haired, good-looking in a rather heavy Middle Eastern way, but with ivory skin; Basil Artimanoff, a good six-foot-three, slim but powerfully built; and in contrast Antonius Modiano, short, pudgy and wearing thick glasses.

"Our group," Nadia said, "except for Selim, whose family owns this house. He had to go down to the farm, where there is some kind of labor dispute, and he asks to be forgiven for not being here."

"Sit down," Nicole Leigh said, motioning to a cushion, and they all resumed their places.

"Nicole is an archaeologist," Nadia said, sitting down next to him, "and she leads our little weekend expeditions."

There was a period of silence, and then Nicole said, "Nadia tells us you were born in Egypt."

He was taken completely by surprise. He shot a glance at Nadia, but she had her eyes closed and was drawing on the amber mouthpiece of the hashish-laden *nargileh.*

"Yes."

"Tell," said the ivory-skinned Artemesia, with the heavily kohl-lined eyes.

"There's not much to tell. My father was a cotton broker in Cairo. My mother died when I was three, and my father returned with me to America. That's about all I know, because my father died when I was only six."

"How did an American come to be a cotton broker in Egypt?" Antonius Modiano said.

"Cotton was the family business, and my grandfather was a broker here as well. He came over originally to help train the Egyptian army. He had been an officer in the Confederate army. You know about Confederate . . ."

"Yes, we know our American history," Nicole said.

"I represent an American company, even," Antonius Modiano added.

"Oh?"

"The Radio Corporation of America."

"So," Nadia said, "why don't we go around the circle and the rest of you tell Alex who you are and what you do."

"I teach riding at the Gezira Club and also play a little polo," Artimanoff said.

There was a pause and Nadia said, as though she were adding a footnote, "Actually Basil is a polo professional, a hired gun. He is paid, and paid well, to play in a match where a team needs a leg up to gain the trophy. He is so good that they call him the centaur, half-horse and half-human."

It was at this point that it occurred to him that he was being let into a very private matter, and that he would not have been had not the group, or whoever led it—and he suspected this was Nadia—decided to admit him, and he felt a rush of adrenaline as though he had been invited to join an exclusive fraternity at college. He knew this was silly, and he knew it even more the next day, but that is how he felt.

"A jeweler," Artemesia said, "an ancient and honorable Armenian craft and profession, though most of my income comes from molding dental bridges."

"And the finest appraiser of ancient Egyptian and Graeco-

Roman jewelry and gold work in Egypt," Nadia footnoted.

"I sell and maintain commercial radios," Antonius Modiano said, "and I am a Sephardic Jew on my father's side and Greek on my mother's, from Constantinople. I speak Ladino, Greek, Italian, Arabic, French, English, Spanish, and Catalan, but this is for historical and familial reasons, and otherwise I have no distinctions of any sort."

"And then," Nadia said, "there is Nicole, who speaks heiroglyphic and demotic ancient Egyptian."

"I am an Egyptologist, obviously, French, married to an English diplomat with whom I do not live. Shall we have something other than smoke?"

The two men brought trays of Egyptian hors d'oeuvres, and Nicole brought him a glass of wine. As she handed it to him he saw on the inside of her left wrist a tiny blue tattoo, hieroglyphs in a cartouche.

That was how it began, and before the evening was over he had smoked hashish for the first time and had been invited to join the group on an outing the following weekend to the Fayum. It was past midnight when the taxi dropped him off at his building in Gezira and took Nadia on to her place—and he realized that he had no idea where that was. He stayed up for another hour or so, reading up on the Fayum in the 1929 Baedeker to Egypt and the Sudan that he had bought in a second-hand bookstore in Washington. Then he was drawn irresistibly to the suitcase that contained his mother's things, where he sought out the letter that contained the remembered phrase, "our Fayum days." Next, he opened the leather case containing the gold ring, and the stone with the floral engraving. He tried it on. It fit perfectly, but he was sure it would have been too large for his mother's hand. It had belonged to a man. He left it on his finger.

★ ★ ★ ★ ★

Nadia had said that they would go to the Fayum by boat, and he was not too surprised that the boat turned out to be the long, elegant motor launch that he had seen transporting the midnight-blue Packard up the Nile at twilight. He said nothing about that to Nadia or her friends. He had had a lonely childhood and had developed the habit of keeping his own counsel, not asking too many questions, and just waiting to see how things turned out.

The mystery was somewhat cleared up when Nadia told him that the launch belonged to Selim's father, who had long ago tired of it, and it was available pretty much anytime the group wanted it. She also told him that the group jokingly referred to itself as the Narcissians, taken from the name of Selim's father's yacht, the *Narcissus*, "and because in Greek legend Narcissus was vain and considered himself superior to others." She laughed. "Like we do. Want to join us?"

"Of course. Particularly if it means I'm considered superior."

"Oh, yes. You have been thoroughly discussed within the group."

This last comment made him slightly uncomfortable. Not only did he not like being discussed but he had the feeling it was being implied he was committing himself to something more than just weekend trips.

"Maybe we will induct you this weekend at the Essabis'."

He had not been told exactly what their destination in the Fayum was, and he had not asked.

"So we are going to Selim Essabi's farm. What about the labor dispute?"

"It's settled," she said.

"How do you know?"

"We have telephones, even in benighted Egypt."

He laughed. They were sitting on the bow of the launch, their legs hanging over the edge, watching the swift craft cut through the brown water of the Nile, and the villages go by. Nadia had her skirt pulled up to her thighs, exposing her slim shapely legs. Like Nefertiti's must have been, he thought, regretting the signal that Nadia had telegraphed that she was not available. Now the green strip of cultivation along the banks had narrowed to a couple of miles on each side of the river, as the desert closed in.

"What kind of farm?" he said.

"You'll be surprised," and before he could say anything more, "so let it be a surprise."

It was. He had speculated on cotton, grain, vegetables, fruit trees. The Fayum was a kind of oasis, but too grand for that, a huge depression in the Western desert where the Nile's water flowed in, immensely fertile, resort of the Pharaohs, breadbasket of the Greek successors of Alexander the Great, and of the Romans. What "the farm" produced was flowers, vast fields of roses and gladioli, lilies, geraniums and peonies, and narcissi—hence the name of the yacht.

Selim Essabi met them at the dock with three old, open, horse-drawn carriages. He was tall and dark-skinned, with a hawk-like nose, quiet and gentle in his manner. Alex reckoned him to be about twenty-eight years old. In fact, all of them were in their late twenties, and all single, that is, never married, or separated, or divorced, thus free of encumbrances for the kinds of adventures he was beginning to imagine such a group might have.

"I thought, Basil," Selim said, as he assigned them and their valises to the carriages, "that we might visit the horse farm first, since it is on the way and they're working with the two-year-olds this afternoon."

"Good. I would like to see how they are getting on."

The carriages moved out and along a eucalyptus-shaded dirt road that ran alongside a large canal. Huge old water-wheels were spaced along the canal, lifting water into wooden flumes that fed the fields where white egrets stepped daintily in the muddy water. Beyond could be seen the bands of white, pink and gold that were the flower fields. On the horizon a sandy escarpment rose above palm trees.

They all got down at a large fenced enclosure where the young horses were being turned from colts and fillies into polo ponies. Arab boys as small as jockeys, shouting, cursing and whipping their mounts, maneuvered the small horses in intricate ballet-like patterns, mimicking the action of the polo field. He found himself leaning against the fence next to Selim Essabi.

"You ride, Mr. Fraser?"

"A bit," he said, not wanting to raise expectations. Actually, he rode pretty well and had since he was a child. It was a thing one did in Thebes, Georgia, if you were from "good family."

"You'll be joining us, as your duties permit, on some outings, I believe."

"Yes, and at this point my duties will permit me considerable time off."

"Good, because we do go on horseback quite a bit."

It seemed to him that this was about the right moment, and he said, "What, actually, is the purpose of your outings, other than seeing sights, if there is any other purpose?"

Selim Essabi seemed taken a bit off guard. "Seeing sights, yes, beyond that not much, except we try to see sights others haven't, take a few more risks than the average tourist would dare. Adventuresome tourism, perhaps that's the best way to describe it."

Alex wondered if this accounted for the member he was

apparently to replace, drowning in the Red Sea, but he followed his usual policy of not asking too many questions.

"The flowers," he said, "I suppose you sell them on the Cairo market."

"Mostly not. We raise too many for the local market. Mostly they go to perfume makers in France, the cut flowers to various cities in Europe, even to New York. That phase of our business is fairly new, as it depends on air transport. We have a couple of planes of our own now, since airline schedules don't always accommodate our needs."

"It sounds like you're in the forefront of the industry."

"We try to stay a step ahead, but growing the flowers is always the key, and there's long experience in the Fayum. From ancient papyri that have been found, we know that in Roman times thousands of Fayum roses and narcissi would be ordered for a wedding. Your family was in the cotton business in Egypt, wasn't it?"

"For a while," he said, "but in the end it didn't work out."

"Yes, my family was hit hard by the crash of 1913 as well."

Again, there was a question he could have asked, but didn't.

His room was small as a monk's cell and whitewashed, as was the entire dilapidated old villa, inside and out. He took a shower in the tiny tiled bathroom, by pulling a chain that brought down a cascade of water from a grating in the ceiling. Then he went down to the terrace where the others had gathered, the women in caftans, the men in loose shirts, as at the Gezira Club, all with freshly washed hair plastered back on their heads. Once again he felt part of something, a feeling he had rarely had in his life.

"Cigarette?" Nicole Leigh held out a round container and he took a cigarette. He rarely smoked, but if he could smoke hashish, why not a cigarette? He examined the cigarette, curious. It was long, oval in shape, and the mouthpiece seemed to be of gold leaf.

"Giannaclis," Antonius Modiano said, who was smoking one. "They invented the cigarette, making them hardly benefactors of mankind, but it made them rich. Greeks, from Istanbul, like my family, then they emigrated to Egypt, where they now make bad wine."

Nadia lit his cigarette with a table lighter.

"Greeks, yes," Artemesia said, "and swindlers and crooks."

"Ah, my dear," said Modiano, "but you know the old saying, ten Jews to out-trade a Greek, ten Greeks to out-trade an Armenian."

"We Russians," Basil Artimanoff said, "are not given to trade, we ride horses, fight with guns and swords, that's more our style."

"Except you aren't," Nadia said.

"Aren't what?"

"Russian. You're Georgian."

"Yes, and we have produced our share of heroes."

"Like Joseph Stalin."

"An aberration."

"Ha!" Nadia said.

"And you Copts, what heroes?"

"We don't have heroes. We prefer working behind the scenes."

"What you have in common," Selim Essabi said, "is that you are losers, minorities, the defeated."

I expected an uncomfortable silence, but there was none.

"While the Muslim empire will rule the world, or at least the Middle East," Nicole said.

"You know better. Sunnis and Shiites, Moroccans and

Yemenis, Turks and Iranians. They are just bits and pieces of what long ago was an empire. In the Moslem world just one division now matters, between the privileged and the rest. My family belongs to the former class, and we will soon be joining you among the losers."

"Come the revolution."

"Exactly. Of course, you North Americans are exempt from all this."

"If you think French-Canadians are not among the losers," Catherine Molyneux said, "you are reading from the wrong text. I can't speak for Alex."

"If you come from the American South," he said, "you understand what losing means, even if it was seventy-five years ago."

A servant in starched white and an enormous white turban came out onto the terrace, just as the sun was going down in pyrotechnics of red, orange and gold.

"The horses are ready."

"What's this?" Nadia said.

"I've arranged a little supper in the desert," Selim replied.

"I'm not sure Alex rides."

"He tells me he does."

"Or that he has riding clothes with him."

"Oh, we'll fit him out. There's a whole roomful of riding clothes and tack left here by guests over the years."

Chapter Six

They rode out at dusk, four men and four women, on Arab
horses caparisoned with multicolored, woven bridles—hard-to-
handle horses—and stallions mixed with mares, a thing that
would never have been done where he came from. A stallion
trying to mount a mare, potentially crushing the mare's rider,
was the commonsense reason for not mixing the sexes. But here
things were apparently different, and Alex thought of Selim
Essabi's statement that he and his friends took a few more risks
than the average tourist would dare.

What happened next bore that out. From moving single
file along a path, which seemed to be ancient, through fields
of flowers, their odors heavy on the evening air, they came out
on the desert, and the eight horses and riders drew abreast.
Who started it he did not know, perhaps no one did, it just
happened. But suddenly the horses and riders moved out together, the pace increasing until they were riding at a full
gallop, heedlessly, caught up in the spirit of the thing, like it
must have felt to have been in a cavalry charge at Marengo or
Austerlitz, except a cavalry charge at night, for now it was
dark and there was no moon. He could not even tell which
rider was to each side of him. There were wild cries in the
night.

This is insane, he thought. Now we are on hard-packed
sand, but at any moment this could change, or there could be
rocks or holes in the path of our charge, and someone could

61

be thrown, killed. And then it happened. A horse went down, and a woman screamed. The other horses were reined in, and they came raggedly to a halt like sweaty mounts and jockeys who have passed the finish line. A *saïs,* one of the grooms who were riding behind them, came up and a lantern was lit.

It was Catherine Molyneux who had gone down. She was sitting on the sand in the pool of lantern light, stunned. Nadia knelt beside her, felt her joints, her head, raised her eyelids and looked into her eyes, talked in a low voice to her, stood up and signaled that Catherine was not seriously injured. The horse lay beside her, thrashing pitifully. Its broken leg bone had ruptured the skin and glistened like ivory in the lamplight. Basil Artimanoff came up to the horse, looked at it briefly and said something to the *saïs.* The next thing Alex knew, Basil had fired a pistol, and where the horse's eye had been was a black hole. This was his initiation, he supposed, into the Narcissians.

Selim took Catherine up behind him on his horse, and they proceeded on, but now at a walk and silently. In the distance the tent that was their destination glowed with lights like a ship at sea. Servants in *galabiyas* moved about, preparing dinner. A whole lamb was being turned on a spit over a wood fire. Even after they had dismounted and formed a circle in the half-open tent around a charcoal brazier, sitting on cushions, the silence continued. Finally Catherine spoke.

"That was a very foolish thing I did."

"That we all did," Selim said.

"And that poor horse."

"I would have spared you that," Basil said, "but I couldn't stand to see her suffer. I guess I *am* part horse. At least I spend more time with horses than with people."

"I've seen worse," Catherine said. "I've seen it done to men."

In the silence that followed, Catherine looked around at the rest of them.

"I'm sorry. I shouldn't have said that, but it's true. In the war in Spain it was usual for buddies to have a pact, that if one of them were so badly wounded he was bound to be captured by the enemy, the other would shoot him. I've witnessed it."

She's going out of control, Alex thought, and searching to change the subject, he said, "How did you get so involved with horses, Basil?"

"It's in my blood. My father and grandfather were cavalry officers."

"In Russia?"

"Yes. Although my family is Georgian, there was a long tradition of serving in the Czar's army. My father was a dashing figure in his dress uniform with his sword, tall like me, with black eyes and big black mustaches, that's how I remember him, and always around horses. He taught me to ride when I was only five years old.

"When I was eight the Revolution broke out. My father was stationed at Odessa on the Black Sea. The Reds descended on the city, and the fighting was savage. Women and children were mowed down along with the men. Finally, a number of the women were rounded up, with their children, and brought down to the port, including my mother, who was pregnant, and me, while the men, regular army, like my father, and armed civilians, tried to hold back the Bolsheviks, fighting street by street.

"There was a British cruiser in port, and pleas were made to the commander to take aboard the women and children, who otherwise would be slaughtered. Finally, they did. Just as the Red army stormed the port area the British cruiser sailed out to sea. I never heard of my father again. I suppose he was killed in the fighting, as almost all of the defenders were, but I don't know for sure . . ."

Basil's voice trailed off, as though he were lost in some ancestral dream, and Alex had a first glimmer of all the separate worlds that existed, beyond Egypt, in the ancient Middle East, like planets in a far space he knew nothing of. Then Basil resumed.

"From the Black Sea we passed through the Bosphorus and the Dardanelles into the Mediterranean, and the refugees were dropped off at any port that would accept them. We made it, my pregnant mother and I, to Alexandria, where my mother died in childbirth, the child too, and I was shipped off to Cairo, where there was a Russian community, of which I was made the ward. At age twelve I began as a groom at the Gezira Club, where I have worked ever since. My life that began so dramatically has become rather mundane."

There began a kind of Arabian Nights of stories from the exotic pasts of the members of the group, subtly directed by Nadia. He would have thought it was all being put on for his benefit, but Catherine's near-tragic fall and the death of her horse were certainly not staged.

"War," Nadia said, "it's what's brought most of you to Egypt, one way or another. Ours has not been a tranquil century."

"And it's by no means over yet," Selim said, drinking Scotch over ice.

"A shitty century," Artemesia said. "Some crazy patriot shoots the archduke in Sarajevo and all Europe goes to war, and Turkey too. In my village on the shore of Lake Van beneath Mount Ararat, we had our own crazy Armenian patriots, which the Turks would hang a few of now and then, but life went on pretty normal, for years, for centuries, then suddenly it's all over for Armenians. My father is shot along with most of the village men, and the women and children, the old men, take a long walk to Russia, eh, Basil, which your family is trying to get away from. We walk and walk, and each day we leave the dead by the side of the road, my mother included. And then, miracle of miracles, some of us do make it across the mountains to Yerevan, in Russian Armenia, I riding on my uncle's back when I couldn't walk anymore. And then, another miracle, there is an uncle in Brookline, Massachusetts, who sends money . . . You know Brookline, Massachussetts, Mr. Fraser?"

"Georgia is far from Massachussetts. Brookline is close to Boston, isn't it?"

"I don't know. All I know is that my uncle sent money to get us as far as Egypt, where we wait for American visas, but then my uncle decides to marry a rich Armenian widow, and we all move to Cairo. Good-bye America. I go to the Armenian gymnasium, and then my uncle says, 'You see what happens to us Armenians. You must have a profession, just in case it happens again, and you have to be able to make it on your own.'

"So, he and the rich Armenian widow send me to dental school, but I am not much interested in putting my hands in people's mouths, so I become a specialist in molding dental bridges, and then I say better to use this knowledge to make jewelry. This leads me to meeting the kind of men who have jewelry made for their women, and so that's how I find myself among you in a tent in the desert tonight. Any stranger story than that?"

"Maybe," said Nicole Leigh. "My story, I think, none of you have heard. It's about war too."

She fell silent, as though feeling over with her hands the fabric of something that had happened to her in a past time and place. He knew from Nadia that Nicole came from the old French aristocracy, which by definition meant your ancestors went on the Crusades, great swords, chain mail. And for those who could trace their lineage back to the time of Charlemagne, who had had an ancestor die with Roland at the pass of Roncevalles, Nadia had said, their lives were determined. The men went to the military academy of St. Cyr and became generals, or lacking that, to the seminary, and became priests and then bishops. The women married into one of the other great families of the French aristocracy, or lacking that, became nuns. But the Great War had swept all that away, along with most of the young men of the old aristocracy.

The rules were abolished, but the imperiousness that went with a social status that few understood, even in France, remained. Nicole was, Nadia said, farouche, that untranslatable French word that means both ferocious and shy, unapproachable, except on their own terms, a concept taken from the animal world.

"My father and my grandfather, and his father, were generals in the French army," Nicole began, "and in the spring of 1925 my father was sent as one of the leaders of a major expedition—which one day will be little remembered—to put down the Riffian rebellion in Morocco, led by a brilliant man, Abd-el-Krim. In the end France had to put 150,000 men in the field to defeat him.

"That spring I was kidnapped from the fine villa that was my father's quarters, and taken up into the Rif mountains as a hostage, ransom to the cessation of the French offensive. Well, of course, in the society from which my family comes, one does not give in to demands for ransom. Men, and women, are supposed to die for honor, without protest or fear. That, however, was not my view of things. In my place of captivity, a whitewashed old building among mountain pines, I was attended by a Berber girl of my age named Aisha, about sixteen, who wanted to know had I been raped, as she had been, as a matter of course . . ."

Catherine rose unsteadily to her feet, one eye nearly swollen closed by the fall she had taken, and went out of the tent into the desert night. The others looked uneasily after her, and it was clear to Alex that Nicole had just said something better left unsaid.

"Go on, Nicole," Nadia said.

"I told Aisha I was too valuable to my captors for them to damage the commodity they held. That impressed her, and she became my companion and co-conspirator. One night the two of us simply walked out of our place of captivity and started the descent of the wooded mountain. I wore native clothes, and Aisha had dyed my hands and face with some kind of brown vegetable extract. We slept in the woods, ate berries and roots that Aisha knew to be edible.

"After six days we arrived at the French lines, where I *would* have been raped, had I not screamed out in French my name and the position of my father. Despite my protests the soldiers took Aisha away, and I was never able to locate her again. My father was extremely proud of my exploit and wanted to know what reward I would claim. I said to be left alone to live my life as I wished."

Catherine had come back into the tent and sat down.

"What are you thinking, Catherine?" Nadia dropped into the silence that followed.

"I was thinking what strange patterns lives make," Catherine Molyneux said. "Here we all sit in a tent in the Egyptian desert, and each of us is here for a different reason. I certainly never expected to be living in Egypt."

She paused, and I was afraid she was about to launch into

an account of her experiences in the Spanish Civil War, and I suspected that seeing a wounded man killed by a friend was not the worst of the horrors she had witnessed. But what followed was quite different.

"I was born in Montreal, and my grandfather was rich. He had gone into the paper business and owned several paper mills. And then he died and my parents moved into his huge old house, which I barely remember. What I remember most is the cottage where we spent our summers, on an island in the St. Lawrence River. It was very beautiful there. But then the Great War came, and my father joined the Canadian army and became an officer, and my mother trained as a nurse, so she would be able to go to France with him. But my father was assigned to a desk job in Paris, and my mother never did any nursing. After the war my parents stayed on in France. My father was a painter and my mother a writer, except he never sold a painting and my mother never sold a story, hardly ever finished one. What they actually did was the Paris and Riviera social scene."

"What was it like?" Alex said, as he saw Catherine pausing, seemingly disoriented by her accident, feeling a sudden rush of sympathy for her, wanting her story to continue.

"When I was a child I met the Hemingways and the Fitzgeralds, Picasso and Matisse, the Duke of Windsor when he was heir to the throne. I called him David. It was all very glamorous, but I got precious little attention, and pretty much grew up as I pleased. By the time I was sixteen I was passing for twenty-one at the casinos in Monte Carlo and well on my way to turning out like my parents.

"Then it all came crashing down. The Great Depression saved me from a life of idle depravity. The Americans in France, even those without much money, lived through the twenties on a fantastic exchange rate. Most had to go home and find jobs. The rich ones, like my parents, found themselves suddenly not rich. The investments on which their trust fund was based shriveled up, and life without money was a different story. My parents divorced, my father went back to live in the family summer place on the St. Lawrence and Mother remarried and moved to Florida. She died a couple of years later.

"By then I was nineteen and decided to go back to France. My father gave me a few thousand out of what remained to him, and I went through it fast." She paused.

"After that?" Alex said.

"I met a photographer, one of the finest in France. I was very attracted to him and eventually moved in with him. He taught me everything I know about photography. When we broke up, I found I had the professional skills to support myself, and in time I became a sort of celebrity. That led to my being asked to cover the war in Spain, then becoming ill and being sent to Egypt to recuperate. Not what I would have expected for myself at all."

It was growing cold now as the desert does at night, no matter how hot it has been during the day, and the reason for the brazier became clear. Some large bird zoomed through an opening in the tent and out the other side. They were drinking from a well-stocked bar made from a donkey cart, a carved and painted box on two wheels. A little drunk, it occurred to Alex again that all these exotic tales he had just heard, might be nothing more than that, spun or at least embroidered, except for Catherine's. Both he and she were newly arrived in Egypt, and perhaps the evening had been a show, put on not just for him but for Catherine as well. Why this might be he could not imagine, but it was a feeling he had.

After they had eaten, and drunk a good bit more, it was agreed that riding back on a moonless night was out of the question, and that they would prolong their stay in the desert to the next day and visit the Ptolemaic temple that was nearby but hidden by the night.

He awoke at dawn, and the temple, rectangular and austere, was close at hand. In front of it, a hundred feet or so away from where he lay among the sprawled sleeping bodies, Catherine was kneeling, adjusting a Rolleiflex camera, focusing on Nadia, who was sitting in the sand, her caftan pulled down, baring her upper body, her thick red-brown hair falling over her bare shoulders, her small perfect breasts golden in the first rays of the sun, the nipples coral.

The other members of the group were asleep on carpets beneath the big tent, except for Nicole Leigh who, half-covered with a blanket, was propped up on one elbow reading a book. He got to his feet and she looked up from her book.

"How do you feel?"

"Fine," he said, "but I think we all got a little drunk last night."

"As befits a *thiasos*."

"*Thiasos?*"

"That's what our group really is. A *thiasos* was, in the ancient Greek world, a nocturnal revel of the followers of Dionysos, the god of wine. Drunkenness and orgies." She smiled. "But don't expect the latter of this *thiasos*."

He laughed, but it had crossed his mind there might be a sexual element to this intimate grouping of unattached young people.

"Tell me more."

"What the *thiasoi* had in common was that their initiates were completely liberated from convention. In ancient

70

Greece the women would put on animal skins and garlands of ivy and wander in the mountains in a state of ecstatic frenzy. It is said they killed wild animals with their bare hands and ate their flesh raw. We don't do that either.

"The *thiasoi* spread to Egypt with the Greeks under Alexander, then to Rome, where Dionysos was known as Bacchus. Cleopatra and Anthony founded a *thiasos* in Alexandria. They and their friends called their *thiasos* The Inimitables, and their revels were so noisy that those living near the palace could get no sleep. But then Augustus—or Octavian as he was called at that time—came as conqueror, and Anthony fell on his sword and Cleopatra killed herself with the bite of an asp, although I don't believe that. I think Augustus had her murdered. The Roman Senate tried to suppress the *thiasoi* because they were 'a threat to public order,' as you would expect of those prigs. But they never quite succeeded. You can't suppress the subconscious, and that's what the *thiasoi* were, the wild and irrational in human nature, organized, and with initiation rites and passwords. Pretty dangerous stuff, that."

"And today, just 'adventuresome tourism,' or so Selim says." He knew now that he did not believe Selim.

Nicole gave him a sphinx-like look that he could not even begin to interpret.

"Are the Narcissians a threat to public order?"

She shrugged. "I suppose that if liberation from convention is, we are."

Chapter Seven

An hour later they were all having breakfast on the roof of the temple, scrambled eggs, coffee, and flat peasant bread filled with *foul* beans, tomatoes and onions.

"Well, Alex, how do you feel about breakfasting at an Egyptian temple with our gang," Nadia said, "just a week after arriving in our ancient land? You must find it a bit strange."

"I like it just fine," he said, "and I don't find it strange. I feel like I've come home."

This was not really true, but he felt that the others were not being honest with him, had some use for him in mind. His reaction to such a perception had always been to become duplicitous himself, even as a schoolboy.

"Actually," Nicole said, "this isn't strictly an Egyptian temple. Although the architecture and the carving are traditional, it was built by the Ptolemies, who were Greek, or Macedonian to be more exact. The Greek inscriptions I will show you after breakfast aren't graffiti, they were put there as part of the plan. When Alexander the Great died in Egypt and his general Ptolemy stayed on to rule from Alexandria, the Greeks were an occupying power, but then, as she always does, Egypt seduced them.

"They tried to resist. Greeks were not allowed to marry Egyptians, were supposed to live in separate towns, but soon they were worshiping the old Egyptian gods under Greek names, were mummifying their dead. Their last line of defense was the Greek language, which they never gave up, and no Egyptian could hope to rise in the social order unless he mastered Greek. Cleopatra, the last of the Ptolemies, was the first of these Greek rulers able to speak Egyptian."

"Who knows," Antonius Modiano said, "perhaps my mother's people came from Ptolemaic Egypt. On both sides of my family I come from races that have wandered much, Greeks and Jews. They go away to escape persecution or poverty, and then a hundred or a thousand years later, they come back to the same places. With the fall of the Temple to the Romans in Jerusalem, my ancestors went west, settled in Spain, and in the Middle Ages became merchants trading with Constantinople. Then in 1492 all hell broke loose in Spain. The Moors were driven out, Columbus discovered America, and the Jews were expelled, all in the same year. My ancestor sailed away to a place he knew well, Constantinople—or Istanbul, as we now call it—and my family remained there until we left for Egypt."

"What made you leave?" Alex said.

"To save our skins. My father was in the business of importing safes, first from England, and then from America, installing them, maintaining them, which included changing the combinations when there were changes in personnel. He did business not only with merchants but with the Turkish government. Then in 1922, during the worst part of the war between Turkey and Greece, a number of plans were found to be missing from a safe in the War Ministry, apparently given to the Greeks.

"I have no doubt some Turkish officer sold them, but that wouldn't be nice for the authorities to admit. A scapegoat was needed. My father had supplied the safe in question, and my mother was Greek. What could be more convenient? My father was tipped off, and the next evening we were on a Brazilian freighter bound for Alexandria. We settled in Cairo, and through his American contacts my father became the representative of RCA. He's retired now and living in Palestine, so the circle is complete."

"War again has brought one of us here," Nadia said. "And you, Alex?"

"I suppose you could say war. If the South had not lost the Civil War, I doubt that my grandfather would have come to Egypt. And if there hadn't been that connection, probably I wouldn't have chosen Cairo when I was offered a post overseas. But only my subconscious knows for sure."

"War," Basil said, "it is like roulette. Men and nations plod along, saving and scrimping, planning and playing it safe. Then one day something gets into them and they decide to see if they can't help fate along with one big gamble. They put everything they have on a spin of the wheel. The Russians are much addicted to gambling. Life becomes boring and they ignore the odds. Many an army officer has blown his brains out because he lost more in one night than he could hope to pay back in a lifetime."

"There are different ways to gamble," Catherine said, and lit a cigarette. One side of her face bore a large bruise from the fall from her horse the night before. "You can take a reckless chance, but it can sometimes be just as reckless to do nothing. England and France have gambled recklessly with Hitler in Spain and over Czechoslovakia by doing nothing. The wheel will soon come to a stop, and I think on a losing number."

"But none of us is going to war," Artemesia said. "Four women and four men, of whom two are stateless, one Egyptian and one American, and I don't imagine any of us are interested in volunteering for war."

74

"But remember what Trotsky said," Basil said. " 'You may not be interested in war, but war is interested in you.' "

"That accursed Suez Canal," Selim said, "that's going to be our downfall if war comes. It has caused us nothing but grief since we were foolish enough to let the British and the French put it there."

"Let's not talk of war," Artemesia said. "Let's talk of what we are going to do after Nicole has lectured us through the temple."

"Well," Selim said, "when the *saïs* gets here with another mount for Catherine, we could ride over to a village I know where the villagers have lots of ancient things they have dug up for sale, once they're sure you're not from the Antiquities Department. They know me."

"Jewelry?" Artemesia said.

"Almost certainly."

"Speaking of which, Alex, that's an interesting ring you're wearing. Might I look at it?"

"Of course," he said and took off the ring and handed it to Artemesia.

She took a jeweler's loupe out of her caftan and screwed it into her eye. "Very interesting, indeed. The stone, a carnelian, is ancient, but not Egyptian, Graeco-Roman."

"I can't quite make out what the floral design is supposed to be," he said.

"Not floral, a grapevine with a grape leaf and a bunch of grapes, and a butterfly on the vine. But the gold ring is modern, made in Cairo. Where did you buy it?"

"I didn't buy it. I found it among some old family things."

"Your father's or your grandfather's?" Nadia asked.

"My mother's."

The Village of the Grave Robbers, as Selim called it, was a

large one, with green cultivation washing up against one end of it, sand flowing into it from the other side. There was a *souk,* or traditional market, a narrow street vaulted in mud brick, its darkness penetrated by narrow shafts of light let in by rounds of green, brown and blue glass.

"Romantic, isn't it?" Nadia said. "Right out of the Arabian Nights, weren't you thinking?"

"I was, yes."

"Do you know what those round pieces of glass that let in the light are made of?"

"What?"

"The bottoms of wine, beer and milk of magnesia bottles."

"So much for romance."

She laughed, and it was then that she took his hand. And it was then that the conundrum of Nadia's feelings for him came fully to the surface of his consciousness. She seemed to like him as a person, was comfortable with him as her employer, yet the feel of her cool hand in his was neutral. Nadia exuded sexuality, but there was not a hint of it in the feel of her hand in his. What then? His suspicious self whispered that she was testing whether he was being taken in. But taken in by what and for what purpose?

They went in and out of a dozen dark shops where ancient coins and ceramic objects, and things that were shielded from the view of the rest of them, were shown to Artemesia, after Selim had said a few words to the proprietor. Artemesia did not bring out her loupe, no more, he thought, than a cardsharp would exhibit his skill at shuffling and dealing cards. One of the merchants, an elderly man, kissed Selim's hand, which Nadia said was a thing no longer done, but probably it was because the merchant's grandfather had been accustomed to kissing Selim's grandfather's hand.

★ ★ ★ ★ ★

By the time they came out the other end of the covered bazaar the sun was high in the sky, and even in October the desert heat was stifling. They rode back to the Essabi farm and a cold lunch and the obligatory siesta that he was soon to become addicted to. But that was later. Egypt had not yet taken sway over his psyche, and he wandered about the extensive gardens that buffered the Essabi villa from the harsh, dry, dusty world beyond its walls.

There was a large fountain in which papyrus grew and goldfish swam, and paths that snaked through a tropical jungle brought into being by a network of channels of water flowing through the vegetation like the veins and capillaries of a body. Up against the perimeter wall, three meters high and topped with broken bottles set in mortar, was a long shed. A door was open and he stepped inside. The interior was lit by skylights, and there was the midnight-blue Packard convertible, and half a dozen other cars, a Rolls-Royce, a Hispano-Suiza, a Bugatti, and others.

When he had seen the Packard being transported up the Nile on the *Narcissus*, he had likened it to a royal sarcophagus being taken to some Pharaonic tomb, and perhaps that was not too far wrong. None of these cars showed much sign of use, and it was as if they had been bought with the express purpose of entombing them in all their costly glitter. He would have liked to have met Selim's father, who grew flowers and bought yachts that he tired of and luxurious cars that he seldom if ever used, but he was in Biarritz, Selim said, and when he would return to Egypt was quite unpredictable. Where Selim's mother was was not said, but a mistress with his father in Biarritz was implied.

They returned to the Nile as they had arrived, in ancient

carriages, at twilight, and went aboard the launch, its engine idling. By the time they were moving downstream toward Cairo, darkness had enveloped Egypt and, lacking electricity, the villages along the shore could be distinguished only by dim, firefly-like clusters of oil lamps.

For a while he watched the pilot in the pilothouse, lit only by the dial of a nautical compass, steering the launch down the Nile. Over his *galabiya* he wore a naval officer's gold-braided jacket with a cap to match, both dirty and ragged, and Alex imagined that he had bought them at some used clothing market to give himself distinction. Then he went forward and found Catherine sitting cross-legged in the bow, and he sat down beside her.

"Did you enjoy this weekend?" she said.

"Very much. I guess I can now consider myself a Narcissian."

"Good, because they do want you to join."

"They?"

"Oh, I'm an outsider too, not one of the inner circle."

"How did you get involved?"

"My psychiatrist in Paris is from Egypt originally, Jewish, from Alexandria. He and Nadia's father, and Selim's father too, all went to school together, in Switzerland. He called Nadia's father and said I was in need of a rest cure, and he thought Egypt would be a good place, and could he keep an eye on me? That's how I met Nadia."

"What do you think of the others?"

"Sophisticated, subtle, more to all of them than meets the eye."

"Do you have the feeling that maybe they think we can be of use to them?"

Catherine laughed. "Well, of course. This is the Middle East, Alex. That's a given. The stories that they told about themselves are straight out of the Arabian Nights, even if they are mostly true. One thing you don't know, that I discovered quite by chance, is that all of them belong to an amateur theatrical group started by the local Brits—as the expats always do—and I imagine that's where they met."

"Actors," he said, gratified to have his suspicion confirmed.

"What do you think of them?" Catherine said.

"Individually, I can't really say. I don't know enough about them yet. But as a group, it seems to me that Selim is right, that aside from himself and Nadia the rest are outsiders, alienated in one way or another from the race or nation to which they belong."

"Don't assume, Alex, that Selim and Nadia are not outsiders too. I was hoping that you would spin some tale about yourself, but you didn't. You must have some story, even if it's not as dramatic as being rescued from Odessa by a British cruiser or walking from Lake Van to Russian Armenia."

"I have a story, but I don't yet know what it is."

He found himself fingering the ring that had been among his mother's things, and it occurred to him that if there were the hallmark of a firm of Cairo goldsmiths inside it, then the firm might still have some record of who had ordered the ancient seal stone set in a gold ring.

"I won't ask you to elaborate on that cryptic statement," Catherine said. "We all have secrets, or at least leave things unsaid, which comes to the same thing. I'm very bad in that way. For instance, I didn't tell you what exactly led to my breakdown in Spain."

"No, you didn't."

Catherine turned and looked back to where the rest of the party was ensconced in the stern, drinking and smoking and laughing.

"I was captured by the Franco forces, illiterate peasant boys, and repeatedly raped in the most brutal way."

"Oh."

"That's why I am in Egypt, trying to bring myself back from the edge of madness. I still cannot let a man touch me any way, though, God knows, I need affection. Just so you know."

"I understand," he said. It was a lame response, but he couldn't think of anything else to say.

"Why don't we join the others," she said, putting an end to their conversation, and getting to her feet.

When they reached the stern the others were lying about on cushions, listening to some family story of Selim's.

"When the Mamelukes ruled Egypt they imported their wives from the Caucasus Mountains, because the Circassian women were considered the most beautiful in the world. When Mohammed Ali, who was an Albanian adventurer, seized Egypt, the practice continued among the ruling class and only came to an end in the late 1800s, when it began to be considered barbaric. My grandfather, whose father had come to Egypt as an officer with Mohammed Ali, was one of the last to import a Circassian woman, as his father had done. His agent simply bought my grandmother from her family, and she certainly had the legendary Circassian beauty.

"Most foreigners assume I am an Arab, but my mother is Italian, so I don't have a drop of Arab blood."

"Nor do any of us," Antonius Modiano said, "except Nadia must have some."

"I don't think so," Nadia said, "at least that is what my family would like to believe, that our ancestors all married within the Coptic church, so our blood is purely that of ancient Egypt."

"And with our new American recruit, we have yet another

facet to our cosmopolitanism," Antonius said.

Again Alex found himself wondering about the identity of the man who had drowned in the Red Sea, whose place he was taking. He looked out across the Nile and the desert and the mountains, now only vague shapes, and without warning the feeling that had haunted him as a child, that he was being stalked by something dark from ancient Egypt, returned.

Chapter Eight

He awoke the next morning in his Pharaonic bed as though he were awakening from a dream, a voyage to the Fayum with seven characters from a myth, a dream within a dream, in which his mother's lover had spoken in a letter of "our Fayum days." For a few moments the image of Catherine Molyneux's face in the twilight, as she spoke of what had happened to her in Spain, floated through the dream and then vanished.

He was fully awake now and his old logical, calculating self, a bit given to philosophizing. He looked at his bare feet sticking out from under the sheet and thought of the feet of mummies protruding from loosened wrappings, and of how death comes to us all but only the ancient Egyptians had found it worthwhile to preserve for at least a bit of eternity the body from which the spirit had departed, unless of course you counted monks of the Middle Ages and the Bolsheviks. There was probably a connection between the display of Lenin's embalmed body in the Kremlin wall and ancient Egyptian funerary practices, but it was a thought too boring to pursue.

Shakespeare said that the past is prologue, which someone had considered a profound enough thought to have carved in granite at the entrance to the National Archives, a few blocks down from the White House, beneath a lugubrious statue that he supposed was meant to represent the Past. It was true though that, at any point in your life, what has come before is just the lead-in, as they said in journalism, to what follows.

Certainly all that had happened in his life until he arrived in Alexandria by flying boat could be seen as a prologue to the main story that seemed likely now to unfold, and the weekend in the Fayum an introduction to the action. It was Monday morning, when the action might now begin.

He turned over in bed and looked at the card set in a sandalwood stand by the telephone on his bedside table, on which Nadia had typed his schedule for the week. His first appointment was at eleven with the American minister to Egypt, at the legation in Garden City. He had given Nadia the day off on the grounds that she had already put in far too many hours arranging for and attending his arrival. But the truth was that he wanted to be alone for a day. He'd had too much of the company of strong, unusual personalities, not the least of which was Nadia's.

He walked over the Qasr-el-Nil Bridge to his appointment at the legation. Garden City looked more like Paris than Cairo, with Beaux-Arts villas built around the turn of the century, in the same blond stone as the pyramids. The streets ran in arabesques through a park-like setting lush with Mediterranean vegetation, more like the Riviera than Egypt, both Paris and the Riviera places that he knew from accompanying his grandmother on a European tour when he was sixteen.

He was met at the wrought-iron gate by a *kawass*, one of the tarboosh-wearing accompaniers of ambassadors and ministers and other dignitaries, whose job seemed to be mainly to open doors for these dignitaries. He was led into an elaborate hall floored in lozenges of black and white marble, with potted palms, and from there into the outer office of the minister.

It came as no surprise that the minister's personal assistant, Chris Weston, was in the outer office, discussing some piece of paper with two young American women, presumably secretaries. Weston introduced Alex to them. As one of them led him into the minister's office, Weston put his hand on his shoulder.

"Why don't you stop by my office on the way out, Alex? Fran will show you where it is."

The minister had the same first name, but he was Alex and the minister was unquestionably Alexander and nothing else. Alexander Kirk was tall and handsome, an older version of Chris Weston, not a hair out of place, not a word misspoken. He was delighted that the American Newspaper Consortium had decided to put a correspondent in the Middle East, where big things were likely to happen soon, and he was equally delighted to have sponsored Alex's application for membership in the Gezira Club. He would see that Alex was included in one of his upcoming dinner parties, assumed that he had brought with him the accoutrements of black tie, and would, in the after-dinner gathering of the men in his study for cognac and cigars, introduce him to some who might be helpful to him in his work. If he had any problems, professional or personal, he was to let Chris Weston know. In twenty minutes Alex was back in the minister's outer office.

Chris Weston had a tiny cubicle just off the minister's office, but he had learned from the Roosevelt White House that the importance of aides was determined not by the size of their offices but by their proximity to the boss.

"Well, Alex, first impressions?"

"A blur. My first week in Cairo has been like a film run fast."

"Yes, even a trip to the Fayum, I gather."

Expressions like "I gather" had always annoyed him, with their overtones of simulated English aristocracy, of knowing more than the speaker needs or wants to reveal. He reacted in his usual way.

"Just how do you gather?"

"It's our job to keep up with what's going on, both because that's our job and because watching out for American citizens is one of our obligations."

Weston wasn't to be shaken, and he should have remembered that from their lunch at the Occidental in Washington. He changed tack.

"Quite an interesting weekend," he said.

"I should imagine. Not every new arrival gets invited to the Essabi farm, a much sought-after invitation. What did you think of the other guests?"

"Not a straightforward Egyptian among them."

"Right, but that's not all that unusual. It's still the outsiders who run things here."

Weston had recognized that his companions of the weekend were outsiders, but in the society that Alex came from that was an indicator of weakness, not strength. He began making another reassessment, of which there were sure to be many more in the weeks and months to come.

"Have any opinions of the other guests?" Alex said, and this time he did penetrate Weston's defenses. He couldn't admit that he didn't know who the other guests were or that he didn't know something about them without losing face, but in offering opinions he couldn't be sure just how far Alex's relations with them had gone. Weston made a good comeback, and the analogy of contract bridge occurred to him again.

"Remind me who they are."

"My colleague, Nadia Simatha, Basil Artimanoff, the polo player, Antonius Modiano, the RCA man, Nicole Leigh, an archaeologist, Artemesia Chakerian, dentist cum jeweler, Catherine Molyneux, whom I'm sure you've heard of, and, of course, our host, Selim Essabi."

For a few seconds Chris Weston seemed to reflect, as though he were looking at a hand of seven cards and contemplating how best to play it.

"Your colleague's family," and he pronounced "colleague" as though Alex had used the word in some odd way, "is very rich. International bankers. It's from them that the Essabis' flower-growing business gets the capital to keep expanding its operations. Basil Artimanoff is Cairo's leading ladies' man. Several of these ladies are rumored even to be Artimanoff's bankers. Modiano does quite a good job for an American company, and we see that he gets some exposure at the minister's social functions.

"Nicole Leigh is apparently a dead-serious archaeologist, respected in her profession, but something of an embarrassment to the British embassy since she chooses not to live with her husband, one of the rising stars of the British Foreign Service. There are rumors there, as well."

As well as what, Chris Weston did not say.

"Artemesia Chakerian I don't know anything about, but who does about Armenians, except that she is under some kind of inept Egyptian surveillance for alleged 'unauthorized' dealing in antiquities. Catherine Molyneux, of course, I know, a household name, at least in the world of fashion photography. They say she has a screw loose, or at least has been in mental hospitals. There, now you know all I know."

He very much doubted that Chris Weston had told him all that he knew about his weekend companions, and as at their lunch at the Occidental, he had the impression that Weston had told him as much as he had because he wanted something in return.

"Want some gratuitous advice, Alex?"

"Depends on what it is."

"Your house party guests are together a lot, and it is said that British intelligence is scratching its head as to what they are up to. And since Nadia Simatha is, it is said, pretty much the guiding spirit of the group, there are some implications for you."

"What are they up to?"

"I haven't the slightest idea, if they're up to anything at all. The gossip ranges from drugs, either on a commercial scale or as part of a self-indulgent way of life, smuggling of antiquities—or some form of espionage. Only the last would be of any interest to British intelligence, but espionage and that crowd is a connection I find hard to make."

"Then why are you interested?"

"Because whatever concerns the British concerns us. Be clear about one thing, Alex: British interests and our interests are not at all the same. War's probably coming, but in any case the natives are restless, and it's not at all clear that the British are going to be able to stay in control in Egypt and the Middle East. We have no intention of going down with them. When the smoke clears we want to have some assurance that Middle Eastern oil will still be available to us, whatever happens to the Brits."

"Why are you telling me this?"

"Because, as the sole American foreign correspondent in Egypt, you will be in a unique position to learn things."

"I have no intention of becoming a spy."

"I'm not suggesting that. I'm just suggesting that our interests may coincide from time to time."

"Tell me, Chris, how did you learn that I was born in Egypt?"

"You put that on your application for White House press credentials. Every once in a while the White House actually shares information with the State Department."

As he left Chris Weston's tiny office, the secretary named Fran came up to him.

"Excuse me, sir. You've had a message from a Mr. Drummond, who wants to know if you might be free for lunch today."

"At what time?" He had afternoon appointments.

"One o'clock."

"Yes, I could do that. Where?"

"The Russian Club."

"Where's that?"

"I don't know exactly. You have a car?"

"No, I'd have to go by taxi."

"I'll have the *kawass* give the taxi driver directions."

"Okay then. Please tell Mr. Drummond I'll be there."

He left the American legation perplexed. Gardeners in baggy Turkish pants were flooding the emerald-green lawn with Nile water from a big hose pipe, and the ubiquitous hoopoe birds were bobbing their heads up and down in search of insects. He was now almost convinced that he was being used in some kind of game that was being played, but by whom and for what reason he had no idea, and he didn't like it. It was time he began to untangle the strands of this mystery, beginning with what the Narcissians were really up to. This appealed to him both because he badly wanted some adventure in his life and because he needed to understand why Nadia Simatha was, seemingly, so indifferent to him as a man.

Then there was the not quite believably explained connection between Arvid Dahlsted, the White House and Chris Weston, who was obviously something more than the American minister's personal assistant. There was also the question of his paternity, which conceivably could have some connection with why he was the object of so much interest, why he had been plucked, with his own connivance, from his comfortable job as a Washington correspondent for a Southern newspaper and set down in Egypt.

But the more immediate question was why Arthur Drummond, head of "navigational security" for the Suez Canal Company, had chosen this moment to invite him to lunch at, of all places, the Russian Club, when he could easily have called his office and made the invitation directly through Nadia.

The Russian Club was at the juncture of the old city and the modern one, in a neighborhood that could best be described as seedy, on the second floor of an old wooden building that had not seen paint in a hundred years. He climbed a dark, creaking flight of stairs, to a door with a carved double eagle on it, last gilded twenty years before. But when the door opened light flooded in. A waiter, in a vaguely Russian costume, showed him into the light-filled dining room where Arthur Drummond was seated, in an otherwise empty room, next to a window, caught in a pattern of colored light filtered through the latticework of *mushabiya*, a bowl of caviar on ice and a bottle of vodka on the table beside him. He stood up.

"Thanks for coming on such short notice, Fraser. My schedule is in an awful mess, and I have to, shall we say, improvise."

"Understood. Caviar?"

"The real thing—Beluga."

"But how, out of Communist Russia?"

"We say the Soviet Union now. Because the Bolshies will sell anything they have for hard currency. Their mothers. Want to buy a Matisse? I could probably get you one for ten thousand pounds. Hold it for a few years, and you'd make a fortune."

As Alex had predicted to himself he would, he was again fast reassessing, this time the level of sophistication of Arthur Drummond, who handed him a piece of toast laden with Beluga caviar, chopped hard-boiled egg and raw onion, raising a tiny chilled glass of vodka, thrown back in a swallow.

"The Chicken Kiev's good, proceeded by borscht if you like."

"Yes."

The meal ended with a pastry laced with pistachio nuts and honey, and then Arthur Drummond got down to business.

"The Essabi farm."

"Yes."

"I'd be careful if I were you."

"Oh."

"Both the Simathas and the Essabis are players in the Suez Canal game, enough shares to make themselves a nuisance but not enough to make a play to take over. This isn't going to be allowed to go on."

"Why are you telling me this?"

"I'm director of security for the company, now, aren't I? And besides, I like Americans."

"Right. But I don't suppose you're going to be able to deal with such a combination through baksheesh."

Drummond laughed. "Hardly."

"So other methods?"

Drummond cocked his head as though he were a robin listening for a worm burrowing through the ground beneath him, ready to be plucked up, but said nothing.

When he came down to the office the next morning Nadia was, of course, already there, immaculately groomed, typing at breathtaking speed, her dark eyes flicking back and forth among four pieces of paper, arranged precisely, two on each side of the big office Underwood, her slim, elegant hand throwing back the carriage every two or three seconds.

"Good morning," she said, her fingers continuing to fly over the keys.

"Good morning."

"It went well yesterday?"

"I think so, but I haven't any means of comparison."

She lifted her fingers from the keyboard with the studied grace of an organist completing a prelude.

"What do you mean?"

"I mean I don't know what doing well would be in Egypt."

"It means when, after an interview, you feel for your wallet and it is still there."

She smiled and he laughed.

"Then just not being taken counts as success?"

"It's the best way. Getting the upper hand here just makes you enemies."

"Well, I don't think I made any enemies. The American minister seems awfully detached."

"He's very rich."

"Do you know his personal assistant, Chris Weston?"

"Somewhat."

She stood up, took some typewriter paper from a shelf, and as she bent over to put it in a desk drawer he saw in the low neckline of her dress the curve of a small perfect breast supported by a brassiere strap, and he thought back to awakening in the desert to see Catherine Molyneux photographing Nadia's nude torso in the dawn light.

"As for the heads of the Greek and Italian Chambers of Commerce, you were right, they are overflowing with gossip and not much else. Ahmed Pasha, the head of the Egyptian chamber, implied that he could be of use to me, from duty-free entry of goods, to entrée to ministers and the king, and even, somewhat delicately put, the company of gorgeous singers and belly dancers."

"Of course. All quite predictable."

"And the rest of my calls this week will be equally predictable, I suppose."

"Probably, but that does not exclude the unexpected and interesting development. You have a telegram from Washington, from Arvid."

"Arvid? You know him personally?"

"He was out here last year, and I took him around."

"And what is the message?"

"I don't know. The telegram is in code, and the codebook is locked up in the safe to which I don't have the combination. But you can bet that someone at the telegraph office has already given a copy to British intelligence."

"I imagine they won't have much trouble breaking a commercial code."

"Not this one, at least according to Arvid. It's a one-time code and unbreakable, unless you can get your hands on a codebook, of which there are only two. Arvid holds one, and the other is in the safe."

"So why don't we see what it says?"

"We?"

"*Chère collègue,* we're in this business together, aren't we?"

He took out of his wallet the combination to the old Chubb safe that Nadia had bought along with the used furniture for the office, and handed it to her. Inside the safe had been almost illegible instructions on a piece of cardboard on how to set the safe's combination, and she had insisted that he do it on his own. When he had done so, he had put inside the safe some gold coins, an old Smith & Wesson revolver which the office held for emergency purposes, and the codebook that Arvid Dahlsted had given Nadia for confidential messages, of which so far, she said, there had been only this one.

When Nadia had opened the safe she brought him the codebook and the coded telegram. He handed them back to her.

"Why don't you decipher it?" he said. He figured that showing confidence in her was more important than having revealed something that Dahlsted wanted only him to know. It was a calculated risk, since he did not know what the Narcissians, of which Nadia was supposedly "the guiding spirit," were up to, but sensed it was a risk worth taking.

"Show me how you do it."

She put the book and telegram on the desk between them.

"This number at the beginning of the telegram tells you where to begin in the codebook. The chart on the inside of the front cover gives you the third letter of the triad, the clear-text letter. The first letter of the telegram text is 'A,' the corresponding letter in the codebook is 'G,' and the chart tells you that A plus G gives a clear-text 'F.' That's all there is to it."

Nadia took out pencil and paper and within a few minutes handed him the clear text:

"For your information Lloyd liner arriving Alexandria Wednesday with party of German tourists taking archaeological tour of Mediterranean, but I have a report that some of these tourists are really senior German military in mufti. I leave it to you what use, if any, you make of this info. A.D."

"What do you think of this?" he said.

"Maybe the German generals are taking a close look at the lands they plan to conquer."

"I wouldn't mind breaking a story like that, but I don't see how I could get aboard the ship."

"Actually, according to this morning's *Gazette*, the

German minister to Egypt is giving a reception aboard the ship, to which local dignitaries have been invited. If you just happened to be in Alexandria that evening, I can't imagine we couldn't get you invited."

"And you."

"Why me?"

"You're too clever for me not to have you along—unless you have other plans."

"How could I after a compliment like that?"

"And how about getting Catherine invited too?"

"Why?"

"If she could get a picture of the group—somehow—we'd have positive evidence. If there are really senior German military among this group, some of them will have had their pictures in the press. She'd love to do it. She hates the Nazis."

"I'm not sure that's a good idea," Nadia said with a frown.

"Why not?" He was interested in what her reply would be. His suspicions had been slightly aroused by the fact that Nadia was so adept with the codebook, though it had never been used, and that neither she nor Arvid had told him about Arvid's visit to Cairo the year before.

"It would be dangerous to take pictures . . . wouldn't it?"

"I don't see why. And since when were you afraid of a little danger?"

Her face changed in a way he did not understand. Then she said, "Well, why not?"

"So how will we get to Alexandria?"

"The Essabis have a weekly flight to Alexandria to deliver flowers for shipment to Europe on the Imperial Airways flying boat. We could all go up together with them. Selim's younger brother, Mansour, pilots the plane."

"They wouldn't mind if we go along?"

"Mind? Our group even takes the plane to go exploring sometimes."

"Tell me, Nadia," he said, taking an even larger risk, "are you—to use an old-fashioned expression—seeing anyone?"

"Yes."

"One of the group?"

"No. That's out-of-bounds. It would spoil this special thing we have if we started that among ourselves. But I don't want to say anything more. He's a married man with much to lose if our 'seeing' each other became known."

This would certainly explain her detached attitude toward him, except that he did not believe her.

Two days later, as the sun was coming up from out of the still, lavender-shaded desert, they stood beside a metal shed at a small private airfield, Nadia, Catherine and Alex, waiting for the Essabi plane, a sun-touched speck in the sky.

It was still chill, but in an hour the heat of the day would come with the ascending sun, that for 5,000 years had assured the dwellers of the Nile valley that its passage overhead was unchanging, that Egypt was eternally the same, that the gods would forever perform their rituals of life and death. These were things that perhaps only an Egyptian could comprehend, and perhaps that was why a gulf existed between Nadia and him. On one level she was his friend and efficient employee, but that was on a learned Western level. Beyond was a vast desert landscape in which a young Coptic woman wandered in the land of Isis and Osiris.

The plane, an American DC-3, was on the ground no more than ten minutes, as its owners sent it forward like a greyhound to meet the Imperial Airways flying boat in Alexandria and put aboard the fragile cargo destined for the luxury flower shops of Paris, Rome and London. And then he found himself in a space packed with cardboard boxes with breathing holes emitting all the perfumes of Araby, and individual cellophane-wrapped sprays and bouquets bearing tags with names such as Rothschild, Orsini and Devonshire.

He was brought up to the cockpit by Mansour to occupy the empty copilot's seat, while Nadia and Catherine, whose badly bruised face now showed only a network of yellow and purple veins, stayed with the cargo of flowers for, Nadia said, "women's talk."

Mansour was the quintessential younger brother, smaller, slimmer, and handsomer than Selim, without the gravity that older brothers assume. He wore a khaki bush jacket and khaki shorts and sported a beard so short that perhaps it was only that he hadn't shaved in several days. He was silent and concentrated as he took the plane down the runway. They lifted off, banked and had the pyramids beneath them. Then he relaxed, smiled and offered Alex a cigarette. He declined and Mansour lit one for himself.

"Selim's been telling me about you. You were born in Egypt."

Alex repeated the story of how that had come about and of how he had come to be offered a job in Egypt, and this allowed him to bring Nadia into the conversation.

"I'm lucky," he said. "She's efficient, clever, seems to know everybody and is a nice person to boot."

"All of those things," Mansour said. "I've known Nadia Simatha since we were both small children. Our families have been close for many years, and her parents brought her with them when they visited the farm, which was often. At one time Selim was madly in love with her, but her father made it very clear to our father that marriage was out of the question. However close our families might be, in business and as friends, no Simatha had ever married outside the Coptic

96

church. We are Moslems of course, if only nominally, so that was that. Selim was sent off to school in England, and when he came back Nadia was married, to someone her parents had picked out, from another Coptic banking family."

"But now they're separated."

"It's not a pretty story. He treated her very badly."

"So what happens to Nadia now?"

"I don't know. The idea was to marry Nadia, who is an only child, to someone who could manage the family business for her when she inherits the bank and all the rest. But when you choose a husband for your daughter on a basis like that . . ." Mansour shrugged. "The only thing for sure is that one day Nadia will be one of the richest women in Egypt."

There was a pause, and then Mansour answered the question that he had dared not ask.

"Selim would like to start all over again with Nadia—he's unhappily married himself—but she has made it very clear that it is out of the question. But enough of that. Tell me about Roosevelt."

Chapter Nine

They had four rooms that adjoined on the top floor of the Beau Rivage Hotel, and his and Mansour's shared a balcony, as did those of Nadia and Catherine. He took a leisurely bath in an immense tub with lion-clawed feet, a wooden fan turning lazily overhead, and then shaved and put on a fresh white linen suit and a silk tie that he had bought at an Italian shop in one of the narrow shaded streets where they had strolled during the afternoon. He sprayed on a bit of the sandalwood-scented cologne that the hotel provided in a fluted crystal vial, and studied himself in the mirror.

He had a naturally dark complexion, which had already been deepened by the Egyptian sun, and with his dark eyes and dark straight hair, he thought he didn't look bad. But for whom or what? He was accompanied by two beautiful young women, one of whom was sexually wounded, and the other behind a glass wall she had built around herself. He shrugged to his image in the mirror. At twenty-eight he fancied that he had seen enough of life to know that nothing in human relations is static, that all is in constant flux, and this fit in nicely with his philosophy of wait and see.

The phone was ringing, and he turned from the mirror just as his image looked back at him with an ironic smile, having caught him in one of his moments of smug self-satisfaction. It was Nadia on the phone.

"Alex," she said, "are you up and about?"

"I am."

"So is Mansour. Why don't you two join us on our balcony for drinks, and I'll tell you what mischief I've been up to."

"All right."

When they converged on the balcony outside Nadia's and Catherine's rooms, his first thought was that he was not the only one who had taken care with appearance. Mansour also wore a linen suit, but of undyed fabric, that once again reminded him of that afternoon when he was eight and had found his mother's keepsakes in a closet beneath the stairs, wrapped in pieces of an old dress that he thought were mummy wrappings. He later learned that the cloth was, indeed, the same. A paisley handkerchief was stuffed into the breast pocket of Mansour's suit.

The two women were simply stunning in short silk evening dresses with narrow shoulder straps, a style that was much in vogue in the summer of 1939, Nadia's in a dusky plum that perfectly suited her apricot-gold skin and Catherine in a champagne color that was only a shade off her own blond French-Canadian complexion.

"Tiens," Catherine exclaimed on seeing Mansour and him, *"quelle élégance!"*

The doorbell rang and Nadia went to the door to let in the waiter with the drinks. Alex had tried to discuss payment for their rooms and service, but she had said her family enjoyed special rates at the Beau Rivage, and for anyone else to pay would just double the bill.

The waiter, in the ubiquitous white *galabiya* and red tarboosh, brought the drinks tray out onto the balcony, bottles of Campari, Cinzano and Fernet Branca, a charged bottle of soda water and a dish of peanuts in their red skins sprinkled with large grains of sea salt, a dish that he soon came to associate with social life in Egypt as closely as the pyramids with its landscape.

Mansour rolled back the striped awning that had shaded the balcony, for the sun was now sinking into the Mediterranean, and made the drinks. They raised their glasses to each other. This is the real beginning, he thought.

"What mischief?" he said to Nadia.

"Well, I got us all invitations to this evening's reception aboard the *Brandenburg* by browbeating the American vice-consul—the consul's away—and we'll go with him and his wife for protective cover. He has a squeaky voice and sounds like he's twelve years old. The consul would have been, maybe, a bit more difficult."

"But you would have browbeat him too."

"Well, yes, probably. I was ready to call the American embassy in Cairo if I didn't get my way."

Yes, and it would have been Chris Weston, whom she knew "somewhat," that she would have called. The setting sun spun gold in Nadia's auburn hair and flashed from her rolled-back eyes and teeth as she laughed. What am I going to do with you, he thought, my accomplice and adversary?

"Where is your camera, Catherine?" Nadia said.

"It's in my handbag. I have one of those sneaky little things that I use for taking photos at fashion showings where cameras aren't permitted."

Nadia saw the look of surprise on his face that she had said this in front of Mansour. They had had to let Catherine in on the contents of his telegram from Arvid if they were to get any photographs on the *Brandenburg*, but he had imagined Nadia would draw the line there.

"It's all right, Alex," she said. "Mansour is now in our group, and that means he's sworn to silence, or *omertá,* as they say in Sicily. In fact he's taking Selim's place, who no

100

longer can spare the time from the family business for our es-
capades."

"Yes," Mansour said, "he's getting a paunch and beginning to lose his hair. Soon he will be wearing glasses and sitting behind father's desk and going 'harumpf.' "

He laughed and white teeth showed in his black beard. He
was extremely handsome and Alex could not avoid the
thought that Selim may have been rejected because Nadia
now was enamoured of his younger brother, and that the
"married man with much to lose" might be a smokescreen to
protect her and Mansour.

"Am I sworn to silence too?" Alex said.

"Not yet," Nadia said, and smiled ambiguously. "You
haven't been through your initiation yet."

He would have liked to have said that witnessing Basil
killing Catherine's horse with a bullet through the eye seemed
like an initiation to him, but he couldn't say that with
Catherine present, and probably he wouldn't have said it
anyway.

He had the feeling that Mansour and Nadia were smiling
in the same ambiguous way, as though there was plenty he
didn't yet understand. He looked out to sea. The sun was setting into the Mediterranean, the sea as smooth and immobile
as a slab of polished marble, and the Moslem call to prayer
was rising from a score of mosques whose still sunlit minarets
pierced the twilight sky above the dusty, ragged city.

He had the odd thought that this moment had been repeated thousands of times in this ancient port city of intrigue
and commerce and sensual pleasures, since the Greeks who
had followed Alexander found themselves stranded by his
death between desert and sea . . . Seduced as always by Egypt,
Nicole had said. And here he was facing the ambiguous
smiles within a closed group of friends like the *thiasos* that

Anthony and Cleopatra had founded 2,000 years before. He had looked up the word in a Greek-English dictionary, and even the look of it was of something secret and strange—θιασος. He should have known that he of all people would be seduced by Egypt.

"Is something wrong, Alex?"

"No, nothing's wrong. I just had a strange thought."

"Alexandria does that," she said, as though she had read his mind, and for the first time he really stopped to think that his name, which was his grandfather's, was the same as that of a Macedonian king who had conquered the world. And across from him sat a woman of ancient Egyptian blood with dark, almond-shaped eyes.

"When do we go?" he said.

"Anytime now."

The Lloyd liner *Brandenburg* was long and sleek and freshly painted white. Spotlights from the dock played upon her, making the ship look like a stage setting, with its strings of colored flags that were brought out for special occasions, and every porthole lighted. A band in the stern was playing something German and faintly martial. They were caught up in the crush of the arriving crowd, which Nadia said was a good thing.

The American vice-consul indeed had a squeaky voice and appeared to be just out of college. He had red curly hair and wore a seersucker suit. His name was Bannister Carleton, which seemed about right, and his wife was Anne, and she wore a flowered print dress. They both gave the impression of a kind of fragile innocence. But in a few years, he judged by his experience with the foreign diplomatic corps in Washington, that would have been replaced by a suave exterior and an inner hardness and cynicism.

The receiving line was composed of the ship's officers and several *Herr Professors* of archaeology. Beyond in the first-class salon local dignitaries mingled with the German passengers, a number of whom wore lederhosen and other provincial garb, which he found both comical and slightly unsettling, as though the wearer didn't really believe in the validity of the modern world.

He made his way around the room, as he was used to doing at receptions and cocktail parties in Washington, looking for someone who might have something out of the ordinary to tell, something that could be spun into a story for his papers. He steered clear of the lederhosen crowd, as he would the out-of-towners at a Washington party, and the Egyptian officials of lesser rank, what they called at home the food and booze crowd. That left the Germans in suits, a few with monocles and even dueling scars, and of the age to be senior generals. He approached one who said that he had been in the military but had retired and was now teaching drawing at a *gymnasium* in Dresden, where they worked much from casts of ancient Greek statues, and therefore . . .

He moved on and spotted a man of about forty, of medium height, his dark copper hair swept back, his perfectly tailored suit out of Bond Street. Alex approached him and held out his hand.

"Alexander Fraser," he said. "Nice party."

"Ah, you are American," and this came out in a flawless upper-class English accent.

"I'm the Middle Eastern correspondent of the American Newspaper Consortium, but you won't have heard of them."

"Ah, but I have. Your consortium provides stories to the newspapers in small-town America, in the heartland I think you call it. I'm Gerhard Kolb-Tinius . . . I see you've heard my name."

"Yes, the largest chemical complex in Germany."

"Exactly. You may wonder what I am doing on a cruise like this, and I will tell you. I am a collector of Greek antiquities and I am taking a sentimental tour of my lands. With dark clouds gathering over Europe, it may not be possible—although I hope this will not be the case—to make a cruise like this until these dark clouds have passed. Tell me, Mr. Fraser, do you have views on the European situation?"

"I do, but they don't come from my experience in the Middle East. I've only been here a short while."

"So, where do your views come from?"

"Before I came to Egypt, I was a White House correspondent."

"Ah. Then you must have some opinion of President Roosevelt."

"I do."

"Will he keep America out of the European situation? On the one hand Middle America has no wish to become involved, but his class is rather disposed to. What do you think?"

"I think it is impossible to say. He is a consummate politician. Publicly, he knows how to work the crowd to perfection, privately, he is a poker player, and even people close to him do not know what he will do next."

"Rather like our own dear leader."

"What is your opinion of him?"

"A very flawed person, but he's all we have for now."

"Why?"

"The alternative is chaos, which is where Weimar was leading us, or Communism, neither of which, I should think, would be very palatable to America."

"But then neither is your treatment of the Jews."

"I do not condone it, but I do understand it, given our history. The English understand this, or at least the rulers in England today do. By the way, I am a graduate of Oxford. Many mock the Munich Accords, but they are a way out of the hellish situation in which we find ourselves. What they amount to is an understanding that Eastern Europe is Germany's business, and in return Germany will undertake to leave Western Europe, and the colonies, to England and France. It is not an elegant solution, but it is a solution. Do you think that will be understood in America?"

"I doubt it."

"Well, it's been nice talking to you, Mr. Fraser, but now I think I'd better go speak to the governor of Alexandria."

He reached into an inside breast pocket and brought out a card, turned it over and wrote on the back of it.

"This is my private number, and will be answered at any hour. If you should come to Germany I would be glad to continue our conversation."

"I doubt that I would have much to offer you."

"One never knows, Mr. Fraser."

Alex continued his circuit of the room and near the entrance he found Catherine talking to a middle-aged man, clearly of Mediterranean ancestry, whose face was very familiar. Catherine turned to introduce him, but the man had in the intervening seconds slipped away.

"Anything worthwhile, Alex?" Catherine said.

"In a way. Did you get pictures?"

"I did."

"I never saw you take any," Alex said.

"But that's the idea, isn't it?" Catherine responded.

"Who was that you were talking to?"

"Sir George Mavroyannis."

"Ah, that's it. A big Greek shipowner of dubious reputation, but who has bought himself a knighthood with contributions to charitable causes favored by the British royal family."

"That's him."

"What's he doing here?"

"I have no idea, but he is a director of the Suez Canal Company, so he's someone important. Nadia seems to know him, but money usually does run with other money."

As Catherine was speaking, over her shoulder he saw Nadia talking to Mavroyannis and Kolb-Tinius, a conversation being watched from across the room by Arthur Drummond.

Mansour, with Nadia at his side, approached them. "Is everybody ready to go now? We have to be up very early in the morning. I've confirmed with the airport authorities that I will be following our usual flight plan, which means taking off at first light. And besides we have to pick up the American vice-consul and his wife. They want to fly back with us."

"What?" Alex said.

"It's the price I had to pay to get us all invited aboard the German ship," Nadia said. "So, *andiamo.*"

They were airborne by the time there was just enough light to see the runway clearly, and Mansour headed the plane due east toward Port Said, which they reached within a few minutes. Then he banked and they were heading south along the canal, its course marked by the lights of ships passing through. There was enough light now to see the ships themselves, which from their angle seemed to be sailing through a sea of sand. This little channel, he thought, so insignificant from the air, is now being studied in the war rooms of London and Paris and Berlin.

They were all quiet, as they watched, fascinated, the landscape unroll beneath them. Nadia and Catherine had changed to bell-bottomed slacks, also much in vogue, and the

Carletons were dressed in tan cotton outfits that made them look as though they were going on safari, and perhaps that was how they saw this little adventure.

They passed over the little port of Suez at the southern end of the canal, and then they followed the coast of the Gulf of Suez south. Mansour had said that he always flew this route without navigational aids, and he preferred it that way. He knew where he was, but no one else did. His marker south of Suez was the Ras Zafarana lighthouse, visible day and night, and he kept it in his sights as would the ships' captains for whom it was designed. From there he would make a turn inland to the Nile and the Fayum, and they would have a late breakfast at the Essabi farm. Then he would have his guests sent back to Cairo by car.

Nadia had gotten out of her seat and gone up to where the Carletons were seated. She pointed out a mountain in the distance on the far side, now lit by the rising sun.

"Mount Sinai."

"You mean Moses and all that?" Anne Carleton said.

"And all that."

Then she went forward into the cockpit. When she came back she sat down beside Alex.

"I've asked Mansour to land at Ras Zafarana."

"How?"

"There's a wide beach of hard sand there. We've done it several times."

"Then, why?"

"For breakfast. No point in going all the way to the farm. Catherine and I have brought eggs and bacon and bread for toast, a spirit lamp to cook over, and coffee."

"I'm astonished."

"Good," Nadia said and went back to her seat beside Catherine Molyneux.

★ ★ ★ ★ ★

They landed smoothly a few hundred yards from the light-house, its light turning at regular intervals as it must have done for many years, and he found himself wondering if it were one of the lighthouses that his military engineer grand-father had built for the Egyptian government—and that was now maintained by Arthur Drummond's company. The deep blue sea lapped softly on the hard white sand.

As they were taking things out of the plane, in the distance two white camels came down the beach bearing uniformed men with old-fashioned rifles slung over their shoulders. The camels were huge and ugly, but they moved with the grace of ballet dancers. The men saluted Mansour and continued on until they disappeared in the opposite direction.

"Border guards," Mansour said. "Lots of hashish brought ashore along this coast."

The breakfast, prepared by Nadia and Catherine, was excellent, and afterwards they lay back on their elbows, and some smoked cigarettes, and they looked out on the blue sea and the red mountains on the opposite shore, and felt like gods.

"Do you have undersea masks on the plane, Mansour?" Nadia said.

"Oh, yes."

"Then why don't we have a swim before we go?" She turned to Alex and the Carltons. "There is a coral reef here, and the undersea life is fantastic."

"We didn't bring swimsuits," Anne Carleton said.

"Then we'll just swim in our underwear," Nadia said. "Nobody else around, so who cares?"

Anne Carleton looked as if she cared a good bit, but after a pause she said, "Well, right."

A first step down the road of the diplomatic life, he

thought. She doesn't dare not do something that the more experienced don't seem to attach much importance to.

Mansour brought the masks and breathing tubes from the plane, and they all stripped down to their underwear. In fact, there wasn't all that much difference between underwear and swimsuits. Then they waded into the water and paddled out to the coral reef. Beneath them was another world from the austere one of sand and sea and sky, a world of strange shapes and vivid colors, masses of coral as big as trees, striped fish that glowed incandescently, and menacing-looking spiny fish and eels.

After about half an hour Mansour called out, "We'd better go ashore now. The sun's up, and you can get an awful burn in just a few minutes."

They went ashore, and then the difference between underwear and swimsuits became all too clear. Even the men exhibited more than they may have anticipated, but the three women showed everything they had, including dark triangles of pubic hair and the pink circles of nipples. Certainly Nadia—and Catherine, which surprised him—had realized this would occur. Perhaps, he thought, it is I more than Anne Carleton who is the prude.

In any case, they walked along the beach to dry their underwear and restore their decency before putting their clothes back on. Catherine and he walked together, a little behind the others. She stopped beside a pile of stones on the edge of the beach.

"That cairn marks where Mireille died."

"Mireille?"

"The one we lost."

"I imagined the one who drowned was a man."

"No, a Belgian baroness, and she didn't exactly drown. We were floating over the reef just as we did this morning, and when we came ashore she just kept floating. Someone went out to get her, and she was just floating there in the water, dead, twenty-five years old. It seems she had a congenital heart defect, and her heart just stopped. It was late in the afternoon, the sun was going down, and we didn't know what to do.

"There are two police checkpoints between Ras Zafarana and Cairo. You don't yet know Egypt, but it was an impossible situation. If we had a dead body in one of our cars, there's no telling what would have happened: blackmail, being dragged before a magistrate, murder charges . . ."

"So what did you do?"

"We put her body in the trunk of one of the cars and just prayed we wouldn't be asked to open it. We weren't. When we got to Cairo we called the Belgian legation and explained what had happened. They sent the legation doctor, who took the body. Two days later there was a notice in the paper that Mireille had died in her sleep in her apartment in Zamalek. It was as though what happened here never occurred. I began thinking there might be more to the story than I realized."

"Like what?"

"Of course this was a traumatic experience for all of us, but the others, or let's say Nadia and Selim, were frantic not so much about the trouble we might get in, it seemed to me, but that something more sinister they were involved in might be exposed."

"Sounds sort of far-fetched to me," he said, to stop the conversation.

What was it Chris Weston had said? That Catherine Molyneux was supposed to have a screw loose or at least had been in mental hospitals. Nadia, too, had said that Catherine had been hospitalized for two weeks after arriving in Egypt. Well, he thought, after what happened to her in Spain, why wouldn't she be unbalanced, imagine dark conspiracies? And, on the other hand, maybe there was a dark conspiracy.

She turned to him, this beautiful young French-Canadian woman in her wet underwear. "I'm sure you are right. Anyway, that is whose place you are taking. I guess this is your initiation."

"Thanks a lot," he said.

On the last leg of their flight he sat next to Bannister Carleton, who was bright pink from the Red Sea sun.

"Why are you going to Cairo?" Alex said.

"Chris Weston wants to see me."

"Oh?"

"I sent a telegram to the legation saying that your newspaper consortium wanted my help in getting you invited to the reception, and I got a reply from Chris saying that was fine, but he wanted me to come to Cairo the next day."

Young man, Alex thought, you have a lot to learn.

When they landed at the Fayum, the midnight-blue Packard was waiting beside the landing strip, and the Carletons, Nadia, Catherine and he piled into the big car. In a couple of hours they were back in Cairo.

Chapter Ten

They dropped off Catherine at the Gezira Club and the Carletons at the American legation in Garden City. Then he and Nadia had a late lunch on the terrace of a Greek restaurant on the top floor of an apartment building across the way, looking down on the lateen-rigged *faluccas* plying the Nile.

"Their sails are like white seabirds," he said.

"And they haven't changed since ancient times."

"Nothing changes here, does it?"

"No, Alex, things change, but you have to understand how they do."

"You will explain, of course."

A waiter intervened with their lunch—cold boiled shrimp, Kalamata olives and feta cheese, *baladi* bread, and dishes of *baba ganouj* and *hummus bi tahini,* spreads made of eggplant and garbanzos, both blended with sesame seed paste. He dribbled olive oil over these.

"Do you know Ibn Khaldun?"

"No," he said.

"An Arab historian of medieval times. He explained history as being like a clock that runs and runs and then runs down, at which point Allah rewinds the clock and it all begins again. Then Allah withdraws, for centuries or millennia, until the clock needs another rewinding. Egypt ticked along for a very long time, and then time began to wind down, and the

Pharaohs became weak and decadent.

"So the mechanism of history had to be rewound again, and that brought Alexander, again, and that brought the followers of Mohammed, but the winding down occurred once more after a thousand years, and that rewinding brought Napoleon, and Mohammed Ali and the English. But the spring of the clock this time is still not completely unwound, and there is more to come. Another world war? A rising of the Arabs in the Middle East? It is too early to say. All I know for sure is that we Copts, as every time in the past, must take steps to protect ourselves."

This sounded to him like some kind of warning to justify something that was going to be done—or had already been done.

"I see," he said, but he didn't want to say more until he thought about the possibilities. So, as he often did, he changed tack.

"Catherine Molyneux."

"Yes?"

"She told me what happened to her in Spain."

"She told you?"

He had penetrated Nadia's defenses, as he had with a well-aimed question to Chris Weston. Penetrating defenses was a journalist's first tool.

"Repeatedly raped, she said, in a most brutal way, meaning . . ."

"Meaning sodomy, Alex."

He could not imagine an American woman saying that over lunch to a man she did not yet know well, and saying it in a cool, matter-of-fact way. But as Nadia had told him the first day, his country was 200 years old and hers 5,000. Nothing shocked.

"As a result, she says, she cannot endure the thought of

physical contact with a man. What do you make of that?"

"I have no idea. I'm not a psychiatrist, Alex. Why don't you ask her?"

And like Chris Weston, she knew how to parry a thrust. As if by agreement they turned to other and mundane things. They had a crème caramel and Turkish coffee, and then Nadia looked at her watch.

"Shall we go?" she said.

"Yes, but you don't need to come back to the office."

"I do. There are some things I must pick up."

So they took a cab back to the office, and a telegram had been slipped under the door. It was from Arvid. He handed it to Nadia.

"It's not in code," she said and read out the clear-text message.

"Reuters has just filed a squib that an ancient Egyptian tomb has been found at the desert oasis of Bahariya. Where were you? Many mummies and much gold, Reuters man says, which sounds like he hasn't actually been there. Mummies and gold are things our readers understand, so why don't you get moving? A.D."

He handed the telegram to Nadia.

"You can take the Packard," she said, as though it belonged to her and not the Essabis. "It's being garaged here in Cairo, and it's a good desert car once you let enough air out of the tires."

"Any other advice?"

"Yes. You might consider taking Catherine along. Bahariya would be perfect for her assignment of photographing 'the unknown Egypt.' And then you would have plenty of time to ask her any questions you want."

He refrained from reminding Nadia that it was not he who had suggested putting questions to Catherine.

114

★ ★ ★ ★ ★

Nadia took a shopping basket, containing several gift-wrapped objects, out of the armoire where she kept her things, waved to him cheerily and went out the door. She was probably going to a birthday party or something of the sort. Her private life was, so far, closed to him, and he still did not even know where she lived.

He walked over to the window. The sun was setting over the Gezira Club and a late afternoon polo match. He could make out Basil Artimanoff by his height and the skill with which he maneuvered his pony. An empty evening stretched before him. He had received several invitations as a result of the calls he had made, but these were a week or two weeks ahead, and he still endured the lonely life of a newcomer. He locked the office, took the elevator down and walked over to the houseboat restaurant where he usually took his evening meal, or at least a drink before walking downtown in search of some entertainment, if only a movie.

He ordered a Campari soda and considered calling Catherine Molyneux and broaching the idea of their going to the Bahariya oasis together and, if she showed interest, suggesting they have dinner later in the evening to discuss it. His drink came and he turned on the bar stool to survey the scene. He instantly saw Chris Weston at a low table in a dark corner of the bar area. He was conversing with a young woman, and a little table lamp lit her face. She was Middle Eastern, but pale-skinned, very slim and very heavily made up. She looked like a model, and he thought that was just the sort of woman Chris would like to be with—or perhaps just like to be seen with.

Chris looked in his direction, said something to his companion, came over and eased onto the bar stool next to his.

"All alone?"

115

"I haven't met many people, and I don't have much of a social life yet."

"That's not what I hear. Ban Carleton tells me he and his wife went with you and some of your chums to a reception last night aboard the *Brandenburg* in Alexandria and then flew on down to the Red Sea for a swim. Sounds like a pretty active social life to me."

He shrugged.

"And flying up to Alexandria for a German cocktail party sounds sort of odd, unless you had heard that some of the Kraut tourists were senior Wehrmacht generals."

He was silent while he considered the possibilities. Either the U.S. embassy in Cairo had cracked the ANC's "unbreakable" code, or Arvid Dahlsted and Chris Weston were hand in glove, or Weston had heard the same story as Arvid had and was just fishing. But in that case, why?

"The rumor about the German generals originated in Washington," he went on, "and I imagine that's where your people picked it up, if they did. The problem is that British intelligence apparently didn't find out until after the ship sailed this morning, right here in their own backyard, with their vital interests involved. They're going to be raked over the coals by London."

"What's that got to do with me?"

"Just this, that if you file a story about whatever you learned last night, the Brits here will appear even bigger fools. Brand-new American correspondent scoops British intelligence in Egypt, of all places. They'll have it out for you from now on, and for the U.S. embassy and me."

"Why you?"

"Because they'll assume you found out information from us that we failed to share with them. Not too good for working relationships."

"What are you driving at, Chris?"

"Assuming you have a story, the minister has asked me to ask you not to file."

"I'll consider it, Chris. If, that is, I have a story."

"Well, I guess I'll have to be satisfied with that, but remember that good relations with the legation could be pretty important to you."

"I know that."

After Chris Weston and his companion left, he did phone Catherine. He told her about the newfound tomb in Bahariya and asked her if she would like to travel with him.

There was a long pause. "Listen, Alex, I'm dying to go, but, for several reasons, I've got to be a little careful."

"It was you who suggested that we travel around Egypt together."

"I know, but before I give you an answer, I want to think about it."

"That's fine, and I can't go for the next three days because I've got a full schedule of calls to make. But the day after that, I plan to leave."

"I understand. You'll hear from me as soon as I've made up my mind."

So he did not invite Catherine to dinner, but he was pretty sure that Catherine would, in the end, come with him.

They started out across the desert at dawn, as travelers do in Egypt to avoid the heat as much as possible, following the track that was dignified on the map with the name "road to Bahariya," the white canvas top of the Packard up against the heat, wind and sand. The car was equipped with military thoroughness: metal vacuum canisters for water and coffee, an insulated ice chest, a large can of extra gasoline, blankets, a shovel, metal treads for getting a vehicle out of the sand,

and other things, including a shotgun for God knew what, re-
sisting bandits or bringing down wildlife, he supposed.
Finally, a porter at the garage loaded into the trunk a small
metal chest painted a drab green with a big steel padlock. No
explanation for the chest was given, but he assumed
Catherine knew what it contained. He asked her.

"I've no idea. Nadia asked me to give it to the owners of
the hotel where we'll be staying."

"Isn't that a bit risky?"

"In what way?'

"It could be full of hashish."

"What do I care?"

She had a point, but he was now wary of what was going
on, and hashish was not what was on his mind. And so they
started off.

Catherine wore a sun helmet with a length of filmy white
silk wound around it, native sandals, canvas slacks and a
coral pink blouse. He could see the picture now in *Vogue*. She
smoked a cigarette of dark Turkish tobacco, an Abdullah No.
3, according to the package, and drank from a half-bottle of
champagne that she had taken from the ice chest. He drove.

"This is what I came to Egypt for," she said.

"I thought you came here to get your head straightened
out."

"That too, but my muse calls. There are photographs out
there that no one has ever taken. Snap, snap, if you know
what you're doing, and you've got an image that in all the
centuries has not been caught before."

"Pretty heady stuff," he said.

"That's what I found out when I was twelve years old and
was given an Eastman Kodak box camera for Christmas. My
course was set."

"You're lucky."

"And your course, Alex?"

"In the course of being set."

They were now out into the true Sahara, where sand dunes hundreds of feet high rose and fell in the distance, like ocean waves frozen in time. A recent sandstorm had deposited what looked like a half-mile of fine, white sand across their path.

"Nadia told me that to cross sand you need to let most of the air out of the tires."

"That's right," Catherine said.

"And how do you get it back in again?"

"There's a pump in the trunk."

Clearly, that would be his problem. The flattened tires of the Packard did grip the sand, and they made it across easily. Then, sweating profusely, he pumped up the tires while Catherine held an umbrella over him.

As the sun began to go down, palm trees appeared on the horizon and cliffs red in the setting sun.

"Bahariya," Catherine said.

The oasis was a piece of rural Egypt able to exist because of underground water that surged up in artesian wells, but the heat of the surrounding desert made the only feasible crop date palms, of which there were tens of thousands. Above the palm trees there improbably hung in the evening dusk pink neon letters, HOTEL SPHINX.

The Hotel Sphinx was plain but clean. It was run by a middle-aged Greek couple, and he wondered how they kept their sanity in a place of such alien culture, with no one else to talk to who spoke their language. It reminded him of those Chinese restaurants one comes across in small Midwestern towns, run by a single family, isolated on the vast American plains.

He repeated his thought to Catherine, and she shrugged

and said, "Simple economics, Alex. Much stranger things are done by people to keep afloat."

The hotel had eight rooms with a single common bath, except for the top floor where two rooms shared a bath and a narrow balcony. This was kept for the occasional visiting dignitary, the owner said, and had been reserved for them.

They were the only guests that night, and they were served dinner by the owner in a cotton waiter's jacket. His wife was presumably in the kitchen. Dinner consisted of soup, a dish of mutton with garbanzos and red peppers that was not bad, and a bowl of fruit for dessert. There was even a bottle of the inevitable Giannaclis wine, barely drinkable.

After they had finished he said he wanted to go out to the car to get his notebooks, and then maybe he would go down to the bazaar and see whether anyone approached the foreign gentleman about the newly found mummies and the gold. Catherine said she would go on up to bed, too tired to wander in the bazaar.

When he opened the trunk of the car, the locked metal chest was there, either forgotten by Catherine or to be delivered to the hotel owners later. On an impulse he took the little chest out and walked with it down to the bazaar, where the business of the evening was just beginning.

After a while he saw a sign shaped like a key hanging over the entrance of a small shop. The proprietor spoke a few words of English and a few words of French.

"I've lost the key," Alex said. "Can you open this lock?"

The dark little man with thick glasses examined the lock. "Maybe." He took out a set of miniature tools and began playing with the keyhole. After several minutes the lock sprung open. Alex prevented the man from satisfying his curiosity about what was inside, paid him generously, and retreated to a nearby coffeehouse where he ordered a coffee *mazbout* and opened the chest casually.

Inside was an RCA shortwave radio that appeared to have been made for military use, the apparatus to construct an antenna, and a codebook identical to the one Nadia claimed that Arvid Dahlsted had left with her the year before, and of which only two copies existed.

After returning the metal chest to the trunk of the Packard, relocked, he went up to his room, sat down at a small table and began writing down impressions of the day. If the newly discovered tomb was worth a story, he would need some local color.

The shuttered doors to Catherine's room opened. She came out on the balcony in a bathrobe, sat down in a chair and lit a cigarette. He went out to her.

"I have some brandy. Would you like a nightcap?"

"I wouldn't mind."

He went back and poured two shots of brandy, came out and sat down beside her.

"I already have my photos for tomorrow set up," she said. "As we were coming into the town we passed a big artesian spring that flows into long stone troughs. There were children playing in the water, women doing their washing, water sellers filling their skins, camels and donkeys drinking. Just what I want. I will need a man to come with me, of course, someone who speaks Arabic."

"I'll see to it. I'm sure the hotel can arrange it."

"And meanwhile, you can go look into this story of a tomb full of mummies and gold."

Over the dark sea of palm trees a new moon had come up, as fine as a paring from a fingernail. Bats flitted in and out of the light from their rooms.

"It was good of you to ask me to come along," Catherine said.

"I don't find it a burden to travel to exotic places with a beautiful woman."

"Listen, Alex. You know that I'm not entirely stable yet."

"You told me."

The next thing she said took him by surprise.

"I'm not a promiscuous woman. But I've had quite a few boyfriends since I was sixteen and able to pass for twenty-one and get into the casino at Monte Carlo. But I've always had a fast rule. Only one at a time. When attraction faded with one or the other of us, I would be alone, but then after a while there would be someone else. I just wanted you to know that if I were able, and God knows when and if that will be, you would have been my next choice."

"I'm flattered . . . and disappointed."

"Thanks," she said. "Well, I'd better turn in now. I'm tired."

He stayed on the balcony until Catherine had closed her shutters and her lights went off, and then he went in, closed his own shutters and took his shaving kit into the bathroom. The door opening into Catherine's room was ajar, and when he went back into his room he left his own bathroom door unlatched. The day that they met at the Gezira Club pool she had told him that she might, if they traveled together, act a little strange, and Nadia and Chris Weston had suggested even more. Being locked apart didn't strike him as a good idea.

Sometime during the night, he was not sure when, he was awakened by a noise in the room. His first thought was that two Westerners arriving in a big expensive car in this isolated, impoverished place was an invitation for burglary. But then a small trembling voice said, "Alex?"

"What is it?"

He turned on the tiny bedside light.

Catherine stood there in her nightgown. She had been crying.

"I need help. Could I stay with you for a while?"

"Of course," he said, and started to get out of bed.

"No," she said, "I want to get in bed with you and have you hold me."

"Of course," he said.

"Do you mind if I open the shutters? I don't want to be shut up in a dark room."

"Go ahead."

After she had opened the shutters she got in bed with him. She was shaking. He reached over and switched off the light and put his arms around her slim body.

"This is an awful thing to ask a man to do."

"It does require a bit of self-discipline," he said and tried to laugh. "What is it, Catherine?"

"I have these terrible dreams and then wake up remembering something awful I suppressed from that film I starred in in Spain. That's the way I see it. Like a film that has parts cut out by the censor, and then they are restored. My doctor said this would happen until all the censored parts are restored, and then, maybe, I would be well again."

"I'll try to help," he said, "but . . ."

"But what, Alex?"

"I've never helped anyone before." For an awful moment he thought he was going to cry. "I've never helped anyone but myself . . . in all my life."

"Then maybe we need to help each other."

At that her body relaxed, and in a few minutes she was asleep. A long time later he finally went to sleep, and when he awoke again she was gone, and the next time he awoke it was light. Across from the hotel there was a tall dovecote made of

123

mud brick, and white pigeons preened in the sun and fluttered about. He felt a surge of happiness.

Catherine came out on the balcony in her bathrobe and he called to her.

"Would you like breakfast up here?"

She nodded, smiling. He picked up an antiquated telephone and ordered breakfast.

As they were eating melon, Catherine said, "Are you still willing to travel around Egypt with me after the way I behaved last night?"

"Yes," he said. He couldn't think of any useful way to elaborate on that.

"You don't know what a weight that lifts off me."

"But one thing, Catherine."

"Yes?"

"If we are going to travel up and down Egypt together, you're going to have to tell me what's going on."

"The Narcissians, you mean?"

"Yes."

"I'll tell you what I know. I imagine it's only the tip of the iceberg . . ."

"Go on."

"It's something that goes back quite a while. To Lausanne in 1908, actually. Selim and Mansour's father, Nadia's father . . . and my doctor . . . they, with some other students from Egypt and Palestine and Lebanon, formed a kind of secret society. Their aim at first was to free the peoples of the Middle East from the Turks, to help overthrow the Ottoman Empire. But the Great War did that for them, and then the British and French replaced the Turks as rulers, behind the fiction of protectorates and such. So they directed their activities against the colonial powers. They were impressed by what Lawrence of Arabia had done, and the power of unconventional means."

"Where did you come across this tip of the iceberg?"

"Some from Nadia, some from my doctor, and some from just being a good journalist and listening to what is being said."

"And the Narcissians are the next generation of this secret society."

"Yes, although there are, of course, other clandestine groups, of all kinds of political persuasions."

"What have we stumbled on?" he said, and was surprised at the "we."

"That's what I asked myself. If I hadn't needed a psychiatrist . . ."

This was more than he could absorb, and raised dozens of questions to which he had no answers. He would leave to another time the matter of what had happened to the locked metal chest and its contents that Catherine had brought to the oasis.

That evening, he found, as he put their things into the trunk of the Packard, that the chest had disappeared. They had gone their separate ways that day and went to bed exhausted, determined to be off by dawn, as the sun sank into the Western desert.

Chapter Eleven

They left even before dawn, having experienced the heat of the desert at midday, the big headlights of the Packard sending beams like twin searchlights down the track and out into the sand dunes, catching night birds and throwing their shadows ahead of them. And then the sky began to lighten and the sand turned pink, as he had first seen it coming into Alexandria on the flying boat. The hotel owners had packed them breakfast and lunch in two cardboard boxes tied with string. They pulled off the track and ate their breakfast from a folding table, sitting on two canvas stools, part of the extensive equipment packed into the big trunk of the car.

"How did it go, do you think?" he said to Catherine.

"For me, awfully well. The key was what Nadia told me, take along someone from the hotel who can communicate in Arabic and give him enough money to pass out to overcome the Moslem fear of photography, the belief that images are works of the devil, and that a camera can catch your image and with it your soul. And you know, they are right in a way."

"In what way?"

"I did catch their images, of all the people and animals and things. They are held on the film until with developing fluids they are brought to life again, and then they take on a life of their own. The image passes from hand to hand, ends up in a magazine or book, or in a shoe box of discards. A hundred

126

years from now someone may open that box or album of magazine clippings, and there will be the image as fresh as the instant it was taken, say of a young woman all in black doing her washing in a trough with palm trees in the background. But that woman will be long dead, her memory lost even in the small place where she grew up and married, had children and died. But her image has a kind of immortality."

"You love photography, don't you?"

"Yes, and perhaps that's why I've never stayed with a man for long. I don't think I could ever love a man as much as my art, except perhaps the man who taught it to me. But once I had taken all his secrets—it was like stealing the secret of fire—I had to get away, be myself, develop my own art. It would have withered in his presence. I knew Picasso when I was in my early teens and old enough to understand what I was seeing. He was like that with women. All they could do was serve him or get away."

Catherine paused and looked out to where a sliver of the red sun was coming over the horizon, soon to bring the fierce heat of the day.

"How was it for you?" she said. "No big find after all?"

"No. That Italian archaeologist, the one with the goatee, told me he had seen the squib filed by the Reuters man, and while it was true that they had found a tomb with lots of mummies and gold, the mummies were of prosperous Egyptians, very late, who could afford mummification, and the gold was gold leaf on the faces and hands of some of the mummy cases. He explained that gold can be beaten so thin that you can literally see through it, and then it is simply pressed against whatever you want to appear as gold. No Pharaohs, no treasure. I'll send my agency a one-liner when we get back to Cairo."

"I'm sorry."

"I'm not. If it weren't for the Reuters man, we wouldn't have had this experience."

Catherine said nothing. They packed up the equipment and continued their journey. The sand that had covered the road was no longer there. Apparently, another autumn wind had come along and blown it away.

"The desert's like that," Catherine said. "Just when you least expect it, it comes to your aid. The next day, however, it may decide to kill you. You haven't been in a sandstorm yet."

After a while Catherine tipped her sun helmet over her face and tried to go to sleep, but the bumpy track kept knocking it off.

"Why don't you get in the backseat and lie down?"

"I think I will. I'm exhausted."

He drove on, from time to time checking on her in the rearview mirror. She seemed to be sound asleep. Her exhaustion was emotional, he thought, and he saw an unwinding of something within her and hoped that he had had something to do with it.

They arrived at Cairo at twilight. Catherine had been awake for a couple of hours but silent, reflective, he thought.

"Do you want to go straight on to the club?"

"Yes," she said, "if you don't mind."

She was staying in one of a half-dozen small apartments that the Gezira Club had for the guests of members, but in the summer of 1939, with war on everyone's mind, the guests had been few and she was allowed to stay on indefinitely.

It was growing dark now, and the lights had been lit along the drive from the front gate to the clubhouse, turning the blossoms of the jacaranda trees that lined it into puffs of lavender smoke.

"The English are an odd lot," she said. "You see that high

hedge there with the lights behind it?"

"Yes."

"That's the croquet lawn, or pitch, or whatever they call it. It has its own membership list, and if you want to join you have to get signatures and all, and you can be blackballed if a member considers you not *pukka* for croquet. They have their own bar, and a room, I'm told, where trophy cups are kept, engraved with the names of winners going back for ages.

"And there, that building, on the second floor are card rooms, and each room has a brass plaque on the door with the terms of play, and you go in and wait until the chairs at the table are filled with other stiff old British types, and then you play."

"I imagine there is a Gezira Club tie," he said.

"Well, of course."

Catherine wanted to stop at the club office, which was still open because there was a dinner dance, to see if she had any mail. He went in with her.

"Any mail in 154?" she said to the man behind the counter, an archetypical clerk-bookkeeper, short and fat, with a few remaining hairs combed across his bald head, a pencil mustache and elastic bands on his sleeves. He got up from the ledger in which he was making entries, and went over to a wall of pigeonholes with names above each printed on slips of paper stuck in metal holders.

"Madame Molyneux?"

"*Oui.*"

"*Il y a une télegramme.*"

The clerk handed Catherine an envelope, and it was at this instant that he realized that the "B.P. 123" on the back flap of Gezira Club stationery containing long-ago letters to his mother stood for *"Boîte Postale 123,"* and that any replies from his mother to her lover—and, it seemed, his father—

would have been placed in one of those pigeonholes against the wall. He had come a long way from the closet beneath the stairs in his grandmother's house in a small town in Georgia.

"Would you like to come over to my place for a drink?" Catherine said. "It's been a long day."

"Yes, I would."

They drove on another hundred yards to a wooden building, something like a barracks, surrounded by eucalyptus trees. There was one light on, on the ground floor. Catherine's apartment was on the second floor, the stairs to it on the outside of the building. She unlocked the door and turned on the lights.

"British colonial," she said of the plain, dark varnished furniture with canvas cushions. She went over to a sideboard. "Scotch or gin?"

"Gin."

"Tonic?"

"Yes."

She opened an old refrigerator on legs, with a coil on top, and brought out an ice tray.

She raised her glass to him. "Thanks for everything."

The light from a big, ugly floor lamp fell on her. She was beautiful. There had been a softening in that tense, threatened face that had made her not so beautiful.

"There's nothing to thank me for."

She gave him a quizzical look then opened her handbag and took out the telegram and opened it.

"Ha," she said and handed him the telegram.

It was from Paris, and the message read, "Five positive (including R.), two probable and one possible."

"I don't understand."

"Among the German tourists on the *Brandenburg* were five positively identified German generals, two who probably are, and one that possibly is. Among the positively identified is General Rommel, who is supposedly being groomed by Hitler for the lead role when they take the war to North Africa."

"I'm still not quite sure . . ."

"I got a number of shots that night with my tiny camera, and sent the film with a journalist I know here—we do that for each other all the time—who was going to Paris. He gave it to a newspaper chum of mine there who gave it to a contact in the French security apparatus. They made the identifications in return for keeping the film. Eventually, I'll get the names of the other generals, but nothing more will be heard of this. Five to one, the French won't share this information with their British allies."

"I'm impressed."

"Before I had my troubles in Spain, I was pretty much on top of things. Given my background, I'm not exactly Little Bo Peep. And I would judge that neither are you."

"A couple of years trying to keep your head above water in the White House press corps does get rid of some youthful illusions."

"It's just that you play your cards close to your chest, don't you, Alex?"

"You observe well, Catherine."

"But that's what we get paid for, isn't it?"

"And now that we have some cards out on the table, why don't you tell me what happened to that metal chest that was in the trunk of the Packard?"

"I gave it to the Greek couple that ran the hotel. I guess they are part of what's going on. Nadia asked me to take it to them."

"You know what was in it?"

"I assume the same as in the others that have been delivered on our 'touristic' visits around Egypt."

"Which is?"

"I wasn't told."

"That's what I understood, so for your safety—and mine—I had the lock picked last night. Inside was an RCA shortwave radio and the paraphernalia that goes with it, and a pad of paper sealed along the edges with glue."

"A codebook."

"Exactly like the one we have in the office, which Nadia says was given her by Arvid Dahlsted for confidential messages between the ANC Cairo and Washington offices—a unique pair."

"So?"

"So, it now appears that whatever is going on, my boss is part of it."

"And it reeks of espionage. Remember, I've just come from the war in Spain where duplicity is the norm."

"But why then would Nadia have wanted me to go aboard a ship in Alexandria full of German generals?"

"Perhaps because the only way she could get there, to do her business without arousing suspicions, was to go there as your aide."

He was astonished at how much he was confessing to Catherine as he delved into his growing suspicions about Nadia Simatha. But he had to make some commitment to someone if he was to break loose from his dry, selfish and, in the end, doomed self. Now he had said it to himself.

"I guess," he said, "that I've got to rethink some assumptions I've made, which seem to always turn out not to be quite right."

"Don't assume anything, Alex. This is a high-stakes game in which lives are not all that important to the house."

"Meaning the casino?"

"Remember, the house never loses, only the gamblers."

That thing from Egypt that had stalked him as a child was back again, somewhere in the dark behind him in the room, or outside in the shadows.

"Would you like me to stay with you tonight, Catherine?"

"No. I don't have hallucinations anymore, as I did at first. I see things as they are, and there isn't a safer place in Cairo than the Gezira Club. The grounds are enclosed by a tall chain-link fence, and the perimeter is patrolled at night by guards with shotguns."

"Why all that?"

"Because all the wealth of Cairo is in the hands of the club members, and they are surrounded by the wretched masses of Egypt."

Alex remembered how Arvid Dahlsted had described the Gezira Sporting Club when recommending that he join it— 600 acres of sybaritic luxury floating in a sea of abject poverty.

He drove the Packard the short distance back to the building that housed the ANC office and his apartment above. The office was lighted. He took the elevator to his apartment, and before turning on the lights he opened the door to the inner spiral staircase. The door to the office storeroom that the stair led down to must have been left open, because he could hear Nadia talking on the phone in Arabic, in a voice that sounded angry or worried or upset, or maybe that was just the way you talked in Arabic over the phone.

He quietly closed the door and lay down on his bed in the dark. He had to rethink everything. With each step he took toward understanding what was going on, the murkier things became. He had thought he was in love with Nadia, but she kept him at arm's length for no apparent reason. That she was having an affair with a married man with "much to lose" didn't ring true. She was the epitome of efficiency and apparently straightforward with him, but she and her friends were involved in something dangerous.

He returned to the metal chest and the others like it. The contents pointed toward a clandestine network to be activated in the event of something. What? War? British intelligence didn't need a bunch of young amateurs to do its work. Was this some German operation? That would be extremely dangerous for anyone involved. In wartime one could be hanged for things like that.

So he didn't try, for the time being, to untangle the obscure pattern that he had uncovered. It had rolled out like an intricate Oriental carpet, the design of which becomes apparent only by looking at it repeatedly for long periods of time. He went about his business, finished making his calls, filed a couple of marginally interesting stories to let ANC know that he was still out here, and sought opportunities to have contact with members of the group other than Nadia, Catherine and the Essabi brothers. He frequented diplomatic receptions, where he would almost always run into Antonius Modiano, the representative of the company that made the radios. Nicole Leigh could always be counted on to be at cultural events, and Basil Artimanoff at the racetrack.

But his first interesting conversation was the result of a toothache, and Nadia making him a dental appointment with Artemesia Chakerian. It was the first of those dark stormy days that occur in Cairo at the end of summer.

Artemesia's *cabinet dentale* was in one of the city's taller buildings, and he ascended to the top floor in a creaking iron cage. He was led by Artemesia's small, frizzy-haired Nubian assistant to a room with an enameled dental chair made in

Germany about the same time as the building's elevator, and left alone.

Rain splashed against the window, and in the distance *faluccas* fought a choppy Nile. On the tops of buildings, neon advertising signs glowed against the dark sky. A metal arm beside the chair held a round of milk glass on which dental instruments were arranged with ritual precision around a blue gas flame. When Artemesia came into the room in a starched white tunic, with her lush features and heavily kohl-lined eyes, it added to his feeling that he was in a kind of Pharaonic chamber.

"So, what's the problem, Alex?" she said, putting a hand on his shoulder.

He opened his mouth and pointed to where the pain was. She picked up a mirror and metal probe, adjusted the light overhead, and felt the place.

"You should have had this attended to earlier," she said.

"I know."

"It's going to take a bit of drilling. I would recommend a painkiller."

"Fine," he said.

She injected the solution and stepped back.

"We'll give it a couple of minutes to take hold," she said, and looked at her watch, then looked out the window at the autumn storm.

"That ring I'm wearing," he said, "it's been nagging at my mind—the grapevine, the leaves and grapes, the butterfly. So I did a little research. It's the emblem of a *thiasos,* one from Graeco-Roman times, first century A.D. The members often wore some piece of jewelry that would identify them to other members. There are a half-dozen just like it in various collections."

"Where did you say you got it?"

135

"I found it in some things of my mother's."

"Ah, yes. I remember now. She had it set in the gold ring at Gulderian's."

"I never said that. My mother died in Egypt of typhoid when I was three. She could have bought it already set in the ring . . ."

He paused and looked out at the rain and the neon signs and the *faluccas* on the Nile. He could feel things moving like pieces on a board.

"Do the Narcissians have an emblem?"

Artemesia laughed, a very shaky laugh.

"Hardly. We don't take all this very seriously. It's more a game for grown-ups, like the Masons. You have Masonic lodges in America, don't you?"

"Yes," he said, "but whether they take themselves seriously, it's hard to say. The secret society that Nadia's father and the Essabis' father belonged to when they were young, was that your group by any chance?"

She could not quite hide her astonishment. "Where did you hear that?"

"Somewhere. I've heard so many things since I've been in Egypt. Your group is an extension of an older one, isn't it?"

Artemesia looked at her watch. "I think we can start drilling now."

Chapter Twelve

His plan to deal with the mysteries around him in a methodical manner was swept aside like so many chips raked in at a roulette table by the croupier, as life has a way of doing. It began with his bedside phone ringing in the middle of the night. It was Catherine.

"Alex, I'm sorry for the hour."

"It's okay."

"I've had a telegram from *Paris Vogue*. They have a fabulous assignment for me—pretty much name my own price—but it involves going to Luxor."

"Oh."

"Could you possibly go with me?"

"When?"

"Day after tomorrow."

Immediately, there came to his mind the image of holding a weeping, frightened Catherine in a bed in the Bahariya oasis. "What's the assignment about?"

"There has been a boom in things Middle Eastern on the Paris fashion scene this season, and my magazine has been caught rather flat-footed. They need to catch up, like a big photo essay, featured on the cover, for next month's edition, which goes to press in a week. They asked rather carefully whether I was up to it, and I said yes, I was coming up out of my problem to where I could do my old thing. You're the very best, they said. And I said, I know that. Talk terms with my agent."

"Yes, I'll go with you." A matter of honor, as his grandfather would have said. "What's involved?"

"They're flying down three of their top models tomorrow, and we'll take the overnight train from Cairo to Luxor. They want the caftans and Turkish pants, the embroidered vests and little red caps, displayed against the monuments and landscape at Luxor."

"Catherine, caftans and all don't have anything to do with ancient Egypt. They're Arab."

"I know that, and so does Paris. But, Alex dear, this is art, not a history lesson."

He laughed. "So it's you and me and three French models. Anybody else?"

"There's a little guy who handles my cameras, the lights and reflectors and all that. But the models aren't French, they're big Slav girls, six feet tall, one Polish, one Russian and one Yugoslav. My editor says they have worked out the visa problems with the Egyptian embassy in Paris."

"I don't get it."

"It's not your world, Alex. French women close-up can be beautiful in a subtle, sophisticated way, but it doesn't come across on film. The Slavs, as they are known in the trade, are skinny but big-boned, with pale skin and large eyes, wide faces and those high Slavic cheekbones. They're the fashion industry's standard. But they're high-strung, and there's often a problem with vodka or men, or both."

"Is that why you want me along?"

"No, I want you along because I want you along. But I thought you ought to know."

Nadia's reaction to his going to Upper Egypt with Catherine, the very kind of thing she had been urging on him, was strangely muted.

"Do you think this is the best use of your time?"

"My time is, so far, not all that valuable."

"Would you like Nicole to go with you? She's in the inner circle of Egyptian archaeology and could open all the doors for you."

"I guess that would be up to Catherine. This is her show."

"Why don't I call Nicole and see if she's available? Then you can decide."

"Okay."

As she was making the call he reflected on Nadia's reaction. Had she and Catherine had a conversation after their return from the Bahariya oasis? Had Catherine told her about coming to his bed and his holding her during one of her bouts with the darkness within? It didn't seem likely, given Catherine's apparent mistrust of Nadia.

In any event Nicole was not available. She was giving a lecture at the Alliance Française. After that Nadia showed some enthusiasm for the trip, or feigned it, and thanked him for "looking out" for Catherine, as she put it. She said she would get together with Nicole, and they would prepare the way with local officials, find them a good guide, all that.

So he returned on the appointed day at twilight to the main Cairo station, huge and dusty and vibrating with every kind of noise, for the first time since he had arrived there from Alexandria and was met by Nadia.

The Slav models were as Catherine had described and more, and all around them men stood openmouthed. They piled aboard the Deluxe Express to Luxor, while the lighting man, with the help of two porters, loaded his metal boxes into the baggage car. By the time the train was speeding past the pyramids, these were but black enigmatic triangles against the last light. Nadia had reserved a single compartment for him and Catherine, and he was unsure what to make of that. But then everything about the relationships between him and the two women was ambiguous.

In the dining car the Slav models were having a noisy dinner with three young European men they had picked up, while Catherine and he were alone at the end of the car, surrounded by empty tables laden with white linen, crystal, silver, and pink roses. Catherine looked down at her place setting and laughed.

"Four knives, four forks and two spoons. It's so British. Make up in display for what is lacking in the food. I'll bet it's awful."

She looked away from him out into the black Egyptian night, punctuated by village lights glittering like children's sparklers. Her appearance now struck him as an assured drawing superimposed on a student's smudged image. When he had first met her there was a washed-out, tentative look to her, as though her features had lost something that once had been there. Now the clear outlines had been restored. Their eyes met in their reflections in the dining car window.

"What is it you see in me, staring so intently?" she said.

"I see you in Paris, as I imagine you were. It was as though . . . you were coming into focus."

"I am."

The headwaiter brought them big, grease-spotted menus, and while Catherine studied hers, he tried to express what he had seen more articulately to himself than he had just expressed it to her. It was, he realized, in part a matter of makeup, applied with the skill, and subtlety, of a professional, the first time he had ever seen her wearing cosmetics. She also wore on her left wrist a wide band of ivory and a link bracelet of chromium repeated in her earrings. Her dress was couturier, of a nubby pale blue linen, and her hair was artfully done, not just hanging loose or pinned up in a chignon, as it usually was.

They both ordered, without much hope that what would be served would bear any relationship to the grand, mis-spelled, French terms used on the menu. And when it came, it didn't.

The coffee was Turkish, and at least that was good. Catherine picked up their empty coffee cups, turned them upside-down on their saucers, spun them a couple of times and lifted them, leaving a swirl of fine grounds on the saucers.

"Our fortunes," she said. "The Egyptians really believe in this. What you see there is what is going to happen. Sort of a Rorschach, I guess. It's how you interpret it. What do you see?"

"A flying bird, big and dark, looks like a vulture. And yours?"

"A person running," Catherine said, "a woman. How do you interpret yours?"

"Does it have to be personal?"

"No, it can be something outside you that's going to happen. The Nile is going to overflow its banks, a horse at fifty to one is going to win tomorrow's race at the Gezira Club."

"I see now that it's not so much a vulture as the shadow of a vulture overhead, an Egyptian vulture like the one in the emblem of ancient Egypt. If it's personal, it's something dark that is pursuing me. If not, it means war is coming. And yours?"

"The woman is either running away from something or toward something. It means either I'm going to get well, or I'm not going to get well. The coffee grounds can't tell which. Is something dark pursuing you, Alex?"

"Yes, but I don't know what, or rather I haven't wanted to find out."

"It doesn't pay to take this seriously. Some Egyptians do. They bet a lot of money on the fifty to one shot and lose. Shall we go?"

He had no idea what to expect as they made their way down the corridor. Catherine had said not a word about their being booked in the same compartment. The lights were on in the compartment, and while they had dined the two plush seats had been turned into two beds with the covers folded back. He closed the door behind them. They both stood there, mute as statues.

Finally Catherine said, "I'm sorry, Alex. When I saw the reservations Nadia had made, I thought the time had come to just be carefree and let things happen as they did or not. It's going to have to be not. You probably don't even know what I'm talking about, but if you do, you must be thinking, how arrogant of her to assume . . ." Her voice trailed off. "Which bed do you want?"

"Against the wall, that would be fine."

At the foot of the other bed was a frosted glass door to a small private bath. She took her travel case inside and he took the opportunity to get into pajamas. When she came out she was wearing a nightgown and matching robe.

"Could we turn out the lights?" she said.

They both turned off the little brass lamps with red shades over the heads of the two beds, and the train hurtled through the black Egyptian night, the car swaying back and forth as the train gained speed on the long straight run to Luxor.

"Alex?"

"Yes?"

"Could I tell you more of what happened to me?"

"Only if you have a very good reason."

"I think I do. Only my doctor in Paris and an army doctor in Spain know it all, and that doesn't do me any good now. One did what he could, with men dying in the hospital all around me. My psychiatrist did, I think, all that he thought useful, and sent me here. Someone needs to know here, where I have to work out my cure, if I can, and it seems that it must be you, if you are willing."

He was about to say that he wasn't sure he was, but she had already continued.

"The outfit I was with ran into a larger force of the enemy and within a few minutes everybody on our side had been killed but me and two others, one of whom was badly wounded. His buddy shot him, and then he was killed. I was captured and given to three peasant soldiers who were left behind to watch the road. One of them grabbed me and tore off my clothes. I fought him hard. They tied me to a tree and whipped me, and after that I didn't fight back anymore. I don't know how many times I was raped, but enough that I required sutures. Do you want me to go on?"

"No, I do not," he said emphatically.

"Anyway, on the third night I crawled out of my blanket— I had no clothes—and snuck off with the uniform and shoes of one of the soldiers. It was just sheer luck that I made it back to the Republican lines. I was half-crazy, but the Spanish doctor said similar things had happened to thousands of women during the Spanish Civil War and most came out of it all right. He implied that I hadn't seen much of the grim side of life, which the Spanish were all too well acquainted with. He also said I was very lucky to get out of it alive . . ."

"Catherine, I wish you hadn't told me this."

"Well, I have, haven't I, Alex, and now it can't be taken back. In some kind of way this makes you responsible for me. I needed to tell this to a man, before I found myself unable to talk about it at all. You see, I thought the act of love was about the finest thing you could experience, and then that same act became an act of torture and degradation. And I thought I could never let a man do that to me again. But if I can't give myself . . . You see? Will you help me?"

"I've already promised that. It's just that I don't know how."

"Just be with me for a while, and then we'll read the coffee grounds again and see what comes next."

The train pulled into the Luxor station, and a mass of people swarmed around it, porters, guides, carriage drivers, kids screaming for baksheesh, sellers of soft drinks and fried doughnuts and wreaths of jasmine blossoms. A suave tour guide arranged by Nadia, large and imposing in an elaborately embroidered *galabiya*, led them through this maelstrom, raising his staff threateningly at anyone who tried to block their way. In their wake came the three Slav models and the young men they had picked up on the train. At the place where the carriages were lined up, they waited for their effects. Catherine went over to the models and came back laughing.

"Our Slavs won't be needing their rooms at the Winter Palace. It turns out that their three young men are French archaeologists, just out of university, working in the Valley of the Kings across the Nile. They have rented a house there together, and they have invited our models to stay with them. These young Frenchmen are about to have an experience they won't forget for a long time."

Catherine laughed again and looked into the distance. It was the look of a woman in a Renaissance painting who turns her head to survey a faraway paradise from which she has been driven.

"I told them that was fine, but they had better show up sober tomorrow morning at the Winter Palace, at eight o'clock. I'd just as soon have them out of the way. I want to look things over, find the places where setting and light will work for what I want to do. Would it bore you to . . ."

"Catherine, when things bore me, I'll let you know."

The suave guide, Youssef, had already sent ahead the luggage and photographic equipment to the Winter Palace with the dazed little French technician, and now he helped everyone into the carriage.

"Youssef, take us to all the principal places, places that people will recall from photographs, especially places with people in costume and local color, palm trees and camels and all that, in the background. I will just take notes today, and I want to visit the Valley of the Kings this afternoon. Tomorrow I will photograph all day. I take it we can count on the weather."

Youssef laughed. "Madame, rain is an event here, and if you go some kilometers out into the Western desert, why, it rains only once in ten to twenty years."

"And while I'm working I can't have children tugging at my clothes and asking for baksheesh."

"Madam, there is only one way to get rid of them, give them all money to go away, to *imshee*. A few Egyptian pounds will buy the whole tribe of those pests."

"Whatever it takes."

For the rest of the morning they drove from one grand monument to another, down avenues of Sphinxes, past columns and obelisks and giant statues, beneath a sky like a glazed blue bowl. Catherine wore slacks and a silk blouse, sandals and dark glasses. From time to time she would have the carriage stop, push the dark glasses back on her blond hair, and make notes and quick sketches. She was quiet, precise and demanding, far from the frightened young woman who was struggling to get back her sanity.

They had lunch in the big, high-ceilinged dining room of the Winter Palace Hotel, a score of overhead fans rustling the long white curtains at the windows. After coffee, this coffee European, Catherine lit a cigarette and leaned back in her bamboo chair.

"Alex, I'd like to go alone with Youssef to the Valley of the Kings this afternoon. I've got so many ideas going that I have to be really focused, and having a handsome man along is distracting, particularly when he is as quiet as you were this morning."

"All right," he said.

"You have an endearing quality, Alex. Unlike most men, you know when to say little."

He did not reply, which seemed appropriate.

She looked at her wristwatch and got up. "Well, till this evening. A drink on the terrace?"

"Sure," he said.

After she had gone he went up to the room that, once again, had been reserved for the two of them. A single fan turned overhead and the shutters were closed, casting bars of intense Egyptian light across a wide bed, what the Italians call a *letto matrimoniale*.

He lay down for a while and was soon asleep. When he awoke from a dream of dark beating wings, it was with the thought that the time had come for him to begin to rid himself of that thing that had pursued him for so long.

He went down to the cavernous lobby of this grand hotel that had been host to crowned heads of Europe, to the czar. There was a wing-collared clerk behind the reception desk, but the lobby was empty at this hour of siesta. A big leather-bound ledger in which guests registered lay open, lighted by a goosenecked lamp.

He approached the desk. The clerk was a Levantine of some sort, Lebanese, Armenian, or any of a number of communities that had led separate existences under the now-defunct Ottoman Empire.

"Sir?"

"I'm a journalist with the *Paris Vogue* party."

"Yes, sir."

He put down his ANC calling card with a five-pound note neatly folded beneath it.

"I'm writing an article on a prominent French politician who supposedly stayed here in 1912, on a . . . private visit. It would be useful if I could verify this. I was wondering if you keep your registration records?"

The clerk picked up his calling card, looked at it, and handed it back to him. The five-pound note had disappeared with the slight-of-hand of a magician.

"We do. They are shelved in the office," and he nodded to an open door behind him, "if you would like to have a look."

He led Alex into the office and took down a huge red leather volume stamped "1912," laid it on a table, turned on a lamp and left him alone.

He flipped through to October 1912. There were hundreds of entries a week, but after a few dozen pages he found it: "(Mrs.) Alice Fraser, 14 Sharia Shagaret el-Dur, Cairo." This was followed by an American passport number. She had been here, and she had been alone. Two readings from coffee grounds. He had begun both a journey into the future with Catherine and a journey into the past alone.

Chapter Thirteen

By the time Catherine returned, twilight was fading into night, the sky that clear, burnished violet of Egyptian desert skies at that hour. The cliffs behind the Valley of the Kings were dark now, the Nile a silver ribbon, the palm trees against the sky silhouettes cut out of black paper. As she came toward him in the light of Japanese lanterns strung over the terrace, he saw that she was disheveled, her hair trailing in dark strings, her silk blouse stained with sweat. She sat down and lit a cigarette.

"I got it all done," she said, "and I could sure use a gin and tonic."

The waiter who brought her drink also brought a telegram. She read it and laughed.

"Nadia got Nicole to call the provincial governor, and he has issued orders that I am to be given every assistance in the cause of promoting tourism. With that, Nadia has been on to the police, who will provide a van tomorrow for the girls to change in, and several policemen to deal with any problems from the locals and their taboos. I wish Nadia worked for me."

"You can't have her," he said.

"Listen, Alex, I'm too keyed up for one of these endless meals they serve here, if you don't mind eating alone. I have an early start tomorrow, and I'll just have a snack sent up to the room, a bath and bed."

"Sure," he said. "Anyway, I may just have a sandwich in the bar."

After she had gone he ordered another drink and had a sandwich brought out with it. Bats flitted in and out of the light from the Japanese lanterns, and a trio of piano, bass and saxophone had begun to play.

When he got to the room it was dark but for a small bed-side lamp. Catherine was sitting up in bed in a nightgown writing in her notebook. She looked up at him.

"Alex, I'm sorry. The bed . . . I thought there would be two."

"It's a wide bed," he said, "and who but we world-weary sophisticates know? Besides, I've already been in bed with you twice, so why not a third time?"

"Alex, you are wonderful. This is very unfair, but there is nothing I can do about it, at least for now. I just hope you have found some female companionship in Cairo."

He said nothing, because he hadn't. It was the longest time he had been without a woman since he was in college, but until he had resolved the conundrum of Nadia and Catherine he had no appetite for alternatives. But now he had begun to despair of solving what he had come to call The Riddle of the Sphinx.

"Ready for bed?"

"Yes," he said, and went into the bathroom to change into pajamas. When he came out the room was dark. He got into bed, and it was so wide that Catherine was an arm's length away. He turned over. The shutters were open, and the moon hung over Luxor, the Valley of the Kings and the silver Nile. This is absurd, he thought and tried to go to sleep.

"Alex?"

"Yes."

"You have become my resident psychiatrist, and I was

wondering if you might want me as yours?"

He was surprised, astonished. "Do I need one?"

"We don't always see ourselves as others see us. Something is holding you in, isn't it, keeping you from being yourself, has for a long time, maybe."

"Is that what you see?"

"Yes. You don't give of yourself, do you?"

That hit home. "I told you that in Bahariya."

"What is this dark thing you saw pursuing you in the coffee grounds?"

He was silent for a long time, thinking about the awful thing she had confessed to him, and what else he knew from Nadia about it. Then he took the step that, like hers, could not be taken back.

"While you were out this afternoon, I checked the hotel records. My mother stayed here a long time ago, when I was barely a year old. There were some letters written to her that I found among her things, from Cairo, from a lover, who I think must be my father."

"Well, those things happen," Catherine said. "It doesn't have to ruin your life."

"I know that, but I have a dread of finding out who he is. He wouldn't be all that old, someone here in Egypt, or an American now back in America. I know it's not rational. There are leads I could follow, but I've avoided doing it."

"I might as well admit to something," Catherine said. "When you and Mansour came out on our balcony that night in Alexandria, I thought for a second or two, well, two good-looking Egyptians, until I realized it was you."

He thought back to looking at himself in the mirror that night in Alexandria, and of course it was true.

"I've suppressed that, I guess. I don't suppose the Egyptian father really bothers me, it's the who exactly."

"Dr. Molyneux's advice is to find out and be rid of the dark thing, though, God knows, who am I to give advice like that?"

Again there was silence, and they were left alone with their thoughts, until he felt Catherine's hand searching for and finding his. It lay there without gripping his hand, or even moving. It was just as clear as if she had said it out loud that what happened next was up to him, and he would bear the responsibility for it. That too was unfair, he thought.

"Catherine, what passes between us is completely private."

"I know that."

"You have been, shall we say, brutally frank with me. I don't know whether I can help you, but I certainly can't unless I am brutally frank with you. Can you take that?"

"I can take anything you say, as long as it's honest."

"That is a given."

"Well, then?"

"What you fear is being penetrated, isn't it?"

"More than fear, a terror."

"Suppose that card is simply taken off the table."

"And?"

"I don't need to tell a sophisticated woman that there are all kinds of hands that can be played without that card."

"Except that I could not respond. Every place that could has been violated. I cannot do anything for you."

"I can handle that. Under those conditions?"

"I could try, but I may have to call it quits at any moment."

"I understand."

Her answer was to sit up in bed and, in the moonlight, pull her nightgown over her head and lie back down.

For a long time he let his hand run as lightly as possible

over her body, her breasts and stomach and thighs. He made no attempt to kiss her, just his hand. She was tense but not rigid, unmoving, her breathing regular and deep. For a while he let his hand rest on her pelvic bone, and then let it glide down into the tangle of hair, put it squarely onto the wet warmth between her legs. She gasped, nothing more.

"I could bring back something you've lost," he said.

He took her silence for acquiescence, and with two fingers felt out that place that has the feel of a sea creature, a place of tides and moon, that when touched quivers, contracts, then swells, and when touched over time in the right way releases spasms that overwhelm every nerve in a woman's body. And it happened just like that, raising Catherine's tightened buttocks off the bed, bringing a cry up from deep within her throat.

After the spasms had subsided, Catherine spoke only once. "At last."

The alarm rang when the sun was not yet up, but the sky was already bright with reflected light from the desert. Catherine got out of bed and, in her nightgown, went to her suitcase and got out some underwear. Before she had lost so much weight, she must have had a superb figure that even now was beginning to reemerge. As she passed the foot of the bed she paused.

"You are a gallant gentleman, Alex."

"My pleasure."

You would have thought he had offered her some refined courtesy rather than what he had done—although he wasn't entirely certain that that was what she was referring to.

"When the time comes—and now I'm beginning to hope I can overcome this thing—I will repay you with interest."

"In this business we don't keep books, Catherine. And

don't feel sorry for me. There is such a thing as psychic satisfaction."

She went into the bathroom and came out fully dressed. She sat down at the dressing table and combed out her hair.

"I'm going to skip breakfast. I want to get some early morning shots, and it's going to take me some time to set up. Join me whenever you like. I'm going to start at the Temple of Luxor."

"I'll be along after a while."

She applied makeup and tied a silk scarf around her head as a bandana. She looked at her wristwatch and put a strap bag over her shoulder.

"*A bientôt.*"

As the door closed behind her he realized that her life, and his, were now changed. Maybe the cure had begun, and his risky proposal of the night before had been the right one at the right time. He had never been a risk taker, but now perhaps he was about to become one. He would have plenty of opportunity.

There was not only the question of his relations with a woman who was having serious emotional problems and the question of his paternity he had revealed to that woman. There was another mystery that could not, for his safety—and Catherine's—be left to just lie there. Why was the group they had been brought into placing shortwave radios in remote parts of Egypt? He recalled something Robert Browning had said, and although he was talking about poetry, Alex felt it applied to him. If you want to succeed you have to get out there on the dangerous edge of things. Maybe that's where he wanted to be.

He had breakfast on the terrace and then walked over past Thos. Cook & Son to the vast Temple of Luxor. Clusters of

tourists had already gathered around their guides in red tarbooshes and *galabiyas*. He arrived at where Catherine and her
technician had their equipment set up just as the three tall
Slavic models in Middle Eastern–inspired fashions emerged
from the police van that was their dressing room. A more sur-
realistic scene you could not have asked for.

Catherine handled the models the way a trainer might
handle horses or prize dogs. Every placement of a limb, every
angle of a jaw had to be exact, and maintained without the
slightest movement. She adjusted their hair, the fall of their
garments, directed her technician in holding up reflectors
that lightened shadows or created contrast.

And then she began shooting with two Rolleiflex cameras
on tripods, taking in one or two or all three of the models. A
group of young Egyptian men in *galabiyas* had gathered, but
the police kept them at a distance. He remembered the saying
that genius is the ability to take infinite pains, and he had the
suspicion that Catherine Molyneux was the genius that some
people said she was.

By the middle of the day they had moved on, and
Catherine finished shooting at the Temple of Karnak. A van
from the Winter Palace arrived, an open tent was set up, a
table and chairs, and a cold lunch was laid out, with champagne in ice buckets, for the six of them. The models went at
the food and champagne as though they were starving refugees. Probably once they had been.

"Well," Catherine said to them, "how was your night in
the Valley of the Kings?"

"The French boys," the Russian said, "much enthusiasm
but not too much experience. Now they have more."

"But was fun," the Pole said.

"More fun when we get back to Cairo. Nightclubs and
dancing there. I know a Russian place."

"If you give me your best after lunch," Catherine said, "down by the Nile, with the *faluccas,* maybe that can be tonight. I've got nine rolls already, and it's good stuff. I have made reservations on the evening flight to Cairo, just in case we could finish today."

They did make the evening flight to Cairo, and as the plane descended toward the lights of the city, he thought again of that tired phrase about past being prologue. But now it was not just time and place and events that were the body of the text of things to come. He had changed, and with that the formula that determined what the future held had been altered, and he did not yet know what the new algorithm was.

Part Two

THE DANGEROUS EDGE

Chapter Fourteen

Whatever the algorithm was that governed the consequences of Alex Fraser's actions—and, presumably, his fate—was already in place by the time he returned to Cairo. Nothing was quite the same, and when he took some action the results were not what he would have expected. He was now part of some new game that was being revealed like a hand of cards dealt out on the table and turned faceup one by one.

The first card was a telegram from Arvid Dahlsted that Nadia handed him in a too offhand way. The new ANC correspondent in Athens—he hadn't known there was one—spoke Hebrew, and it made sense to add coverage of Palestine to his portfolio and take it from Alex's. That left Alex with Egypt, and he was to continue to follow the directions he had been given in Washington. He knew these to be not to file copy just for the sake of filing copy, but to report only stories that ANC's competitors could be counted on to file, to widen and deepen his contacts in Egypt, so as to be ready for the war that Arvid and he—and practically every well-informed person in Egypt—thought would be coming soon. But now he was convinced that when war came, he would be asked to do something more than just report.

"Well, how was it?" Nadia said.

She was wearing a pale green linen blouse, more jewelry that looked as though it had come from an ancient Egyptian tomb, and heavy makeup around the eyes. Nefertiti, he thought again.

"Was what?"

"Upper Egypt, of course."

"Just like the postcards."

"And the Slavic models?"

"They gave three young French archeologists an experience you don't usually get on digs."

Nadia laughed, and he had the impression she already knew this, had already talked with Catherine.

"And Catherine?"

"She's very impressive at work. You can see why she's at the top of her profession."

"What I meant was . . ."

"Her emotional state."

"Yes."

"Getting better, maybe."

"She told me that you were good for her."

So Catherine and Nadia had already been on the phone.

"I don't know about that, but I'm trying—as you asked me to do."

The second card had been turned. The relations between Nadia and him, as tentative as they were, had changed, and it was she who had willed it. He was now part of an other, an other that consisted of Catherine and himself.

And then he turned the third and—he was pretty sure—critical card, win or lose. Since he was a child he had been stalked by something from the land of Egypt, but suddenly he had become the stalker. He couldn't do much better than to begin by finding out who he was.

The goldsmith's shop that had crafted the ring into which the seal stone with a butterfly and grapes had been set was deep in the Muski, the Cairo bazaar that had remained virtually unchanged since the Middle Ages. Merchants sat cross-legged on wooden platforms outside the narrow, dark shops that held their goods, brass and copper, alabaster and amber, woolens and printed cottons. He paused outside the goldsmith's shop. It had a hint of modernity to it, with expensive German cameras and Swiss watches in the window, from which the scrolled, gold leaf name, Gulderian, Purveyors of Jewelry to the Khedive of Egypt, was peeling with age.

His opening the door to the shop rang a bell. A small man with heavy features, wavy, pomaded hair and gold-rimmed glasses emerged from the rear, parting a beaded curtain and revealing a half-open safe door that would have done credit to a metropolitan bank.

"May I be of assistance, sir?"

He took off the ring he was wearing and handed it to the man.

"I believe this ring was made by your firm, around 1912. I am in Cairo for the first time, and I thought I would take the opportunity to try and find out for whom the ring was made. My family is in the cotton trade in America and in those days had several business connections in Egypt. I would like to be in touch with whoever had this ring made as a gift for my father, who is now deceased, and perhaps pay a call on him. I might also want to bring back some nice piece of jewelry for my wife."

He said this with a glance around the glass cases filled with expensive pieces of gold set with gems.

The Armenian jeweler took a loupe out of a vest pocket and screwed it into his eye.

"The year *is* 1912, the month July. Yes, I think I could find a record of the order. I am the fourth Gulderian to head the firm, and we must keep good records. We have sometimes made wedding rings for three generations of a family who are our clients. If you will just wait a moment, I will bring out the records for 1912."

The jeweler disappeared through the beaded curtain and returned in a few minutes with a large ledger. It was like the performance at the Winter Palace Hotel, when he had discovered that his mother had been staying there in October of 1912. This was easier than he had expected.

Gulderian turned the pages of the ledger and then abruptly stopped. His heavy eyebrows shot up.

"One twenty-six . . . and then one twenty-nine. What is this?"

He reinserted the loupe into his eye, examined where the pages joined.

"The pages for the last days of July have been cut out—very carefully. This is extraordinary, unheard of. Only members of my family have access to these records. What is going on here?"

He looked up at Alex as though he were in some way responsible for this desecration of the Gulderian records.

"I'm sorry . . ."

"Might I have your name, sir?"

He decided that lying was not the best policy. He might need Gulderian again, and what he had said so far was mostly true, even if meant to deceive.

He handed Gulderian his business card.

"A foreign correspondent. But you said . . ."

"I have just arrived in Egypt. Should you solve the mystery of the missing page, I would appreciate a call."

"Yes, of course."

He left the shop baffled, but sure of one thing. An Armenian jeweler of Egypt might plumb levels of duplicity that he had not even dreamed of, but the jeweler's astonishment at finding his own records mutilated was not feigned.

He did not phone Catherine after their return to Cairo, because he was no longer so sure what had passed between them that night at Luxor was as positive as he had believed the next morning. And she did not try to get in touch with him, which only fed his doubts that he had done the right thing.

However, the next Sunday he went to the Gezira Club for a swim and the buffet lunch, and Catherine was there and warm and friendly. She was in the same chaise longue by the pool, in the same blue swimsuit and wearing dark glasses. He brought up a stool and sat down beside her.

"What news?" he said.

"Paris is ecstatic about the Luxor photographs. Next month's cover will be the profile of our Russian up against the profile of Queen Hapshetsut carved in honey-colored stone, with a twelve-page spread inside. How's that?"

"I'm very glad for you."

"Was it okay for you?"

"Of course."

"I'm sorry about putting us in bed together all the time. But we had a good talk, didn't we?"

"Yes."

"You are going to look into the question of who your father is, aren't you?"

"Yes."

"After that we talked about something else, but I can't remember just what. I must have been mostly asleep."

"Oh, just this and that."

A cold chill had run through his body. What had passed between them sexually had been erased from her mind. Rather than bringing her back toward reality, he had become a part of the censored film.

"Actually," he said, "I've already begun to follow up on the leads as to whom my father is. You remember the ring of my mother's that Artemesia looked at in the Fayum?"

"Of course."

"I believe it was given to my mother by whoever my father is. I went to the jeweler's where it was made and asked him if he could find a record of the purchase. When he looked at his records, the page where the purchase should have been entered had been torn out."

"I don't like that, Alex."

"Nor do I."

"Do you have other leads?"

"One. I have some letters written to my mother in Luxor on Gezira Club stationery. The return address is a mailbox in the club office, number 123."

"Mine is 154. I suppose I could sneak a look at what name is on 123. Wait here."

Catherine got up, pulled the saffron caftan over her head, put on rope espadrilles and walked in the direction of the club office. Half an hour later she returned.

"I managed to distract the little man at the club office long enough for me to sneak behind the counter and look at the name on Box 123. Ian Stuart. I happen to know him. He's about thirty-five years old and certainly not your father. Then I made up some cock-and-bull story that allowed me to ask the question of whether old member records were kept by the club, including such things as who the mailboxes had belonged to.

"Yes, I was told, all records are kept forever, because this is Egypt, and because this is Egypt no one ever looks again at records once they are stored away. Probably there are hundreds of boxes in the attic of the club office which were just shoved in, one box after another in no kind of order, and finding any specific record would be quite impossible."

"So, why don't we try?"

"What do you mean?"

"A little breaking and entering one night soon."

He had been joking, or rather he had been expressing a wish to do something he knew was not possible. What was preoccupying him was the chilling discovery that what had passed between Catherine and him in a bed in the Winter Palace Hotel had been completely expunged from her memory. He had not only done her no good, he had apparently set back her cure.

He spent the next week in the limbo he had been assigned to, meeting and getting to know people in preparation for what might or might not happen in the weeks and months ahead. The following Sunday he again went to the Gezira Club for a swim and the buffet, and found Catherine doing laps in the pool, in a rubber cap and goggles, with the determination of an athlete in training. He sat on the edge of the pool with his legs dangling in the tepid water until she came out.

"Well, I've got things set up for you," she said, without any introduction.

"In what way?"

"The storeroom where the old club records are kept is the attic space over the club office. The men's and women's dressing rooms are on each side, and there is an outside staircase at the back of the building. I have a copy of the key to the storeroom door . . ."

"How did you . . ."

"Don't ask. I'm a bit nuts, you know. The crazy are granted a kind of cunning not available to the sane. Anyway, the only problem is a night watchman who punches a time clock at the club office at twenty minutes after each hour. You should be able to work around that easily. All you will need is a flashlight, and in a night or two, who knows?"

"But I can't do that."

"Then why did you bring it up?"

"But I wasn't really serious."

"I think you were. You do want to know who had Box 123 in 1912, don't you?"

"Yes."

"Well?"

And so it was that at half-past twelve the next night, after having a drink with Catherine in her apartment in the club guest quarters, he crossed the drive and went through the eucalyptus trees to the rear of the club office. It was a Monday night, when the club closed early, and there was not a sound and no lights but the outside security lights. He climbed the stairs, turned the key in the lock and went inside, turning on his flashlight and locking the door behind him.

There were literally hundreds of boxes the length of the long storeroom, some of cardboard, some light wooden boxes that, from the labels, had originally contained vegetables and fruits for the club kitchen. An aisle had been created down the center of the storeroom. If there was any method in how the boxes were arranged, it was not apparent. But, eventually, he made out that the records had been brought in and dumped at the end of four islands of boxes that began at the door. Two islands had reached the wall in one direction, the other two islands were halfway to the opposite wall.

The completed islands consisted of records from the 1880s to around 1915, the still-incomplete ones of records that ended only the year before. That was the general principle, the path of least resistance for the porters who had hauled the boxes up. But here and there boxes completely out of sequence had been tossed willy-nilly on top of the piles, and a number of boxes had broken open, and their contents had spilled out, revealing the considerable damage done by mice and insects.

By two o'clock in the morning, choking on dust and covered with it, he had staked out an area centered around the year 1912. He had one advantage. The boxes, by and large, contained records from one source: the restaurant; the bar; the sports accounts, polo, tennis, golf; membership; the library and periodicals; employee records; and the postal facility. The last contained receipts for registered mail, purchase and sale of stamps, and bills for box rental.

At ten minutes after four in the morning he came across the record of box rentals for 1912, the silverfish gliding away from the beam of his flashlight. The pages were so ravaged by insects that they looked like lace. Each box number had opposite it a name, followed by initials and the amount due and date paid. All that remained opposite Box 123 was part of a name, "Simaic . . ."

He broke off the fragment of dry paper and ground it to dust between his thumb and forefinger. Now the only record that remained of Box 123, for the year 1912, was locked away in the cells of his brain.

Chapter Fifteen

Over the next several days he pondered his one glance at a fragment of yellowed paper, with part of a name written on it in ink in a script that derived from some school in Egypt where the writer had been taught orthography, probably a French school, since the club records were kept in French. The name might have a different ending from the one that seemed obvious and, even if it didn't, how many Simathas were there in Cairo? And since the initials were missing, which of the Simathas had rented Box 123 for 1912? He would have to settle these questions before he could reach any firm conclusion.

But he knew all this was sophistry. He had repeated on a larger scale in the club attic his experience in the closet under the stairs in his grandmother's house, and the mystery had been solved.

That he had been by chance brought to Egypt to work alongside his half-sister was a coincidence that defied the odds. He had taken a course in astronomy at the University of Virginia, and his professor had made the point that when the odds reach a number of a certain magnitude, the question of coincidence can be dismissed: It would simply not occur. That being clearly the case, who had brought him to Egypt, and why? His professor had also pointed out that when the odds are extremely low, it is perfectly justified to assume that the obvious answer is the correct one.

Why had Nadia Simatha brought him to Egypt, and with

whose assistance? At least Nadia's attitude toward him now made sense. Incest is not lightly regarded in any society. Where did this leave him? That he had visited Gulderian's to try and find out who had had the ring made was now probably known to those who were manipulating his life. That he had actually found the postal box record for 1912 could not be known, and that he had done so involved odds almost as astronomical as those his professor had cited. As far as Catherine was concerned, he saw no choice but to take the line that the task of finding a specific record in the club office attic was as hopeless as it had been described to her.

This left the central question of just what was going on that he had been drawn into. He resolved to confront this directly as soon as there was a good opportunity. Such an opportunity came along sooner than he expected, in fact was thrust on him. He received an invitation from Chris Weston to "a small dinner party" he was giving at his apartment in downtown Cairo.

Since Egypt had begun to be industrialized around the turn of the century, the European companies—and two or three American ones—that had arrived to divide up the pie, had begun to erect office buildings in downtown Cairo for their headquarters, renting out the rest of the space. Atop each building there was usually an apartment with large terraces, what we would call a penthouse, usually occupied by the company's local manager or rented out to someone who could afford it. This apparently included Chris Weston, personal assistant to the American minister to Egypt.

Alex was the first to arrive except for the gorgeous Simira, the pale-skinned Middle Eastern woman, no last name given, who had been with Chris when Alex had last seen him on the houseboat restaurant, and Fran, one of the secretaries he had met at the legation. While they waited for the others—from a glance at the dining table there would be seven more guests—Chris took him out on a terrace laden with exotic plants for a look at Cairo by night.

"It's vast," he said. "Down there are hundreds of thousands of Egyptians milling about in all those lighted streets and dim alleyways, with hardly a clue as to how their lives are being directed by foreigners on our level, where penthouses float like ships in the night. We'll be replaced, of course, by Egyptians, educated enough, or shrewd enough, to take our place, but that's a few years off yet . . . Excuse me. There are some other guests arriving."

And in ones and twos they arrived, Basil, Artemesia, Nicole, Selim Essabi, and then Catherine and Nadia.

While drinks were being passed out by *suffragis,* Chris came up to him.

"I think you already know most of the others."

"I know them all," he said.

He looked across the dimly lit room, with its wall hangings emblazoned with Arabic letters, fragments of Graeco-Roman sculpture, and miniature palms in ceramic urns. He caught Nadia's eye, and her look was the inscrutable sphinx one, and then Catherine's, who gave an almost imperceptible shrug and lifting of the eyebrows, as if she had done something not quite in good form, and had been caught at it.

"Why are they here?"

"Your chums are feeling the heat from unfriendly quarters, and the purpose of this evening—each of them having undoubtedly been followed to the Firestone building—is to make the point that the American legation is not indifferent to the fate of the—what is it that you call yourselves?—the Narcissians."

"And the 'unfriendly quarters'?"

"Why don't we go out on the terrace again? The moon will be coming up over Cairo."

And it was, ragged in the dust over the city, like the skin torn off half an orange.

"Egyptian cigarette?" Chris said, holding out a pack.

He took one, as he usually did when he felt under pressure.

"Perfumed," he said.

"Ground cloves, from the island of Zanzibar, for centuries a source of cloves and slaves for the Omanis, and thence to Egypt . . . The unfriendly quarters? Well, they don't reveal themselves, but I suppose there is some specific organization. There usually is, isn't there? However, the milieu from which the unfriendliness comes is fairly clear."

Chris Weston sighed, as though he regretted having to get into particulars, but then went on. There was a bit of Lawrence of Arabia about this performance.

"French *rentiers,* English owners of stately homes, British and French fascists—manipulated by the first two groups— half-crazy soreheads who fancy they could do for Britain and France what Hitler has done to Germany."

"So the French coupon-clippers and the milords, what are they after?"

"Let me give you two statistics. First, half the land in England, outside the cities, is owned by a mere eight thousand families. Second, Suez Canal Company bonds are by far the most attractive investment in the world."

"How so?"

"No capital expenditures. Unlike the Panama Canal, there are no locks. Suez is just a ditch dug between the Mediterranean and the Persian Gulf, and only minimum maintenance is required. I learned a lot about this when I was vice-consul in Port Said.

"As canal traffic increases year by year, so do revenues, but costs remain more or less the same, decade after decade. Then, your investment is watched over by the French and British governments. The French because it's their baby, the British because it's their lifeline to their colonial empire, that is to say India. So you have an investment that's currently paying a dividend of sixty percent per annum, about ten times what a 'good' investment pays, with virtually no risk . . . unless there is an Arab uprising, or there is war. It makes the ruling classes in France and England nervous about anything that might rock this boat."

"I fail to see what all this has to do with a small group of people too young to be powerful who socialize together."

"Well, it does. Why don't you get Nadia Simatha to explain it to you?"

They had moved back into the main room of the apartment. Chris Weston looked at his wristwatch.

"Now, where's Antonius? He's always on time. I'd better give a call. We can't sit down to dinner with an empty chair," Chris said, walking away.

Alex didn't see why they couldn't sit down to dinner with an empty chair, and he also didn't see why he should get Nadia to explain anything to him. He would approach Nadia only when it was to his advantage. He sat down on a camel saddle converted into a stool, and at that moment Nadia broke away from the others and came over to the dimly lit corner where he sat, his drink on a huge brass tray beside him. Down the hall a phone was ringing. Nadia sat down on a camel saddle opposite him, took a cigarette out of an inlaid wooden box on the round brass table and lit it. She was wearing a black dress with pearls, this assistant of his, who Mansour had said would one day be one of the richest women in Egypt.

172

"Alex," she began, but the sentence was never finished. Chris appeared from the dark hallway and stood above them.

"Antonius," he said. "There's been an accident. Coming here, he was hit by a taxi crossing the Sharia Magrabi."

Both he and Nadia stood up.

"Not badly hurt?" Nadia said.

"Critical."

All three of them sat down.

"I was about to pick up the phone when it rang. It was the legation doctor. Some Egyptian doctor who happened to be at the scene of the accident had determined that Antonius was pretty much smashed to pieces, recovered his papers and, since Antonius headed an American company, called the legation. The Marine guard on duty at the legation, who is given copies of guest lists for the evening, told him that I was giving a dinner party to which Antonius had been invited. But instead of calling here, the Egyptian doctor called our legation doctor . . ."

There was a long silence, while three people pursued their private thoughts.

"Antonius, if he is still alive, is being taken to the American Hospital on Gezira, and both doctors are going there. There is apparently something peculiar about the accident, but our doctor wouldn't say anything more. He said he would call when he knows more . . . maybe in an hour or two."

"So, what do we do now?" Nadia said.

"I think we should go on with the dinner, tell the others after we know more," Chris said. "There's nothing anyone can do now."

Alex found this exchange strangely cold-blooded, as he did the vivacity with which Nadia and Chris carried on conversation with the others during dinner. It was as though what had happened to Antonius Modiano had come as no great surprise to them.

After they had retired to the main room for coffee the phone rang again, and Chris was gone for some time. When he returned he beckoned Nadia and Alex to join him in the alcove with the brass tray and camel saddles. It was the first time he had seen the ever-cool Chris Weston show emotion, his voice breaking.

"Doctor Baker says that there are contusions on Antonius's body that are incompatible with an automobile accident. In fact, Antonius was already badly injured when he was hit by the taxi. His body must have been thrown in its way."

"The contusions?" Alex said.

"The doctor said they were deliberately made, and for lack of a better explanation, he would say they are the result of Antonius being tortured."

An image came to his mind of several of them sitting on the sand at Ras Zafarana on the Red Sea, where the Belgian woman had died while floating on the water, an image of the surf coming in, hissing across the dry sand and withdrawing, leaving a glistening surface quite unlike what had been there a few seconds before.

"*Quel horreur,*" Nadia said in a choked voice.

Well, Alex thought, we've come to the heart of the matter now. Two phone calls and his newfound friends' evasions and intrigues had been swept away like dry sand.

"What are we going to do?" Chris said, his composure now utterly shattered.

"You might begin by telling the truth," Alex said.

"Yes," Chris said in a vague voice. "I'll leave that to Nadia. I had better go tell the others."

"Wait," Nadia said sharply. "Somebody must get over to

Antonius's apartment straight away."

"Right," Chris said, "but who?"

"Basil," Nadia said, "he's strong and fearless. He carries a pistol, you know—it's a Russian thing."

"Right. I'll speak to him."

When Chris had left them, Nadia and he sat looking at each other, each waiting for the other to speak. Finally, he did.

"Why don't you put all the cards out on the table, Nadia, faceup? It will save time."

"There are an awful lot of cards," she said and smiled. "What is it mainly you want to know, Alex?"

"First, what is a social club, the Narcissians, up to that would lead to one of its members being attacked in this way?"

"Yes. Actually, one of the purposes of this evening was to bring you fully into what's going on . . . but then . . ."

"Go on, and it might help to start at the beginning."

"The beginning, yes." She looked through the open doors on Cairo by night as though she were looking into the past.

"The University of Lausanne, on Lake Geneva, 1908. There were a number of students from Middle Eastern countries, from various minority communities within the Ottoman Empire, Jews, Greeks, Armenians, Lebanese Christians, Copts, although our status was somewhat different. An organization was formed with the purpose of promoting the overthrow of the Ottoman Empire. The representatives from Egypt were my father, the father of Selim and Mansour, and Victor Halevy, who went on to study under Freud and became Catherine's psychiatrist."

This was so close to the version Catherine had given him, based partly on what Nadia had told her, that Alex could only assume this was the line Nadia put out when pressed.

"But then the Ottoman Empire collapsed, there was the

debacle of the Great War in the Middle East, and the minorities found themselves subjects of so-called protectorates of the British and French in Lebanon and Syria, Palestine and Egypt. The objective changed to getting the British and French out of the Middle East, which meant joining cause with like-minded Arabs."

But at this point Nadia's version veered off from that of Catherine.

"Then came the rise of Hitler and Mussolini," she went on, "and if they conquered Europe, the fate of the minorities in the Middle East became even more menacing. So the objective changed once again. By then the active role had been passed to a new generation—in Egypt the code name was the Narcissians—and we began taking measures to ready ourselves for the war we saw coming."

"Such as placing shortwave radios in obscure places in Egypt."

"Yes," she said as though she were aware that he had already discovered this. "That's why Antonius was brought in. He represented two of the minorities, but more important, he represented the American company RCA in Egypt. The radios are only one of many things that have been done in the last few years to position ourselves."

"In relation to what?"

"The Suez Canal, of course. That's what it's all about, has been for the last seventy years. The British and the French—and the Germans—don't give a damn about Egypt or Palestine or Syria. These are just chips in the game of the canal, who controls it, whether it stays open or is closed. All the rest is just dust kicked in the eyes of the public, the press, other governments."

"Chris Weston?"

"American oil interests. Six years ago a new nation was

created, Saudi Arabia, and the American companies moved in, found vast quantities of oil, began drilling. The first shipments from the Dhahran fields are now beginning to pass through the Suez Canal. Our organization has made common cause with you Americans, secretly and at the highest level . . . Isn't that enough for now? After all, what has happened tonight should be uppermost in our minds."

This seemed to him the moment when Nadia's defenses were as down as they were likely to get. By tomorrow the ramparts of deception and evasion would be repaired.

"Yes, I agree. But there is one other thing. You know who my father is."

He had to admire the calm coolness with which she said, "A cotton broker, I believe."

"My real father."

He thought that the jolt this gave her was at least as powerful as that of the news about Antonius.

"How did you find out?" she said without any discernible emotion, but incredulously.

"There were letters that my mother kept, written on Gezira Club stationery."

She could not know that the letters were unsigned, that he had only found a name a few nights before in a pile of crumbling records in a Gezira Club storeroom.

"Yes, 1913. It was tragic."

"And my father?"

"Your father, why dead."

"Dead? What are you talking about, dead?"

"My Uncle Simon—I was assuming you must know—died in the same typhoid epidemic that killed your mother."

Chapter Sixteen

And so in one evening all was swept away, as though a *khamseen*—the wind that comes out of the Libyan desert and for days on end ravages the Nile valley—had scourged his life. It was as though such a wind had overturned one of those large Egyptian storage jars and scattered its contents across a tiled floor, bits and pieces of things as strange as the contents of his mother's trunk had been to him. But now these objects could be picked up one by one and made to yield their secrets.

Now he knew that Nadia Simatha—if they were indeed down to the bedrock of truth—was not his sister. She was, however, his cousin, and why that should have led to his being lured to Egypt could be examined with less of a sense of emotional urgency than before. That the Narcissians were involved in something deadly serious was no longer in question. Basil Artimanoff had gone to Antonius's apartment and found a wall safe open and empty. It was an American Diebold safe, made by the firm that Antonius's father had represented in Istanbul, and beyond the capabilities of local safecrackers. Antonius had been made to open it, and whatever its contents they were now known to the enemy, and who or what this force might be was still unclear.

He went down to the office the next morning and was informed by Hassan that Nadia had phoned in sick. This did not surprise him. Her glittering crystal armor had been shattered. There was someone else whose façade of cool cynicism had been breached—Chris Weston. Alex figured he would start there, and he phoned the American legation. The phone was answered by Fran, who said she had been told to anticipate a call from him, and Chris had said that if Alex wanted to talk to him, they could meet at Groppi's, a Swiss-owned ice cream parlor and patisserie where Cairo society was accustomed to going for tea. It was a place to be seen, not a place where one would expect to be invited to discuss secret matters, so perhaps it was a good place for just that.

The hour chosen for their meeting was toward the end of teatime at Groppi's, the sky over Cairo pink, with shoals of salmon-colored little clouds riffled across it. The last tables of Egyptian and foreign ladies were folding their napkins, putting out their cigarettes in heavy glass ashtrays bearing the names of various French and Italian aperitifs. As he came through the glass doors, the headwaiter motioned Alex to follow him, and they went down a corridor to a small dining room where Chris Weston was waiting for him.

They exchanged some inconsequential remarks, then Chris said, "I have to go to the men's room."

Then he put a finger across his lips, took Alex by the wrist and led him out the door, closing it behind them.

Once outside, he released Alex's wrist and said in a low voice, "The room will have a listening device planted somewhere. They'll be listening to a lot of silence for the next hour or two."

At the end of the dark corridor there was a door with a sign, "Emergency Exit," in French, English and Arabic. Chris leaned against it and they were out in a narrow alley malodorous from piles of garbage. From there they went on to a wider alley, a narrow street, a boulevard where no Europeans were to be seen, then into another narrow street, another narrow alley. There they entered an Arab eating place where small dark cakes danced in a big copper pot of boiling oil.

"Tahamiya," Chris said, "broad beans ground into paste and fried. You break them open and they're bright green inside. Why don't we have a plateful as appetizers? You can have beer too, if you like. This is a Copt-owned place."

"Yes to both," he said.

Chris spoke to a man who appeared to be the owner in Arabic, of which Alex understood not a word, and they were led to a table at the back of the long narrow room. The beer and the bean cakes arrived almost instantly, along with pieces of flat *balady* bread and a bowl of sesame seed paste covered in olive oil and decorated with a design in paprika.

"Well," Chris said, breaking open a bean cake, which was indeed bright green inside, "what do you want to know?"

"The truth, the whole truth, and all that."

He was feeling very confident now, and he was in no mood to be gentle with Chris Weston or any of the others who had deceived and used him.

"I'm afraid I can't do that. I don't have access to the whole truth."

"You certainly gave the impression that you did."

"I didn't have much choice, a junior foreign service officer sucked into something much bigger than I knew existed. What you have been seeing is someone treading water, trying to keep afloat."

This sounded very like the truth to Alex, and he said, "How did you get into this?"

"Harry Hopkins."

"Harry Hopkins?" Alex was too stunned to say more. As a White House correspondent he had, only occasionally, been given access to Hopkins, FDR's most trusted adviser, for a background briefing on some issue.

180

"I was on loan to the White House from the State Department, because I speak Arabic, and the President was getting interested in the whole question of Middle Eastern oil. Then one day Ickes called."

"Harold Ickes, the Secretary of the Interior?"

"Who else? He's responsible for federal lands and any mineral resources they may contain. A very sensitive area, ever since Warren Harding and the Teapot Dome scandal. Ickes had been approached by a representative of a consortium of American oil companies that had been exploring for oil in the Arabian peninsula, under an agreement with the Saud family, who had defeated their tribal opponents and had formed a government in what is now known as Saudi Arabia, that was recognized by the League of Nations. George Crane would have been gratified. You do know George Crane?"

"I don't think so."

"Well, if you've used a urinal or a toilet in America, you know George Crane."

"The plumbing fixture Crane."

"The Versailles peace treaty after the Germans were defeated in the Great War, provided not only for self-determination for the small ethnic entities of southeastern Europe, but also for the minorities of the now-defunct Ottoman Empire. This was Wilson's doing, and to say that his vision was naïve and impractical now seems obvious. But then it wasn't all that obvious. No one knew what would come out of the breakup of the old order in the Middle East.

"In any case a commission was set up to work out the future of Syria, Lebanon and Palestine. George Crane was named by Wilson as the American representative, and he was, of course, snookered by the British and the French, who had troops on the ground in those places. The British had promised Abdullah, the Grand Mufti of Mecca, who had fought with Lawrence of Arabia to this end, Palestine. The problem was that the British had also promised Palestine to British Zionists, who had contributed financially to the Allied cause.

"The end result was that a piece of desert back of Palestine, that they named Transjordan, was given to Abdullah's family, and Palestine was left in limbo, the British being too conscious of the importance of Arab oil to just hand Palestine over to the Jews. George Crane left the proceedings a very angry man, and he decided to try to do something for the Arabs with his considerable private fortune. What he did was to send out a team to Arabia to drill for water, in hopes of making a better life for the desert Arabs. What they found, of course, was not water but oil.

"Thereafter the story becomes murky until American companies found what is probably the largest reserve of petroleum in the world. People kill for such things, you know."

"And now the oil of Saudi Arabia is beginning to flow out through the Suez Canal."

"Yes."

"And Antonius Modiano has been tortured, his safe broken into."

"Not by our side."

"By who then?"

Chris Weston shrugged.

"By British milords and French *rentiers* and British and French fascists?"

"The truth may be somewhere in there."

"But why?"

"It has to do with the canal."

"By now I understand that, but why exactly?"

"Frankly, Alex, I don't know. Look, I was given leave of

absence by the State Department, at the White House's request, to represent the American oil companies' interests, as 'personal assistant' to the American minister in Cairo. I was flown to Texas and California and Indiana to be briefed by the companies, and then I found myself in Cairo, with instructions to get in touch with a clandestine group of wealthy and influential representatives of minority communities in the Middle East. I work with this group, but I'm not part of the inner circle."

"Who is?"

"The Simathas, the Essabis and Halevy."

"Which explains Catherine's involvement."

"I suppose."

"What about Artemesia Chakerian and Basil Artimanoff?"

"They wanted the Armenians and Georgians represented."

"Would Artemesia be related to the Gulderians who own a string of jewelry stores?"

"All Armenians are related to each other."

"That leaves Nicole Leigh, married to an Englishman and the daughter of a French general. Hardly a Middle Eastern minority."

"Her father served in Syria. Her mother is a Lebanese Christian."

The owner of the restaurant approached their table and spoke softly to Chris in Arabic.

"There is someone watching the front of the restaurant, Hakim says."

"Then out the back door again?"

"No, there'll be somebody there as well. But there's another way."

The man called Hakim led them up a narrow staircase, along a corridor, and then down another narrow staircase that led to a door opening onto another street. They came out on a busy *midan* and parted ways.

The next Sunday morning, the eight of them—the Narcissians less Antonius Modiano and plus Chris Weston— got onto one of the Essabis' DC-3s at their private airfield outside Cairo and flew up to Alexandria and then veered west along the Mediterranean coast to Mersa Matruh, two-thirds of the way to the Libyan border, above what, Alex thought, had to be one of the most spectacular shorelines in the world, completely bare, completely flat, nothing but ribbons of color, but what colors! The beach was an unbroken swath of pure white for a hundred miles, backed by a swath of beige inland, sprinkled with spots of sage green, and then the sand color of the desert, a thousand miles deep behind. On the sea side the shallowest water was the purest turquoise, the next stripe a brilliant green and then the deep blue of the Mediterranean.

At the airstrip, no more than packed sand with a windsock, they were met by the midnight-blue Packard convertible and another luxury car. They drove through the little town of Mersa Matruh, where, according to Nadia, the only economic activity was diving for sponges, throughout the Mediterranean the preserve of Greeks, but there was enough of that to support a little Greek Orthodox church. Beyond the village, on a rocky point that formed one side of the harbor of Mersa Matruh, was a handful of whitewashed villas built around a spring providing enough water for violet-flowered bougainvillea vines, fig and lemon trees, and a few palms. One of the villas belonged to Nadia's family.

There were servants there, and a cook, apparently brought in the two cars, and they were served a chilled seafood salad of octopus and squid, dorade and rascasse, shrimp and sea urchins. There was a refrigerator, Nadia said, run by a gasoline generator that also pumped fresh water from the spring, drinkable but brackish and tasting of sulfur.

Afterwards they put on swimsuits and swam in the warm sea, the water as limpid and crystalline as the air above Mersa Matruh, and they bought sponges from Arab boys working for the Greek sponge divers. By the time they had showered and put on fresh cotton clothes, the sun was low in the sky. In the late afternoon light a plume of dust arose in the west, from a vehicle being driven fast along the coast road from Libya. Selim came out of the house with a large pair of nautical binoculars hanging from his neck.

"It looks like our Italian. I let him know Nicole would be here, but I don't want him here with all of us together like this. We'd better go out and meet him, Nicole."

Nicole got up without a word, and she and Selim went into the house. A couple of minutes later the Packard was speeding down the coast road. Two plumes of dust approached each other, met, and the dust subsided. Three tiny figures moved down the beach, two together and one following some distance behind.

"Our Italian?" Alex said.

"An Italian officer assigned to Libya. He's on the quartermaster side of things, and he knows precisely what the Italian army has on hand, in the way of arms, food and supplies, along the Libyan-Egyptian border, and why. He provides information at intervals to Nicole, thinking he's aiding the cause of international Communism. He's been told that Nicole is a member of the French Communist Party."

"Is she?"

"Oh, yes." Nadia laughed. "She says it was the worst thing she could do to her father. Also, she says, it's useful in blackmailing her husband. If the British Foreign Office ever found

185

out it would be the end of his career."

What Nadia had just said apparently came as no surprise to the others, except for Chris Weston, who looked surprised.

"The information that is provided by our Italian is, if appropriate, turned over to British intelligence in return for whatever is useful to us at the time, sometimes for them just leaving us alone. It's yours for free, Chris, provided it goes no further than the White House."

"Yes," Chris said, apparently too astonished to venture more.

There was a good bit of eating and drinking, and even dancing to a windup phonograph, that evening on the terrace, under a moon that shimmered on both sea and white sand, but no serious conversation, no reference to the violent attack on one of their number. And one by one the others drifted off to bed, leaving only Nadia and him on the candlelit terrace, the candles guttering out one by one. He went over to the bar that had been set up and brought over two glasses of brandy.

"We have some unfinished business, I believe," he said.

Nadia reached defensively for a scented Egyptian cigarette, and he lit it for her with a wax match.

"That's for you to say, Alex. If you think so."

"Let me put it as starkly as I know how. Why was I brought to Egypt?"

She pulled on the cigarette and her classic Egyptian face was for an instant set aglow.

"You are not going to let go of this, are you?"

"Of course not."

"Well, then, it was because of a promise made when Simon and your mother were dying of typhoid, a promise that, no matter what, their child—you—would be taken care of."

"A promise made by whom?"

"His brother—my father. Alex, such things are very serious in the closed society to which my family belongs. Promises like that are absolute, totally binding . . ."

"And then?"

"And then my father followed you, every step of the way. He knew of the death of the cotton broker, your mother's husband, he knew that you were raised by your grandmother, that you went to the University of . . ."

"Virginia."

"Yes. He knew that you found employment with a newspaper in Georgia."

"The *Atlanta Journal.*"

"Yes. He decided that you were made for greater things. He intervened in your life."

"Are you saying that it was your father who arranged for my employment by the American Newspaper Consortium, had you put in place as my assistant in Cairo?"

"Yes," and she put her hand on his wrist as one might do with a child one was telling about life being more complicated than the child had imagined. "I understand how you must feel."

"And after this, what does he have in mind?" He was confused, angry, wanting to strike out.

"I'm not sure. Once he spoke of bringing you into our business. It's vast, Alex. I was asked to form some kind of judgment on that, but I'm not sure you are ready or willing."

"And now what am I supposed to do?"

"I think you should talk to my father."

"He's vacationing in Europe."

"Not exactly. He's attending to our work. He and Selim's father and Victor Halevy are all in Montreux in Switzerland,

187

a few miles from where they went to the University of Lausanne together, for the annual meeting of the Near East Philanthropic Society, as our organization is publicly known."

Chapter Seventeen

He was up early the next morning, sitting on the terrace mulling over all that he now knew, or thought he knew, when Catherine came out of the French doors.

"Hello," she said, "I thought I would take a walk along the beach before breakfast. Would you like to join me?"

"Yes," he said.

They walked along the beach, the gentle Mediterranean tide lapping over their bare feet, and Catherine took his hand.

"I've recalled what happened that night at the Winter Palace Hotel in Luxor," she said. "It came to me in my sleep a couple of nights ago, in place of one of those terrible nightmares about Spain I have. It did happen, didn't it?"

"The Winter Palace?"

"Yes."

"It did."

"It's a good sign, I think, that it came back, even though I suppressed it for a while."

The weird logic of her thinking baffled him, and he said nothing.

"But I can't do anything like that again anytime very soon. I'm not ready yet, it seems."

Again, he said nothing.

"But now that we have been intimate, I think I can talk to you more frankly."

He couldn't think of anything more frank than telling him

of being repeatedly raped, but then he was in strange and unknown territory.

"You told me that there was 'psychic satisfaction' for you
in what we did, didn't you?"

"I did."

"Then I don't feel quite so bad about what I've put you
through, but now I'm going to ask you to do more for me,
something more difficult, maybe."

Catherine walked a few paces toward the incoming sea
and let the frothy little waves break around her ankles.

"Go on."

"I want you to be my friend, my gentle male friend who
asks nothing of me, is tolerant of my behavior, of my demands, while I finish ridding myself of my demons."

"I can do that," he said.

"Are you sure? You told me once that you had never
helped anyone."

"And you told me that perhaps we could help each other."

"Yes, I did. And now I'm going to do something that is
very difficult for me."

She turned and put her face close to his. He could smell
her female scent blended with the residue of last night's perfume. And then she kissed him gently on the lips.

"There, I've done it."

They walked along in silence for some time, and when
they turned to go back to the villa and the others and breakfast, he was surprised at how far they had come. He was about
to do something that was very difficult for him, but now he
felt he had to be honest with Catherine, not hold back anything.

"Catherine, you haven't asked me what I found in the attic
of the Gezira Club."

"I figured you would tell me if and when you wanted."

"In 1912, Box 123 belonged to a Simatha."

She said nothing.

"I confronted Nadia with this. She says an uncle of hers, now dead, is my father, and her father lured me to Egypt to bring me back into the family . . ."

He had put this very badly, but he didn't want to elaborate, he just wanted to be honest with Catherine.

"The Copts are a rather strange crowd," she said. "I guess I'm not surprised."

"Strange enough to be involved in something that has resulted in Antonius Modiano's near death, and God knows what else is in store. Where does that leave us, Catherine?"

Suddenly, he realized that he had made his choice, and that Catherine's fate and his fate were now inextricably entwined.

"In Spain," she replied cryptically, "they make some of the finest swords and knives in the world, a skill they learned from the Arabs in their seven hundred years of fighting each other. I've watched them make swords. I had always assumed that it was the pounding and grinding of the metal that gave the sword its quality, but that's not it at all, it's the annealing, when the red-hot sword is plunged into cold water, that's what determines the blade's quality.

"I was well annealed in Spain, Alex, and it made me tough . . . or I will be once I get over the trauma, and I will. My doctor said that if a woman doesn't go completely to pieces in the first few days, she will recover with time, the healer of most things."

They had now covered about half the distance back to the villa, and he didn't know what to say.

"But there's something else." She paused and then began to speak quickly, as though she wanted to get it over with. "There was something much worse that I saw in Spain, pho-

tographed, than what happened to me. The film is still unde-
veloped, stored in Cairo. I know that I should develop it, but I
can't bring myself to do it. And it was done by our side. Our
side? The Republican side was composed of Liberals, Social-
ists, Communists, Trotskyites and Anarchists. Some were capable of nobility and great self-sacrifice, some of the most
appalling atrocities imaginable. It's the latter I have on film.
Tell me what to do."

"Give the film to me," he said. "I got interested in photography at the university. I can develop the film and make contact sheets. I'll look at them and tell you what I think. Then
you can tell me to turn them over to you or destroy both
prints and negatives. How does that sound?"

"It sounds just fine."

They were approaching the villa now, and he could see the
others on the terrace.

There was a big breakfast laid out on a sideboard, scrambled eggs and fried tomatoes, toasted bread and fig jam,
white cheese and black olives, little fish fried whole, a pot of
yogurt, and a large metal jug of coffee over a spirit lamp.
They ate breakfast, the eight of them, more coffee was
brought, and some lit cigarettes. Well, now, he thought, we
get down to business, and they did. It was, of course, Nadia
who began.

"One of you spoke to me of putting cards out on the table,
faceup, and I think that's where we now are." She did not
look at Alex. "Antonius Modiano is going to live, but it was a
close thing, and any of us could be next. Nothing like this has
ever happened to us before. Would any of you like to speak to
it?"

He looked around the room. Four men and four women
lounged on the cushions scattered on the tile floor, leaned

against the plain whitewashed walls of the room, holding coffee cups.

"We are at the end game," Nicole Leigh said. "They see themselves losing and have decided to move."

"Who is they?" Chris Weston said.

"First," Nadia intervened, "we had better make clear for you—and Alex . . . and Catherine—just what is at stake out there on the table. Our Society now holds a critical block of stock in the Suez Canal Company, through a very complex series of acquisitions over many years, that will only become apparent when a crucial vote is taken by the board of directors in Paris.

" 'They' is a core group of old-line Canal Company shareholders who have been under the illusion that they were invincible. Now they will learn better."

"And for that Antonius Modiano was tortured."

"Listen, Alex, we have to be hard. Don't think we are uncaring about what happened, but the last time around we were soft, we believed the British and the French—and the Americans—and hundreds of thousands of our people died in the years around the Great War. This time we are going to play our cards carefully and close to our chests—or is it vests you say?"

He said nothing, but he thought back to the first time the metaphor of a game of bridge had been used and his lunch with Chris Weston at the Occidental Restaurant in Washington, a long, long time ago.

"It doesn't strike me," he said, "that Canal Company bond holders would be very adept at doing what was done to Antonius."

"Of course not. You hire someone for such things, and not common criminals. That is not to say that what was done to Antonius was not the work of gangsters brought in from Marseille or Palermo, but in between there will be someone who understands both how to do such things and how the game we are engaged in works."

"And who would that be?"

Nadia shrugged. "I would just caution all of you to be extremely careful from now on. We won't be taking any more jaunts into the desert."

After breakfast they packed their bags and waited on the terrace or in the dining room for the cars to come to take them to the plane. Chris and Alex were sitting on the low wall that surrounded the terrace, saying nothing, lost in their own thoughts. Beyond was the sand and the sea, and it was possible to hear the hissing of the Mediterranean surf against the dry sand. Then Basil Artimanoff approached, sat down on the wall beside them.

"I think we who are not in the inner circle need to take precautions."

"In what way?" Chris said.

"To protect ourselves from what comes next. I think Nadia and Selim have a pretty good idea, from Montreux, of who is responsible for what happened to Antonius. Antonius called me that day and wanted to talk. I was involved with horses at the club at the time and told him I would come over the next day. That was a mistake I don't want to make again."

"But what can we do?" Alex said.

"If I were you I would do what I'm going to do, get the hell out of Egypt."

"What do you make of that?" he said to Chris as Basil walked away.

"Alex, I've already told you, I'm way over my head."

It was at that moment that he wrote off Chris Weston as anyone to turn to if they really were on the dangerous edge of things, and it was at that moment that it also occurred to him that Basil must frequent the Russian Club.

The DC-3 was waiting for them on the airstrip of packed sand. Mansour was standing beside the metal stairs up into the plane.

"I've just had some news," he said, to the group as a whole, "over the plane's radio. The Germans invaded Poland this morning, at dawn."

"Well," Nadia said, "there's no turning back now."

She did not elaborate on this cryptic remark.

The next morning when he came down to the office Nadia was already there, her usual assured, immaculately groomed self, but with a look around her eyes of someone who has not slept well.

"Have you turned on the radio?" she said.

"Not yet."

"I have. It's clear that Warsaw is doomed, and that the British and French have no choice now but to declare war on Germany."

"Well, at least that will give us some work to do."

"Maybe."

"Anything else?"

"You have a telegram from Thebes," she said, and he was for a few seconds disoriented, thinking of the Winter Palace Hotel in Luxor, which was part of the larger sacred city that the ancient Greeks had named Thebes.

But the telegram was from Thebes, Georgia, from the family lawyer, informing him that his grandmother's house and the large plot of land on which it stood had been sold for an astonishing amount of money, and this sum, less commissions and taxes, had been deposited in his local bank account. If not rich, he was suddenly very well-off.

"I own a whole island in the St. Lawrence, where the

family summer cottage is," Catherine said, when he told her over dinner that evening. "It's worth a lot of money too, but I don't think I could sell it. Perhaps someday I can . . . Do you have any regrets?"

"Of course," he said. "It's my childhood and youth, and it will be torn down. Nobody lives in huge old houses like that anymore. It's the land the developers want. But I would never have gone back. Whether it's torn down or not, all I will have of it is memories. You can't live in the past."

"You can't live in the future either," Catherine said.

"But you can make provisions for it. What about you and me?"

"It's 'us' then?"

"Could you want that, given everything?"

"Yes, I could."

When he arrived at work the next morning, he found Nadia dressed in a light woolen suit, but however light, not what one wore in Cairo in the fall. She was as intense as he had ever seen her, like a coiled spring, her eyes sparkling with that adrenaline look she got when under pressure and wanting to achieve something, a quivering of the nostrils.

"Well," he said, "I suppose it's Montreux."

"You've come a long way in a short time, Alex."

"Good bloodline," he said, and they both laughed ironically. Yes, he had come a long way in a few weeks.

"Want to tell me why Montreux?" he added.

"A vote has just been taken in the British Parliament. If Hitler does not agree to withdraw from Poland by eleven o'clock this morning, a state of war will exist between England and Germany. The French are expected to follow suit by this evening. I understand that German nationals in Egypt are to be interned, and others on a list prepared by

British intelligence will be arrested."

"Like you."

"Possibly. There are certain things my family and others have done that could be subject to misinterpretation."

"Where does this leave me?"

"I don't know, Alex. You have the choice of coming to Switzerland and discussing that with Papa, except that . . ."

"There is Catherine."

"Yes."

"And the Narcissians?"

"Disbanded. Antonius is out of hospital, and he and Artemesia are already on their way to Switzerland."

"Together."

"Yes."

"Basil?"

"Disappeared." She shrugged. "Perhaps he was working for the other side."

"Nicole?"

"Working for the British, I've always assumed. She's gone back to her husband, now that everything's blown, and he's to get an ambassadorship in an Arab country."

"Chris Weston?"

"He's being transferred to the American consulate in Dhahran, Saudi Arabia."

"That leaves Selim."

"He's taking the same flight as I am to Geneva, now that certain assets of both our families have been transferred out of Egypt. I told you the truth, Alex. He is the married man with much to lose if our relationship had been found out."

"So that leaves me and Catherine all alone."

"You and Catherine had better get out too, while there's time. We can see that you are given protection in Switzerland."

"No thanks, Nadia. I have no intention of becoming the relative who lives on a stipend from the Simatha clan. I prefer to make it on my own."

"And I'm sure you will. What do you intend to do now?"

"That, Nadia, is none of your business."

She recoiled. The Simathas were not used to being talked to in that way.

"Alex, it's going to be dangerous for you here."

"It may even be dangerous for you in Switzerland. You don't know just who you are facing, do you?"

"We have a general idea."

"General ideas don't stop bullets, Nadia. Only the specific does, and I intend to find out just what that is, for my own sake and Catherine's."

"Please, Alex, let me know if you do. I can give you several ways of reaching me in Switzerland."

"Yes, of course," he said.

Nadia Simatha—and all the wealth and power that lay behind her—had bowed her neck to him. Not bad for a boy from Thebes, Georgia . . . if he survived.

"Good-bye, Alex," she said, opened a desk drawer, took out a package and handed it to him. "I think this should be yours."

He took the package from her. "Good-bye, Nadia."

She paused at the door. "Things didn't work out too well, did they?"

"Things aren't over yet."

Chapter Eighteen

They rented a houseboat. Catherine kept her quarters at the Gezira Club, having the switchboard tell callers that she had left but they could leave a message if they wished. They had gone incognito but not, he supposed, from assassins sent from the Marseille or Palermo underworld.

"I had a talk with Antonius yesterday at the hospital," Catherine said over a public phone the next day. "He is out of danger now and talking. He told Basil that we are all in danger. It seems that 'our' people in Montreux do have some idea who may be the other side. Have you heard of Calouste Gulbenkian?"

"Mr. Five Percent."

"Yes."

"Surely not him?"

"No, he's far too well-known, but perhaps someone who operates in the same way."

"Which is?"

"A cut of the profits in return for doing all the behind-the-scenes stuff that the principals don't have the skills to handle. Gulbenkian was in on the beginning of the oil business in the Ottoman Empire before it fell apart, from Turkey to Persia to Egypt, and through political change and war and shifting petroleum cartels he's held onto his five percent, and is now perhaps the richest man in the world."

"And our Mr. Five Percent?"

"Someone who has come up from dark alleyways of the Middle East, knows the intricacies of political intrigue, the uses of violence . . . but who also knows how the Suez Canal Company is run from its elegant building in a good, quiet quarter of Paris."

"How much of this is your idea, and how much what you have picked up from Nadia and Basil and Nicole, and our other sophisticates?"

Catherine put her hand on his wrist as Nadia had done at another such moment a few days before.

"Alex, dear, I was brought up in the world I'm talking about, where all that counts is the means to buy pleasure at whatever it costs."

"By the way," he said, "I've developed and printed your film at a Lebanese place in the Muski, where they let outsiders do their photographic work, which is almost invariably of a personal and pornographic nature that the owners would not want to see in the hands of potential blackmailers."

"And?"

"A field of the dead," he said, "but . . ."

"Yes?"

"They're all women."

"Should I look at the contacts?"

"I don't know, Catherine. It's for you to decide. I don't even know what it's about, but when people are cut down by gunfire it's not just neat little bullet holes in the bodies. What happened?"

"Prostitutes, more than two hundred of them, camp followers as they say, camp followers of the Anarchist battalions, a very effective force for the Republican side, but the prostitutes were spreading venereal disease that was sapping the strength of the battalions. The Anarchist leader knew that if they were just sent back to Barcelona they would soon return to the front, so he had them rounded up and taken in trucks to a remote place where they were machine-gunned. This was Durruti, who was himself assassinated shortly afterwards. And shortly after that, what happened to me happened, and you can see now why love and sex and violence and death are all mixed up and drove me crazy."

He held Catherine to him and said, "I'll have the negatives and prints put away in some absolutely safe place, and we'll let time and history and all that tell us what will happen to your photographs. Okay?"

The next several days, days of perfect early autumn weather on the Nile, were the only idyll he had ever known. He was proud of himself and hopeful of Catherine's recovery, and the dark shadow of the vulture's wing, in the form of the unknown personage from the world of Middle Eastern intrigue, only made these days in their houseboat hideaway the sweeter. During those nights Catherine allowed him to touch her more, and she began tentatively to put her slim hands on him. It was the kind of thing that young inexperienced lovers begin with, which they certainly were not, but it had that kind of feeling of youthful awakening that he had never known and now cherished. He was, in other words, very happy. He was also in love. He had thought, briefly, that he was in love with Nadia Simatha, but that was because he badly needed something beyond what he had had with Nancy and Dorothy and other women, and because Nadia was extremely skilled at manipulating the feelings of others.

For these few days they idled, ate in exotic restaurants at night, went dancing, spent their days visiting museums, leafing through newspapers and magazines on the little stern deck of the houseboat, where the leaves of the giant eucalyptus trees that lined the canal spiraled down. They went shopping for clothes, ancient artifacts, the ceramics and glasswork of the Muski. Then one morning, lying in bed, Catherine and he faced the fact that they were going to have to get to work, identify the enemy, if they were to protect themselves before they met a worse fate than what had happened to Antonius Modiano.

They began in the reading room of the Gezira Sporting Club. They were mostly alone there, except for an occasional elderly Egyptian or Englishman consulting a reference work in pursuit of some memory of past events. If they were observed by anyone with a reason to wonder what two people of their age were doing there, he hoped their known professional links to journalism would provide an adequate answer.

They began with various reference works containing biographical summaries of prominent persons of the Western world. He found that Catherine and he had a similar mindset for investigation, what she called the Sherlock Holmes method. After everything else has been eliminated what remains is the answer, however unlikely it may seem. Their parameters for identifying their prey were that he was already powerful, with the ability to make things happen, and powerful meant rich. He would have come up from an environment where the only rule was to win, and he would have an intimate knowledge of how things worked in the old Ottoman Empire. That would mean that he came from a minority community, the Turks not having had reason or inclination for taking initiatives.

Three days of labor brought forth some interesting types from the dry summaries of lives lived, but it was clear that their parameters were too wide. He recalled to Catherine the old saying that Artemesia had thrown out to Basil that weekend in the Fayum, that it takes ten Jews to outwit a Greek, and ten Greeks to outwit an Armenian.

"Well, why not," Catherine said, closing the big red book she had been consulting.

"Why not what?"

"Why not a Greek? Stavisky was Jewish, Gulbenkian is Armenian. Why not a Greek?"

"But why?"

"Ever since ancient times the Greeks have been mariners, they are still very much in the shipping business, they care about things like canals for the use of oceangoing vessels. Those in the trade prospered under the Ottoman Empire, knew how to get things done with bribes, and I suppose even rough stuff when that was called for . . ."

"How did you get to be so expert on this subject?"

"Actually, I had a Greek boyfriend for a while. His family was in the shipping business. They had residences in Paris and London and cut a wide swath socially."

"So people of their background wouldn't have felt shy about walking in the front door of the Suez Canal Company in Paris?"

"Not in the least. Why don't I call Stelios and get a few names from him? We're still on good terms."

She rummaged in her handbag and brought out a leather address book and then stood up.

"You mean call him now?"

"Alex, you've signed on with me, so you had better be prepared for things like this."

In fifteen minutes she was back, smiling broadly.

"By luck Stelios was in his Paris office. He gave the names of three Greek magnates that he thought met the description of whom I was interested in, the reality of my interest as disguised as I could make it. One is quite old, the second has become involved in some business growing out of the war in China, the third is Sir George Mavroyannis."

"The man you were talking to on the German cruise ship."

"Exactly. Want to know more? George Mavroyannis made his fortune by selling arms to both sides in the Greek-Turkish war of 1922–23. Then he went back into the family shipping business, and a few years ago he bought a large block of shares in the Suez Canal Company from the British government, enough shares to make him a director."

"The chase is now on, I reckon."

"It could be a wild goose chase, Alex."

"The only way to find out whether or not it is is to pursue our leads, and we're both professionally equipped to do that."

From various books and old magazines in the club library, they soon found out that Mavroyannis was born into a family, in the Greek islands under Turkish rule, that had been in the shipping business for a couple of hundred years. His father and grandfather had specialized in recruiting Greek fishermen and peasants to sign on as seamen aboard the ships owned by the dozen or so families that controlled the Greek-owned maritime trade in the Mediterranean and beyond.

When work was begun on the Suez Canal around 1860, the Mavroyannis family recruited the Greek workers who supplied the bulk of the skills needed to supplement the brute force of the Egyptian peasants digging the canal. And when the canal was opened the Mavroyannis family were among the first to exploit it for trade with the Persian Gulf, down the African coast and into the Far East. This included the supply of arms to tribal leaders and warlords from Arabia to China.

The experience gained by his family in the arms business allowed George Mavroyannis to move quickly when the Greek-Turkish war broke out in 1922, supplying arms to both sides. He was not without competitors, but some of these either disappeared or met violent deaths. After the war he moved to London, where a segment of the popular press branded him a "merchant of death." To counter this, Mavroyannis became an important contributor to certain charities favored by members of the royal family. He was rewarded with a knighthood.

"Do we have enough to go on?"

"We do."

"So what next?" Catherine said.

"We know a good bit about the past now, but what about the present? Where are his residences, who are his friends, mistresses, what further ambitions does a man who has achieved so much still have?"

"I can tell you one thing, Alex, from growing up among the set my parents ran with, that the more you have the more you want."

"So where do we turn?"

"I could find out lots from Stelios, but I don't think that would be a good idea. Relationships between the Greek shipping families are a web too subtly woven for us to untangle."

"So where?"

"The one thing that Stelios did say about Mavroyannis is that he likes to shine on the international social scene. I have a female friend who writes a gossip column for a Paris daily and another for a London magazine, both under pseudonyms, and she will either know the details of Mavroyannis's social life or be able to find out. I'll give her a call."

"We'd better move fast. We've been left holding the bag by our former friends."

"Let's face it, dear boy. We've been taken."

"I don't know exactly who has been taken. This troupe calling itself the Narcissians appears and then disappears, like strolling players, like *A Midsummer Night's Dream*."

"That's poetry, Alex, not life."

"Life is where you get killed."

"You don't need to tell me that."

That evening Suzie or Suzanne returned Catherine's call to a room they had taken in the Semiramis Hotel. She said she had gone through her file of clippings on George Mavroyannis, of which there were many. Some were only a few lines, some several paragraphs, some whole pages torn from a magazine, almost all accompanied by photographs. In some Mavroyannis was in evening dress, in others in a bathing suit, aboard a yacht or on a beach. In most a young beautiful woman, or women, hovered about him. But he was ugly, Suzie said, with thick graying hair, bushy eyebrows, a barrel chest, overly long arms, bandy legs. And except for those taken on a beach he wore heavy-rimmed thick glasses. Obviously, what all these young beauties saw in Sir George was dollars and pounds and discreet apartments in Paris and villas tucked away behind Cannes and Nice, and fast cars and large yachts.

One woman occurred most often in the photos, a dark, intense one. Olga Danilova, prima ballerina, Ballets Russes de Monte Carlo, current mistress number one. As for friends he seemed to have none. The lone wolf.

"So are we any better off for what we now know?"

"It's we then."

"Yes, we both are getting well now, Alex."

"What am I getting well from?"

"A narrow selfishness."

"Then I have you to thank, Catherine."

"Yes, you do. I suppose there have been other women who thought that about you, but perhaps they didn't tell you to your face."

"Yes, perhaps," he said, thinking of Nancy and Dorothy.

"But for now what we need to do is stay alive."

"Yes."

"That's all. The rest will work itself out. But staying alive . . . We're caught in a situation where we are wanted by a man without scruples who wants us for what we know, but we don't know much, which makes it even more dangerous. You can't be made to tell what you don't know, as they made Antonius tell what he did know. Those who know, unfortunately for us, have *fouté le camp*—good French expression—fucked off."

"Yes, we are wanted for what we don't know."

"Well, it's your problem, Alex. You're now the man in my life, and that means you're going to have to take care of me."

"All right, I can handle that."

"So, tell me what we do."

"We leave on the lights in the houseboat, to buy us a little time, and I will put a chair close to the door, so that if it's opened the chair will move a bit, and we'll know, if we return, that we've had visitors."

"Where did you learn that trick?"

"From a movie. I'm operating with very little real experience."

"And right now?"

"Right now we go to my apartment above the ANC office, and we don't answer the phone. Tomorrow I'll see what I can do to make our situation more secure."

"Why don't we just get out of Egypt now?"

"Running won't help. They'll find us."

"What will help?"

"Cunning," he said, and he knew he had that part right.

There was a battered taxi waiting alongside the quay, opposite the houseboat restaurant, and they took it to the back of his building and lugged their bags up the servants' stairwell. He pulled the heavy curtains that had been installed by the former owner, the Lebanese, before turning on a bedside lamp. Catherine looked around the bedroom with its mirrors and laughed, went into the bathroom with its blue mirror and sunken tub and laughed again.

"Not your doing, I trust."

"No."

Within ten minutes they were under the covers of the Pharaonic bed, and within another few minutes sleeping the sleep of forgetfulness, of those who will themselves not to be where they know they are going to be the next morning.

"So, having slept on it, what do you think about what we know?" he asked her over breakfast.

"There's one thing I know that I haven't told you. Antonius is setting up a radio transmitter in the Swiss Alps, that will broadcast Christian evangelical stuff to the heathen of the Middle East, under a contract that is supposed to make him a lot of money. Radio transmitter, radios buried in various remote places in Egypt . . . what does that suggest?"

"What?"

"That our friends have struck some kind of deal with the Germans that will facilitate their seizure of the canal in return for a major role in running it under German rule."

"That's pretty strong stuff you're saying."

"That's why it's so dangerous."

"And Mavroyannis?"

"That's the other side, representing the old-line canal shareholders, the Brits, the French, et cetera. Big money."

"Yes," Alex said, recalling what Chris Weston had said about Saudi Arabian oil, "the kind of money people kill for, and the muscle is on Mavroyannis's side."

After breakfast they went down to the office and Catherine

continued her pursuit of Sir George Mavroyannis through international phone calls she placed over an unlisted telephone that ANC had had installed before he arrived in Egypt, running up a bill he would have difficulty explaining to Arvid Dahlsted. But then Arvid had some things he was going to have a great deal of difficulty in explaining to Alexander Fraser.

He went to his desk and took out the package that Nadia had handed him before leaving for Switzerland. Inside it was another package tied with cord and sealed with red wax impressed with the same gemstone that had sealed the packet of letters from his mother's lover, a gemstone set in a ring that he now wore on his finger. He took out a penknife and cut the cord. Inside was a leather book with gold-leafed edges to the pages. It was a blank book meant for use as a diary or journal, and less than half of the pages were filled, with what appeared to be his mother's handwriting. The first entry was dated May 23, 1904, when his mother would have been nineteen, and began, *"My aunt Sarah Joyce has given me this book and strongly urged me to keep a diary of my marriage in Egypt and my life there . . ."*

He flipped the pages with his thumb and found a few references to family and friends in Thebes, Georgia. Whatever else this diary might be, it was not a forgery. Not only was he fairly certain that the handwriting was his mother's, but no one from outside Thebes could possibly concoct something he wouldn't instantly spot as fraudulent. He began to read.

Chapter Nineteen

May 23, 1904

    My Aunt Sarah has given me this book and strongly urged me to keep a diary of my marriage in Egypt and my life there. I don't think I will do that, for to do so would mean I could not put down my true thoughts and feelings. My aunt clearly wants some record of my stay in Egypt that can be read by members of the family and made a part of the family archives, a record of the exotic interlude of one of its own. Neither she nor any of the others understand that although I can be located on the family tree on my aunt's study wall, I have no part in what they stand for or believe in.

    I think my Aunt Sarah understands that I do not love Howell Fraser, and she has as much as said so, recalling that she was not in love with my Uncle Adolph when they married, but that love had come with time and proximity, as it usually does. I do not believe this. I think what happens is that we make the best of whatever situation fate has thrown us into and give a name to the situation that causes the least pain.

    That is not my way. I became engaged to Howell Fraser because this was the surest means of knocking the sand of Thebes, Georgia, off my sandals forever. What happens after I have no idea, and I make no commitments to any course of action. If I do write in this fine diary that my aunt has given me, it will have to be kept in a secure and secret place.

    I have arrived in Alexandria in what I am told is the worst of the hot, humid season, but I don't care. I suppose I shall make entries in my diary from time to time, because there are certain impressions I would not like to lose the exact flavor of, as they follow one upon another, day by unfolding day.

I was met at the docks by an officious Greek dragoman in a red fez, or tarboosh as they are called here, and put on the train for Cairo. I shared the compartment with three English ladies returning from leave in England, and their immediate aim was to find out where I fit in the social order, but when they discovered that I was American they lost interest. This left me to regard the strange and exotic landscape, the camels turning wooden machines that brought up water from the canals to the fields, the first date palms that I had ever seen, small boys in nightshirts driving water buffalo that must have weighed a ton or two with a stick, men driving donkey carts loaded with watermelons or crates of chickens or a sheep marked with a streak of red dye that one of the women told me meant it was being taken to slaughter.

To my surprise I was met at the Cairo train station not by my husband-to-be but by a young Lebanese clerk from his office. It seemed there had been some business matter in Port Said of an urgent nature, but Mr. Fraser would call on me the next day at the hotel where I would be staying until the marriage could take place since, I gathered, it was not considered proper that I stay in the house we would be occupying on the island of Gezira in the Nile until then. I would have been crushed, I suppose, had I come to Egypt with high expectations, but I had not.

The hotel was a nice one run by a Swiss couple, and my room overlooked the Nile and its boats with white sails that looked like doves' wings. At breakfast a servant brought me an envelope that contained a note I supposed would be from my fiancé, but it was from Alexander Fraser, my prospective father-in-law, inquiring if he might call on me at noon. If that were convenient, I could inform the hotel desk and they would get word to him.

I watched from a chair beside a window in the sitting room as an open horse-drawn carriage pulled up before the hotel steps promptly at noon. An elderly man got down. He wore an old-fashioned frock coat and carried a gold-headed black cane. This would be Alexander Fraser, formerly a colonel in the army of the Confederate States of America. I knew his age to be seventy-two, but he did not look it, trim and moving with ease and wearing a neat white beard. When he entered the sitting room I rose and he, of course, kissed my hand. We sat down opposite each other over a small table of intricate Arab woodwork that held a bowl of pink roses.

"My dear, we have never met, but I feel I know you well," he said. "I knew your parents, your grandfather even, your uncles and aunts. Therefore, I feel I can speak to you more directly than I would to someone I was meeting for the first time. I have come here to apologize."

"For what?" I said, my first words to him.

"I was not aware that my son had been called away on business to Port Said, or I would have been at the station to meet you myself. Only last night did I have a telegram from him saying there have been complications and he will not be able to return to Cairo until tomorrow. He asked me to convey his apologies to you, which I have done, but I must say that I am vexed . . ."

"It's not the end of the world," I said.

"No, it's not even the end of anyone's life."

"Nor even, perhaps, a phase of anyone's life," I said.

He gave me a look of shrewd appraisal and seemed to be weighing his next move.

"Would you care to join me for lunch at Shepheard's Hotel?" he said. "The food's reasonably good, the service overwhelming, although the place is a damned sight too pukkha sahib for my taste."

"I would be delighted," I said.

As we drove to Shepheard's in the Colonel's open carriage, the cloth top partly pulled up to provide shade, I tried to remember what I knew about him. He had gone into the War Between the States, as it was called in the South, a lieutenant and emerged as one of the youngest colonels in the CSA. His nickname had been Five-horse Fraser, for his supposedly having five horses shot out from under him in combat. He had tried to go back to farming after the war but times had changed. Eventually, he signed on with an American military mission to train the Egyptian army, but that too had failed in the end. He had stayed on in Egypt brokering cotton and had a son, who was now away on business in Port Said, and thus unable to meet his arriving bride.

Well, it is over. We were married in the Anglican cathedral beside the Nile by an American Episcopalian minister, who is in Egypt hoping to cure his tuberculosis. Our honeymoon to Luxor has been postponed, again for business reasons, and the Colonel tells me that I should not take this too amiss, as my husband Howell finds himself trying desperately to stay afloat in a rapidly declining world cotton market.

I am now ensconced in the Fraser residence on the island of Gezira, which is really quite grand, with palm trees and a brilliant green lawn, gardeners and house servants, and I smile to myself. It is not all that different from the antebellum South. The Colonel has a wing of the house to himself, about which there is no question, since he owns the property.

I am now also a married woman, no longer a virgin, initiated into the secrets of the flesh, liable to pregnancy and all that. I find it a bit strange—in the general sense, that is—that the business between men and women is this thing. Hardly a novel thought, I imagine. But within the generality there is, of course, the specific, but how different this is for different women I'm not sure. In my case, I felt that this could be the most momentous thing in your life, under the right circumstances. Once or twice in the act of love, as it is called, I did feel a surge coming on, but then it faded. Does it take love to make it happen, or is it just a physical, animal thing? I don't imagine I will know until I experience it— if I ever do.

Something unexpected—at least for me—has happened. Howell has been appointed as the American consul in Cairo. While the remuneration is not grand, we now, at least, have a base on which to stand and, Howell says, a social position is worth more than the remuneration. Well, we'll see.

The initial result of my husband's appointment is that we must put out a considerable sum to have dresses made for me and suits for him, so that we can attend various official functions to which we are invited. He takes his new duties with considerable seriousness, wears a gold watch chain, and has himself driven to his office each morning in his father's carriage.

I am pretty much left to my own devices, and after a few mornings of tea and sticky cakes with the wives of other consuls and officials with social pretensions, I have vowed to avoid all such activity as best I can. The only person with whom I can speak with any degree of freedom is my father-in-law, in fact more freedom than I enjoy with my husband, whose amorous overtures have the nature of a duty to be performed, almost an afterthought. This I find shameful and humiliating to me. I sometimes take off all my clothes and stand before the mirror, to confirm that I am an attractive woman.

My husband's appointment as American consul has been something of a mystery to me. He told me immediately afterwards that the position had been vacant for some months and he had thought of applying for it but had not done so. I now have the answer. Old

Alexander Fraser tells me laconically that it perhaps has some-thing to do with his still having a few friends from his West Point days in the upper reaches of the administration in Washington. This leads to a discussion of his military career and the terrible car-nage that he was a witness to, and a participant in. General Sherman had it right, he said. War is hell.

On whether the war was a question of states' rights, as the South maintained, or slavery, in the view of the Yankees, he rather thought neither. What made it unavoidable, in his opinion, was the Southern code of honor. Once the war had begun, how-ever, that code of honor had one mitigating effect on the ensuing horror. By and large women were not assaulted or violated. The Southern gentlemen who made up the officer corps of the Confed-erate army believed firmly that a woman's person was a sacred vessel. On the Yankee side there was a similar, if not quite as fa-natically held, view handed down from the Pilgrim fathers.

Relations between my husband and myself have gone from mildly affectionate to almost hostile. The sticking point is my re-fusal to spend my days in mindless social activity that might ben-efit his career. He now sees a future for himself. The American minister, under whose authority he comes, has taken a shine to him, and the world cotton market has partly righted itself, and he is even making some money from his brokerage business.

We never discuss our problem directly. That is not the way in Thebes, Georgia. I thought I had knocked the sand of Thebes from my sandals forever, but a bit of my hometown has washed up in a house on the island of Gezira in Cairo. Cairo is, indeed, now my hometown, and thus I feel no need to write about its exoticness in my diary. I want out of my situation but have no idea how that might be done.

Physical relations between my husband and myself have simply ceased to exist. I am appalled. I would like to speak to my father-

in-law of this, but even for someone of my liberated spirit that would be quite impossible. I'm sure he would have some sage advice. Despite his age he has a young Lebanese "housekeeper" in his wing of the house, and she is clearly more than that. I don't know where to turn. I made my choice and I will simply have to live with it, I suppose, hoping that fate will somehow rescue me. In any case, I do not have the heart to write in my diary anymore.

It has been nearly two years since I made an entry in my aborted diary, but events both momentous and swiftly moving have taken place that I want to record, so there is no confusion in my mind in the time to come over just what happened and what my feelings were.

Nothing in life is static, and however much you may think you have reached a point where change is excluded, it always comes. My husband was summoned to a meeting of American consular officers in Rome. I was left alone for several weeks, I thought, but my social life became more active than it had been for a long time. The American minister put out the word that the lonely consul's wife was to be invited to social events, and this time, unlike the ladies' teas, I felt an obligation to put in an appearance, usually escorted by one of the young legation officers.

One of the events I was invited to was an elaborate costume party given by a rich Copt family in their villa near the pyramids. The theme of the party was Verdi's opera Aida, *composed for the opening of the Suez Canal, but not performed until two years later. The day of the party marked the fortieth anniversary of the opening of the canal, and I understood that the senior member of the Simatha family, the wealthiest Copts in Egypt, sat on the board of directors of the Canal Company. The invitation was conveyed by a telephone call from the personal assistant to the American minister.*

I already knew some of the Simathas, whom I considered

216

among the more interesting local people with whom the foreign community came in contact, and I accepted the invitation. My acceptance was followed by a slight pause, and then the minister's assistant, whose name is Elmore Wiggins, said something that considerably startled me.

"They would like you to come as Aida."

"Me? Aida? For Pete's sake, why?"

"Well, for one reason, they don't want twelve ladies showing up as Aida, so they are trying to assign roles. One old bearded chap is being asked to come as Giuseppe Verdi."

"Well, all right, but why an American as Aida?"

There was another pause. "Apparently, someone thinks you are the most beautiful 'European' woman in Cairo."

The pause this time was of considerable length. I was at first dumbfounded, but then I remembered regarding my naked body in my dressing mirror, to assure myself that my husband's apparent lack of amorous interest in me could not have a basis in my looks. Well, all right, I thought, if somebody from the privileged classes regards me as beautiful, I'll have to rise to the occasion. I laughed.

"All right, I'll do it, but I'm going to need some advice."

"I thought so."

"Thought so about what?"

"Thought that you would do it, and thought that you would want advice. I've already spoken with the minister's wife. She says if you do it you should do it with style, to the greater glory of the Stars and Stripes. She has spoken with her hairdresser, the best in Cairo, and also a top-notch cosmetician. He says he can turn you into an Aida that will knock them dead. I've made an appointment with him for you the afternoon of the Simatha party."

"Well," I said.

"Mrs. T. has also spoken with the director of the Cairo Opera, and they are lending you their costume for Aida, which will be delivered once it has been properly cleaned and ironed."

"Well," I said again.

"Oh, and I've arranged with the leading Cairo jeweler, the Armenian firm of Gulderian, to lend you appropriate jewelry. It's all the real thing and it's fully insured, so you don't need to be nervous about it."

"Well, then, I guess everything is settled."

"If you have any problems," Elmore Wiggins said, "just call me."

When the hairdresser-cosmetician had finished with me he held up a mirror to the front, back and both sides. I gasped with astonishment. I had not only been made to look like Aida, I was *Aida*. My dark hair had been dressed in numerous tight braids, like those I had seen on the seductive women painted on pieces in the Egyptian Museum. My eyes had been so heavily lined with kohl that they looked like those of a gazelle, my cheeks rouged, my mouth painted a startling pink, and enlarged around the edges to give me a slightly Nubian look.

"Now," my creator said, "just don't touch anything until you leave for the party."

The Simathas' party was at eight, and a car was to call for me. I was as nervous as a cat. At six-thirty the dresser from the Cairo Opera and Aram Gulderian himself arrived together. I was stripped down to my underwear by the dresser, while the jeweler looked thoughtfully out the window. When Aida's heavy silk costume was in place, Gulderian opened the velvet cases on the salon table and adorned my ears and neck and bosom and wrists with diamonds and emeralds, sapphires and rubies. When everything was arranged to his satisfaction, he stepped back and regarded me.

"My God!" he said.

At seven-thirty my car arrived, a Rolls Royce, no less. A young man in a white linen suit escorted me to it and seated himself beside me. I could feel perspiration trickling down my sides.

"Are you one of the Simathas?" I said.

He laughed. "No, I am Mr. Peter Simatha's private secretary."

The head of the clan.

Floodlights dimly lit the pyramids, and the Simatha villa in front, surrounded by palms, was also lit. The house was built in the form of an Egyptian temple enclosed by stone pillars with painted capitals. The car pulled up in front of the entrance, a servant darted inside, and Peter Simatha himself came out to greet me. He was tall and thin, with silver hair, about sixty-five, and not in costume. He too wore a white linen suit, and his heavy glasses gave him a rather owlish look.

For a few seconds he said nothing and then, "Aida in the flesh." He gave me his arm, and we entered the central hall where a number of costumed guests had already gathered and servants were passing with trays of champagne. There was a balcony at the end of the hall, where an orchestra in formal dress played an air from Aida. Eyes were turned on me, and it was at this moment that my life began.

With me on his arm Peter Simatha stopped beside a handsome young man as tall as he, and somewhat resembling him. He too wore a linen suit.

"My son Simon. Simon, Aida."

The son kissed my hand.

"Simon is the black sheep of the family."

The young man gave his father an ironic look.

"He fancies he's an artist rather than a money grubber like the rest of us. He's back for a few weeks to recover from the rigors of Paris. I've written his teacher, that chap Matisse, to get an opinion on whether he can scale the heights. If he can, then I'll back him. If Matisse thinks he's wasting his time, then it's back to money grubbing. Well, I'll leave you young people. Have to play

the host. Simon, do try to say something amusing."

His father walked away, and Simon stared at me. *"You're breathtaking,"* he said.

"I think that could be considered amusing," I said.

"I am having a hard time convincing myself that you are the American consul's wife rather than a Nubian princess."

"Somebody else must, since a message was sent to the American minister asking that I take the part."

"I suppose I'm responsible for that."

"What!?" I said. *"But you don't know me. We've never met before tonight."*

"No, but I've seen you twice at social functions. My father recently mentioned to me that he was in a dilemma. There were a dozen Egyptian ladies invited to his party who considered themselves beauties, and many of them would come dressed as Aida, and that would spoil the party. On the other hand, if he chose one of them for the role, the rest would be furious. I said, why not select a foreign woman for the role, and that should ease the situation. I said I had seen an American woman whom I thought would fit the part perfectly. I hope you don't mind."

"No, I'm enjoying playing the role."

What I did not say was that according to Elmore Wiggins, the person who had asked for me had described me as the most beautiful "European" woman in Cairo.

Before our conversation could go much further, the guests were assembled and paired off, and a procession took place into the dining room to the strains of the "Triumphal March." I led the procession with the man dressed as Radames, a big bronzed man with a prominent nose and black wavy hair. I thought he looked like an Italian tenor, and it turned out that is exactly what he was, flown down from La Scala in Milan for the occasion. After dinner he sang several arias from Aida.

Tables were scattered throughout the Simatha mansion, and as *soon as I had filled my plate with exotic delicacies I was whisked away to the terrace by Simon Simatha before any of the other men who obviously had an eye on me could get to me. Cushions had been laid out the length of the balustrade and we sat on the balustrade and ate from our laps. This effectively prevented anyone else from joining us.*

"Have you been with your husband as consul in other countries?"

I said not and recited the story of the old colonel and the cotton brokerage business and of how my husband had returned for college in America and met me, our families being from the same small town in Georgia.

"I really didn't know my husband very well when I came out to be married," I said. And to my surprise I added, "There have been strains."

Simon Simatha gave me a curious look.

"Who is Matisse?" I said, trying to quickly distance myself from my unwise remark.

"Few people outside of the art world know who he is today, but in a few years he and Picasso will be recognized as the greatest artists in the world."

"Will you make the grade with Matisse?"

"Frankly, I don't know, but I know that he will tell my father the truth. If he discourages my continuing with art, I'm not going back to 'money grubbing' as my father calls it. The family can afford to have one member not in the firm. I'll find something else creative to do, probably in Europe."

"I know almost no one who does creative things."

"Doesn't your husband have a hobby? Most diplomats do."

"My husband has no hobbies."

Simon Simatha gave me another curious look, and this time I could read its meaning. It was the look of someone who has recognized an unhappy wife.

"By creative I don't necessarily mean painting or playing the violin. Travel can be a creative activity, and you're in a good place for that."

"I haven't been outside Cairo," I said.

Simon Simatha looked at me in disbelief.

"How many years have you been in Egypt?"

"Four."

"Not even to Fayum? You can do that in a day. Lots to see and a beautiful lake."

"Not even to Fayum."

"The American minister told me that he wanted you looked after while your husband was away. For how much longer will that be?"

"Two more weeks."

"This weekend I am joining two old school chums who are married now, and their wives, for a trip to Fayum. There is a hunting lodge there mostly used for duck shooting. Would you consider it improper if I asked if you would care to join us, your minister being duly informed?"

"No, I wouldn't consider it improper."

"Will you go?"

"There's no one to tell me I can't, so I suppose I will."

The deed is done. I am now an unfaithful wife, an adulteress. It was done on a bed in a hunting lodge on the edge of Lake Fayum, in the middle of a still, tranquil autumn afternoon, while the others were off shopping for native handicrafts. It was the happiest moment of my life. I cried out during the act, cried for joy afterwards, while Simon held me and rocked my naked body back and forth . . .

He closed his mother's diary. He could read no more. He knew how the story of his mother's search for love had turned out, with the deaths of both her and Simon Simatha, his father. The only fruit of her passion had been a son, a man now her age when she died, a man described by Catherine as possessed by a narrow selfishness. He put his head down on the desk and wept.

He felt Catherine's hand on his shoulder.

"What's wrong, chum?"

"I've been reading my mother's diary. The Simathas had it. I can't go on. It breaks my heart."

"Well, why don't we do like you gallantly did with my photographs of the slaughtered prostitutes? Let me read the rest, and I'll tell you whether you should go on."

"All right," he said. "There's not all that much more."

He went to a sofa and lay down, put an arm over his eyes. He saw his entire life as a wreck, broken pieces of what might have been scattered over the Egyptian sands.

Catherine came over and sat down beside him.

"Look, Alex, be a man, and being able to cry in front of a woman is one sign of a man. We all die, soon or late, and maybe your mother had more happiness in her short life than she would have had had she lived to be ninety."

"Why does any of this matter to you?" he said.

"Because," Catherine said, "I love you."

Chapter Twenty

Never before had anyone said to him that they loved him. Perhaps his mother had, but he was too young to remember. Certainly his father hadn't, nor his grandmother, not Nancy, or Dorothy, or any of the other women he had known, whose company he had enjoyed, whom he had slept with. Nancy he could understand, even though they were engaged, but not Dorothy. It could only have been that she understood he had not wanted to be told he was loved, he had not wanted to be loved. His emotional life had become so desiccated that it was only with the greatest effort that he now said, "I love you too, Catherine," even though it was what he wanted most to say, the one phrase that could save him.

She did not speak, and he opened his eyes and saw that she had left the room. She had not heard him. Perhaps she thought he did not love her, or was too proud or too cold to admit it. The one great chance of his life could be slipping away. He went up the spiral stairs to the apartment two steps at a time, but she was not there. He had to do something before it was too late, but he did not know what. The only place he could think of where she might be was the Gezira Club. He called the club office and asked that she be paged at the pool. He must have waited twenty minutes before she came on the line.

"Hello?"

"Catherine?"

"Alex, is something wrong?"

"I don't know," he said.

"Well, what is it?"

"I love you."

"I know that," and she laughed softly in her throat.

"You do?"

"Of course. I'm not a fool, my dear."

"Can I come to you?"

"You can."

"Now?"

"Yes," she said, and there was a change in her voice, "but I have a visitor. In fact, it would be better if you were here."

"Visitor?"

"Sir George Mavroyannis."

"Oh, my God."

"Yes . . ."

"I'll take a cab right away."

"Good."

Catherine was lying on her usual chaise longue, under a beach umbrella, in her usual blue bathing suit. She had never looked so good to him. But in his usual place George Mavroyannis was sitting, in bathing trunks, long hairy arms and bandy legs, his eyes hidden by dark glasses. He stood up and took Alex's hand.

"Mr. Fraser."

"Sir George."

"Do sit down," and he pulled up a chair as though it were his own private terrace. "I'm in Egypt on business, and I thought I would look up Miss Molyneux. But having you here is an added bonus."

"I'm afraid I don't follow you."

"Well, you and Miss Molyneux have certainly been following me, haven't you?"

Alex said nothing.

"I have had several reports of your inquiries into my background and professional and personal life. You might have saved yourselves the trouble. You could have just asked me directly, and I would have told you that my overriding interest at the moment is the fate of the Suez Canal."

"Yes," Alex said. "That is clear."

"But what is not clear to me is what you two are up to. Are you working for the Society or are you free agents?"

"Does it matter?"

"It does. Until I know what you know and what you are prepared to do with this knowledge, you are an unknown quantity. Otherwise . . ."

"Otherwise, what?"

Mavroyannis looked at his feet as though he had suddenly realized he needed a pedicure.

"Otherwise I could have you killed. But that is an idle thought. Too much risk. You are an American foreign correspondent and Miss Molyneux is a photographer of world renown. No, that wouldn't do. My point is that there is nothing I won't do in pursuit of my aims, if the risk is acceptable."

"I see. So what do you want from us?"

"A deal. Whatever you know that would be useful in the pursuit of my aims in exchange for, well . . . something very worthwhile."

"What exactly do you want to know?"

"It's too early to say. The game has not advanced that far. What I am asking is that you keep in mind that an advantageous deal may be in the offing for you. That's all."

Mavroyannis looked at the clock above the clubhouse entrance.

"Well, I had better be going now."

When he had gone Catherine and he looked at each other.

"What do you think he means?" Alex said.

"I don't know, but one thing I'm sure of. When Mavroyannis says there is nothing he wouldn't do in pursuit of his aims, he is stating a fact."

"So what should we do?"

"Get out of Egypt till all this resolves itself."

"I've already said I thought we would be found, but at this point what other choice do we have? Where?"

"I don't care, as long as it's not Europe . . . but different. It's time we had a little fun."

And then she left and he was alone. On the other side of the pool Antoine Habib was standing, in trunks, a towel thrown over his shoulders. He was smoking a small cigar and rolling it between fingers and thumb with the sensuality that he gave to everything he did. He was one of the Middle East's leading playboys, putting the likes of Basil Artimanoff to shame. Alex went around the pool and approached him.

"Antoine."

"Dear boy."

He called all men "dear boy" and all women *"chère amie."*

"I have a question."

He took a puff on the cheroot. "At your disposal."

"If you were taking a woman in whom you had a very special interest to a place outside Egypt, and she specified 'something different' but not Europe, where would you take her?"

"For how long?"

"For a weekend, a week, I'm not sure."

Antoine took another puff on his cigar. This, for him, was a matter of fundamental seriousness. It was like asking a philosopher a weighty teleological question.

"Egypt is flat, hot and dry. I should think something toward the opposite end of the spectrum. Do you ski?"

"No."

"Not important. I would still suggest the High Lebanon."

"Baalbek."

"Thereabouts. Summer tourism is over, winter tourism still a way off. I'm assuming your lady would find privacy congenial."

"Yes."

"Well, there you are. Those magnificent Roman ruins against the snow-covered mountains, groves of yellow poplars, reddened vines in the courtyards of small, discreet hotels with wood fires in their fireplaces, serving good Lebanese food, warming pans of coals in between the violet linen sheets in the evening, breakfast served to you in bed, with blood-orange juice . . ."

"Thank you, Antoine."

"My pleasure, dear boy."

Now he had every motive for moving fast and decisively, moving before Mavroyannis was aware of their absence, in such a way that tracing them would be difficult. He had bribe money to spend, and as usual in Egypt, it worked. Within the hour they had reservations on the evening plane for Beirut, under false names, the airline staff being inured to such arrangements by the steady flow of adulterous couples for weekends in Lebanon. Their hotel was not one of the luxurious ones but big enough that arrangements could be made, such as a touring car ready right after breakfast, destination unspecified.

Their high-ceilinged room had a balcony facing the Mediterranean, and after dinner they went out on it and watched the last of the light fade over the sea.

"Things are different now," Catherine said, taking his hand in hers.

"I know," he said.

"So why don't we sort it all out tomorrow in the high mountains, and just leave things tonight like they have been. We're too tired and tense . . ."

"I know," he said.

So that night they slept apart in their wide bed with only a chaste kiss when putting out the lights.

Waiting for them after breakfast was a big touring car with two spare tires set in the front fenders. They left Beirut by a back road and headed into the high mountains. Had they shaken Mavroyannis? He rather doubted it.

It was as Antoine Habib had described it, the massive remains of the Roman temple, the snow-covered mountains, the groves of poplars turned gold by the autumn chill. Their little hotel even had red vines—Virginia creeper—on its walls. Perhaps it was the same hotel where Antoine had brought one of his conquests.

A boy brought their bags to their room, opened the shutters to the magnificent view and closed the door softly as he left. A wood fire burned in the grate, and he went to the window and opened it and let in some of the cold mountain air. Catherine came up behind him and put her hand on his shoulder.

"Well done, Alex, even perfect."

"Thank you."

"There's something I have to say." She touched his neck, let her hand rest there. "I would not have said I loved you if I were not a whole woman again. I've loved you for some time, I can't remember exactly when I realized it. But I wasn't going to say it until I was sure I wouldn't disappoint you."

229

"You've not disappointed me," he said, turned and kissed her passionately on the mouth.

"Easy, Alex," she said. "You're splendid in moving decisively when it's needed, like with our friend Mavroyannis. But making love is not one of those occasions. The slower the better."

He held her closely.

"Oh, and another thing. It's also not an occasion for solemnity. I'm not a vestal virgin, you know, just a quite experienced woman who's a bit out of practice."

"I'll try to remember that," he said, closed the window and led her to the bed, the covers already turned back. The sheets *were* of violet linen.

They lay quietly in their clothes on the bed, facing the window where the remains of the Temple of Jupiter were turning gold in the afternoon light. The fire crackled in the grate. Then slowly pieces of clothes began coming off, kisses were planted shamelessly. He let his hand slip beneath the last garment that Catherine wore, felt the warmth and wetness between her legs, let a finger slip inside her. She gasped and frowned.

"Don't worry," he said, "it's going to go well," and he stripped her of her panties.

"Your hair is the color of straw," he said, to ease the tension. "You're darker down there."

"The color of honey, I've been told. Taste." And he did.

And then he was on top of her, within her.

"All *is* well," she whispered, and moved her hips slowly for what seemed a long time before the motion quickened. Muscles inside her closed tightly around him, squeezed rhythmically. He gasped.

"It's a trick ladies never learn," she said and laughed with a laugh that was free of tension.

And then they moved more swiftly, and he had the strange sensation that they were running toward a deadly explosion, not away from it, and that they had to get there in time. And they did.

Lying apart now, he further explored Catherine's body with his hands, felt the ridges across her back.

"Where I was flogged," she said, "the day my agony began. But today, at last, it's over, thanks to you."

"I didn't do anything extraordinary," he said.

"I'll be the judge of that, Alex."

Not only was the agony over, for both of them, but they had entered paradise, a paradise of sensual delight accompanied by the beauty of the High Lebanon by day and Arabic music and dancing in the courtyard below them by night. He sent a telegram to his Washington office saying he had been taken ill and could not return to Cairo when planned, knowing full well that, with a world war just having broken out, this could get him fired.

"*Malish*," Catherine said, which was Arabic for "so what?" or "who cares?" He didn't, just as he hadn't when he jilted his fiancée and took off for Egypt. What a good move that had been.

A couple of days later, after an hour of adventuresome lovemaking, Catherine got out of bed and took something from her suitcase.

"Now that it looks like we're going to be a long-running act, I thought I would show you something. You remember when I gave you the film with the pictures of the executed Spanish prostitutes, and you told me that you wouldn't advise my looking at them? Well, I've looked at the rest of your mother's diary, and I guess I feel the same way about it. But there are a couple of pages that I think you should see.

Before putting the diary away in a safe place, I had a photo-copy made of them."

She handed him two sheets of paper.

When there could no longer be any doubt, according to my doctor, I was both elated that I was carrying Simon's child and frightened of the consequences when my husband finds out, as he eventually must. I will not have an abortion, and I will not entice Howell into sleeping with me to trick him into thinking that the child is his. That least of all!

I had no idea what I was going to do. I needed advice, and the only place I knew to turn, most reluctantly, was to my father-in-law. What a humiliating encounter that would be for us both. But in reality it was something so different that it took my breath away.

I approached Colonel Fraser where he was reading beside the papyrus pond, hidden by bamboo, as he often did.

"Could I have a few words with you, sir?"

"Why indeed. I'm only sorry you don't offer me that privilege more often."

He put down his book and motioned to an empty lawn chair beside his. I sat down, folded my hands and looked down at them. How to begin? Well, no point in beating around the bush.

"Colonel, I'm pregnant."

"How delightful," he said and took my hands in his.

"You've only heard half the story. Your son is not the father."

"I didn't suppose that he was. I may not say much, but I'm not unobservant."

"But the child will be illegitimate, and I disgraced, Howell humiliated."

"Not at all. Your situation borders on the commonplace. If Howell wishes his career in the consular service to prosper, he will

avoid scandal. After all, who is to blame, you or him?"

"I don't know."

"In any case, I would be glad to point out some home truths to my son."

"Don't you want to know who the father is?"

"Young Simatha, I would assume."

"But how did you . . . ?"

"Perhaps I even had a hand in bringing you two together, who knows? Young people should have at least one shot at happiness."

"But that is beyond all the norms . . ."

"I never gave a damn for norms. However, I care a great deal about your happiness."

"I'm flabbergasted."

"Don't be, just get on with your life, knowing that this conversation never took place."

I suppose we talked some more, but I remember only what I have just written down. One shot at happiness. Yes, that's all I had wanted . . .

Three months later Colonel Fraser died and was buried in the Anglican cemetery of Cairo. Now I was on my own, but he had given me the courage to continue the fight for my happiness.

"Thank you," he said to Catherine, "thank you for showing me that."

"It makes you feel better about things, doesn't it?"

"It makes a great difference."

They stretched their stay into two weeks, and all that remained for him to be finally and completely happy and at peace with himself would be for things to go on like they were forever.

But life does not grant such requests. When they got back to Cairo, an envelope had been slipped under the door of their houseboat. He picked it up and opened it with fore-boding.

"Well," Catherine said.

"An invitation to spend the day at the Essabi farm, two days from now. It's initialed 'N. S.' "

"So Nadia is back."

"Yes."

"What do we do?"

"We go, I suppose. Better to walk into the lion's den than hide in the bushes and wait for the lion to sneak up on you."

"You're right. I wish you weren't, but you are."

Chapter Twenty-One

Saddle horses were waiting for them at the landing where the steamer from Cairo came in. The Essabi yacht was tied up at its own dock. Catherine and he rode out to the farm saying little, each of them lost in thought about what they would encounter and the reason, after all that had happened, for the invitation.

"I heard some gossip when I went to the club to pick up my mail," Catherine said. "Nadia and the Essabi brothers were able to venture back to Egypt without fear of being detained by the British because King Farouk let the British ambassador know that he wouldn't tolerate that. The King and all the Egyptian aristocracy want the Germans to win. The British know this and there's going to be a showdown one day, but it won't be over the Narcissians. Besides, they haven't actually *done* anything. The British have even released the two Essabi planes they had impounded."

"Impounded? Why?"

"Part of the operation, along with the radios and who knows what else? You didn't think the Essabis bought two expensive American planes just to deliver flowers."

"This leaves us awfully exposed, and we know too much."

"I don't think we are in any danger. After all, Alex, you're Nadia's uncle's son. And the glue that holds things together in this part of the world is family. There's no loyalty to anything else."

"So, we just wait and see."

Nothing ever changed in the Fayum. The white herons fed in the flooded fields, the waterwheels turned, the kites wheeled overhead, just as they would have 1,000, 2,000 years before.

In the courtyard of the Essabi farm a *saïs* took their horses. There was only one car, the midnight-blue Packard, parked in the early morning shadow of the house. The French doors stood open and they went in.

They were all there, Nadia, Selim, Mansour and, to his surprise, the other side, in the person of Sir George Mavroyannis, his thick gray hair slicked back, his thick glasses removed, emphasizing his bushy eyebrows. He wore starched linen trousers and short-sleeved shirt, espadrilles, and on one hairy wrist a watch that must have contained a pound of gold.

"There's coffee and croissants on the sideboard. Help yourselves," Nadia said, as though this was a business meeting, which of course it was. This also meant that there were no servants present. He went to the sideboard and got coffee and croissants for Catherine and himself, and took them to where she sat on the sofa.

"This would appear to be a business meeting," he said before anyone else could speak. He was not going to let Catherine take the brunt of whatever followed.

"That's not a bad characterization," Selim said. "Most everything was decided yesterday, but there are one or two loose ends, involving you and Miss Molyneux. We need to close the ring, so to speak."

"Close the ring?" He had not the slightest idea what Selim was talking about.

"For a time we needed to have others involved, but now that we have reached an agreement with Sir George to pool our resources, we need to put things back the way they were."

"Have others involved? Was that what the Narcissians was all about?"

"We needed to obscure things a bit."

"From whom? British intelligence?"

Selim did not reply directly.

"In any case we are going to need your help in reclosing the ring."

"Go on."

"Before leaving the Narcissians, one must drink of the waters of Lethe."

"Forget everything we know, you mean. There must be a price for that, since I gather killing us is considered too dangerous." His heart was pounding. He was getting very far out on a limb.

"Just a joke," George Mavroyannis said.

"I suppose what happened to Antonius Modiano was also a joke. As a matter of curiosity, Sir George, why would he now have a contract to build a transmitter, in Switzerland of all places, for some Christian evangelical group?"

"As to where, there are still Calvinists enough in Switzerland to facilitate such a project. As to why, Modiano now won't be disposed to talk about our . . . misunderstanding. The contract is a lucrative one."

"I see." He thought he did see. A powerful transmitter would be needed to control the radio net that had been created in Egypt and, no doubt, other parts of the Middle East. Inserting coded messages—even into Biblical texts—was an old trick. And Mavroyannis had not told him that without a purpose.

Nadia Simatha gave Mavroyannis a malevolent look. Now, at last—perhaps—he was seeing the real Nadia, the lioness who would soon lead her ancient and vastly rich family. She still looked like Nefertiti, but now, like that ancient queen, she could make decisions of life or death with cold indifference.

"Of course you expect some recompense for the inconvenience we have caused you," Mavroyannis continued. "I had in mind Suez Canal Company bearer bonds."

"Bearer bonds?"

"The company is almost completely self-financing, so we rarely issue bonds, but occasionally there is some special reason. Bearer bonds are quite anonymous. There is no name on them, just a serial number, and whoever possesses them can present them at any major bank and receive cash with no questions asked. On the other hand, the bearer is responsible for safeguarding them. If someone were to steal them he could cash them in just as easily as the real owner."

There was some threat in what Mavroyannis said, but it was too subtle for Alex to figure out without some reflection. But Mavroyannis must know they might have deposited an account of all they knew in a safe deposit box in some secure place, which in fact they had.

"The amount?"

"Would a hundred thousand pounds, at prewar exchange, be reasonable?"

He looked at Catherine. Half a million dollars. She nodded her head.

"The amount is acceptable but the arrangement itself . . . We would want to think about that a bit."

"Fine, but can you give us a definite answer today? There is a certain urgency."

"Today?" He looked at Catherine. Again she nodded. "Yes, I think we can give you an answer today. Perhaps I should take a little walk and think about it and then talk it over with Miss Molyneux."

"As you wish."

* * * * *

He went out onto the terrace. A walk around the house was not sufficiently removed from what was going on for him to gather his thoughts. Their horses were tethered in the shade beside the Packard, so he got on one and rode out the gate into the fields and along one of the many farm roads that bordered the canals. He was sure there was some kind of trap, or at least something being held in reserve, in what Mavroyannis had proposed. But clearly, to refuse their offer would put Catherine and him in danger, if not from Nadia and the Essabis, from Mavroyannis.

Down a road in the distance a band of *fellahin* moved, armed with scythes and old swords and staffs, shouting angrily. Even someone as little acquainted with the Fayum as Alex, knew what was going on. Constantly, there were disputes between villages over water rights, and one side or the other would march out to clash with the other and, if successful, destroy the offending dike or lock that had drawn off water they believed rightfully theirs. If things got out of hand the police would arrive and fire over the combatants' heads or, if really out of hand, into the crowd itself.

Far in the distance a column of black smoke rose into the sky. He thought at first that it was peasants burning trash. But then he saw another and then a third column of smoke that were not coming from rubbish heaps but from landowners' houses. He turned his horse just in time to see the angry peasants swarming around the Essabis' farmhouse which was in flames. He spurred his horse forward at a gallop. By the time he reached the house the *fellahin,* anticipating police intervention, were scattering in all directions, laden with the Essabis' valuables.

He leaped from his horse as it went through the gateway. The Packard was ablaze and, from containers lying about, it looked as though its tank had been emptied to ignite the house. He ran toward the French doors but it was too late. The interior of the house was an inferno, and he thought he smelled burning flesh.

"Catherine! Catherine! What have I done? What have I done?" he screamed to himself, and then out loud.

The Essabis' old majordomo was sitting on his accustomed bench, dazed, his beard and turban singed by the fire.

"Where are they!" Alex shouted.

"Too late."

"All of them?"

The Egyptian shrugged. He did not know.

He ran around the courtyard, into the stables, opening the doors of outbuildings, calling Catherine's name.

In the toolshed where she was hiding, he almost missed her. She had burrowed into a pile of burlap sacks, and only a lock of blond hair and an eye showed. He pulled the sack off her face. She had not answered because she had expected to be killed.

He scooped her up and ran out into the courtyard. Her clothes were burned, her face scorched, but she did not seem injured. What this might have done to her fragile mental state he did not want to think about.

A carriage stood in one corner of the courtyard, an old horse harnessed to it. He gently put her down on the floorboards, ran back into the shed to get some burlap sacks to cover her.

"I have to get her back to Cairo, Abdullah," he said to the majordomo.

"They will kill you."

"Not if you help me."

"They would only kill me too."

"A thousand pounds Egyptian—on my word of honor."

Abdullah considered. At his age, his life against a thousand pounds, more than he would earn in his entire lifetime, might be a fair wager.

"What do you want me to do?" he said.

"Get us to the docks, hire a *falucca* to take us to Cairo."

He tilted his head, indicating it could be done.

"Also, can you find a pistol?"

Abdullah nodded his head again. In a minute or two he returned from the house with a shiny, wicked-looking Luger, clearly belonging to one of the Essabis. Alex held it in his hand, and he realized he was prepared to die trying to save Catherine's life. Catherine looked up at him, and he thought she understood this.

And so they made their way to the landing place, a *saïs* sitting beside Abdullah on the driver's seat. They took obscure back roads that skirted the still-marauding mobs, and arrived in about an hour, in time to see the Essabis' burning yacht sink while a large crowd of idlers watched. Abdullah mingled with the onlookers.

Alex pulled back the sack covering Catherine's face. She was conscious.

"You saved me."

"And the others, burned?" he said, feeling sick at the remembrance of the smell of burning flesh.

"The smoke got them first, I think . . . on my stomach . . . through the kitchen . . . hid among the garbage cans . . ."

Her voice trailed off and her eyes closed. For the first time he had a chance to think, and his first thought was that the mob had been provoked. The Essabi-Simatha clan may have reached an agreement with Mavroyannis on the canal, but someone else in this high-stakes game had struck first. Who? British intelligence? The Germans? A bloc of canal shareholders? It didn't help that he didn't know exactly what the game was. He could only assume that Catherine and he were still in danger.

Their departure was delayed until dark, so that they could be gotten aboard the leaky old boat without being seen. The voyage took all night. From time to time he would feel Catherine's forehead and pulse and pour a little water into her mouth. She was still conscious but said nothing more.

They did not reach the Cairo landing place until dawn. He sent the boatman out to find a taxi, and within the hour Catherine was in a bed at the American Hospital on Gezira. He confirmed with her doctor that she was in satisfactory physical condition. Knowing her past history, the doctor would not speculate on what her psychological state might be. Alex then got on the telephone and arranged for a charter flight to take Catherine to Paris. Ironically, the only plane available was one of the Essabi planes that was not making a flower delivery that day.

They arrived at the airport about noon. He rode in the ambulance with Catherine and the nurse who would accompany her. At the stairs to the plane he leaned over the stretcher and kissed her, and she spoke for the second time.

"What you did was very brave," she said.

He shook his head.

"Oh, yes. I experienced some terrible things in Spain, but I also saw some acts of bravery, but none more so than yours. Don't keep shaking your head, Alex. You don't think well enough of yourself. Always remember that I said you were a man, and a brave one."

She was carried up into the plane, and he stood by the ambulance and watched it take off. With it went the only being he had ever cared about on earth, and he had the awful premonition he would never see her or hear her voice again.

Chapter Twenty-Two

Once before he had felt a great wave pass over his life like a *khamseen,* but that had been personal. This was different; it was an impersonal scouring of the earth, that left all barren and desolate, but the same in that the sky above was blue and tranquil after the storm had passed.

It was as though a great avalanche had roared down a mountainside burying all beneath it, or a typhoon had passed, sweeping all human life from a Pacific atoll. The stillness that followed was the more inscrutable because there was no question of right or wrong, no human malevolence behind the event that would help to explain it away. It was just there, as cold and meaningless as the turning of the stars in their courses.

He had been spared the worst horrors of what happened that day by arriving late on the scene. What he had seen had not been self-censored like Catherine's remembrance of what happened to her in Spain, but he had willed himself not to think about it. There were two images, however, that no amount of willpower could expunge, that came back and back to the theater of his mind and hung there like slides in a jammed projector. One was of the midnight-blue Packard aflame in the beaten earth courtyard of the Essabi farm in the Fayum, like some burnt offering to the gods. The other was the image of Catherine's face peering out from a pile of burlap bags in the corner of a toolshed where he had found her, a terrified animal waiting for violent death to take her.

His initial assumption that the Suez conspiracy was behind what had happened was, he thought for a while, made untenable by the information that the mobs had been rioting over the price of bread. They had not only attacked the homes of the landowners, but had also gone through the Fayum seizing bakers and shoving them into their ovens to roast alive.

The mob had, according to that view, borne them no more personal animus than the typhoid epidemic that had borne away his mother and father. But then he had to face the truth that whoever would kill some dangerous opponents would not have had the least hesitation in adding the violent deaths of a few bakers to help cover their tracks.

He only hoped that Nadia and the others died of smoke inhalation and not like the bakers. Nadia may have been duplicitous and cold-blooded, but she was a beautiful young woman, full of life, and the thought of her dying by fire was more than he could contemplate.

And now he waited. He went back to the apartment and threw himself on the bed, not even taking off his shoes. And there he lay for most of the rest of the afternoon, not thinking at all, just watching the Egyptian sun creep across the polished floor and the Oriental carpets, as Cairo and Egypt and the earth turned beneath the sun. And then he slept until the phone rang.

"Hello?"

"Mr. Fraser?"

"Yes."

"Well, she's arrived safely."

"Who has?"

There was a pause. "Why, Catherine Molyneux. We met

the plane with an ambulance as you asked. She's sleeping now."

"Sleeping where?"

There was another pause. "The American Hospital in Neuilly."

"Oh, yes. How is she?"

"It's too early to even hazard a guess, but I wouldn't get my hopes too high."

"Who is this?"

"Dr. Brown, head of psychiatry. Dr. Halevy asked that I call you. He is Miss Molyneux's personal physician, as you may know, and she is in good hands."

"You don't speak with a Viennese accent."

There was a nervous laugh. "Spelled 'B-r-o-w-n.' "

"Oh."

"Mr Fraser, I have a request. Please don't try to phone or write Miss Molyneux. We can't permit her any communication right now."

"I understand."

"And as for visiting her . . . well, we'll just have to wait and see. Certainly, no time soon." He thought he heard implied, ". . . if ever."

It was then that Alex Fraser went astray, took the wrong turning and became lost in the tangle of his own emotions and perceived inadequacies. Trapped in the paradox of needing above all to go down to the underworld where Catherine again dwelt and bring her back up to the light, which he felt he was capable of doing only with Catherine's help, the one thing unavailable to him. He supposed it could be said that he had simply stopped trying.

Intimidated from attempting to get in touch with Catherine, her keepers silent and inscrutable, he went back to work. He even sent a brief message to ANC on the deaths of Sir George Mavroyannis and the Simathas and Essabis, neglecting to mention that he had been present. The reply expressed understanding of his absence in Lebanon, informed him that Arvid Dahlsted was no longer employed by ANC, and offered to extend his contract, which was nearing termination, *sine die,* on the same terms. He took this to mean that in the not too distant future he would find himself without a job. He did not care, in fact he cared about nothing.

He came to equate his situation with that of his mother, who had had her brief time of happiness, before death took her and her lover. Catherine and he were still alive but dead to the world. The words of his mother's diary offered the only hope, a small one, that sustained him. *". . . I don't know where to turn. I made my choice and I will simply have to live with it, I suppose, hoping that fate will somehow rescue me . . ."*

But he did not lose his job, in fact was offered a substantial raise to renew his contract for another three years. War had broken out in Europe, and a knowledgeable correspondent in Cairo was worth his weight in gold. His situation was regularized by the British. He was added to the War Correspondents roster, issued a khaki uniform that included shorts and kneesocks, and even a service revolver, so that he could enter future battle zones, should there be any, and attend confidential briefings.

With space in short supply, he shared his office with a British correspondent. He no longer had an emotional life, or as Shakespeare's Cleopatra had said, "immortal longings." He could hardly believe how pathetic his situation was. He did understand that, with all the drama of the North African war swirling around him, he was only an adequate foreign correspondent. He simply did not have the will to scale the heights around him.

★ ★ ★ ★ ★

And then fate intervened, during the Italian invasion of Egypt in September of 1940, as it had in his mother's life in the form of an invitation to a costume party where she was asked to come dressed as Aida. His fate proved to be very different from hers. It came in the form of his being thrown up into the Saharan night in a ball of fire, then descending in a rain of flaming vehicle and human body parts. He assumed he was dying, and imagined he might have had he not stanched the wound in his side with his knotted shirttail and held it tight against death itself. It was then that he realized he desperately wanted to live, and as the night went on he began to understand why.

He began to understand that what had led him astray was guilt. He should have been there to share the fate of the others when an unseen hand had struck them down, but he had been out riding alone when the columns of black smoke began to ascend into the sky from the burning farms. But now he too had been struck down by an unseen hand. He had paid his dues and now could begin to hope. It made no sense, he knew, but that was the way he felt.

With the coming of the light he could see what had happened. Their desert vehicle had hit a land mine and his three Australian colleagues had been instantly killed. The remains of the vehicle still smoldered, sharing the fate of the midnight-blue Packard. He tried to get up from the sand but the pain in his ribs, which seemed broken loose from his spine, would not allow it. He pulled himself through the sand and found the first-aid kit, still intact. He wrapped his midsection with gauze and wide lengths of tape until at last he could stand with endurable pain.

A pair of binoculars lay in the sand, and he scanned the empty horizon, empty except for an island of rock thrusting up, from which palm trees, date palms laden with dates, grew. That meant food and, more important, water. Their water cans had been blown apart, and he knew that without water he could not survive beyond the coming day. He began to assemble equipment and supplies that he thought might prove useful, and since it was more than he could carry, put them on a desert sledge he constructed of a military stretcher.

It took him the better part of three hours to reach the little oasis, and by then the sun was so fierce and he was so dehydrated that he could not have made it a hundred yards farther. But make it he did, crawled up the little knoll and let his face fall into a pool of bubbling crystal water. His ordeal was over. He lay down in the shadow of the palms and slept through the rest of the day and into the cool night. When he awoke the stars were so numerous and pressed down so low he almost felt suffocated.

The next morning he realized that his ordeal was by no means over. He got out a map and compass and found the dot that he thought must be the little oasis. They had wandered far from the traveled routes, and when a patrol would come by—and he didn't much care whether it was Allied or German—if ever, there was no way of knowing. And then he laughed, and he thought it was that laugh, painful as it was, that saved him. He was like Robinson Crusoe washed up on a desert isle, and like Crusoe his survival depended on the intelligent use of the materials at hand. He went to work.

The spring was a permanent fixture or the palm trees would not have survived for the many years their growth indicated. Dates from the palms, particularly if dried, would provide food rich in sugar for a long time. His problem was not to survive but to be found, and for that purpose he made a lanyard that could raise a square of white cloth with a red cross painted on it with Mercurochrome, to the top of a palm tree, should a plane or vehicle appear on the horizon. Then he constructed an open tent from a tarpaulin. The essentials that he had to do were less arduous than he had expected, and he soon found himself with more time to think than he had ever had in his life, particularly in the starry night, lying wrapped in blankets against the cold.

He thought mostly of Catherine, and he marveled at how he had gone so monstrously astray. But how had their driver, with compass and maps, put them a hundred miles off course? These things happened, and there was no use dwelling on them. He resolved to find Catherine and go to her, no matter what obstacles were put in his way, knowing she could by now be confined to an institution from which she might never emerge.

All he knew for sure was that when France fell in May 1940, Catherine and some others at the American Hospital in Neuilly who had the means, were moved, as citizens of a neutral country, to other facilities outside France, Catherine to a Swiss clinic near Geneva. The ban against communication with her except by immediate family members, of which she had none, was continued, and he wondered if her psychiatrist who had been part of the Montreux student secret society had had something to do with this. It had been nearly a year since he had seen her.

His sojourn on his tiny desert isle, and there was not the slightest difference between a sea of water and a sea of sand, did not last long. Early on the third morning a plume of dust, like a small waterspout, moved along the horizon and then lazily inland toward where their patrol vehicle had met its end, obviously following the single errant set of tracks in the sand. Through the binoculars he could see the patrol car, identical to their own, come to a stop beside the wreckage, three men in Australian uniforms get out and circle the burnt-out vehicle. One of them raised binoculars and spotted the white and Mercurochrome flag that he had already hoisted. Within seconds the rescue vehicle was heading straight as an arrow toward his refuge in the sand sea.

"Well, what have we here?" the first sun-bronzed Australian to descend from the patrol car said. "You're no Aussie."

"No," he said, "American war correspondent. Hitching a ride."

"What happened?"

"Land mine."

"Well, we can see that."

"Directly under us. I was in the right rear seat, the ejection seat, I guess."

"You're damned lucky."

"I know," he said contritely, as though he were somehow responsible for what had happened.

"Well, it's a shame what befell those poor buggers, but there's nothing we can do now. So we'd better get the hell out of here before the Iteys catch up with us."

At the huge Australian encampment there was plenty of cold beer as promised, and also a telegraph wire. He filed a story on his adventures that he thought would make the front pages of the small-town newspapers that depended on ANC for their international news. By early afternoon of the next day he was back in his office in Cairo. The first thing he did was to attempt to get through to Switzerland by phone, which he finally managed after many frustrating delays.

"*Clinique Les Mimosas,*" a female voice said in cool and measured French.

"My name is Alexander Fraser. I am inquiring about Catherine Molyneux."

"Catherine Molyneux?"

"A patient of yours."

"We have no patient with such a name."

"Then she must have been released."

"Not since I have been here."

"Then perhaps it was before your time," he said, now desperate.

"Perhaps."

"Don't you have some kind of file of former patients?"

There was a sigh from the other end of the line.

"I know it's a lot of trouble, but this is a very urgent matter."

There was no reply, but he could hear the sound of cards being riffled.

"I'm sorry, but I find no such name."

"Not even anyone named Catherine?"

"Monsieur, I am very busy . . ." and again a sigh, that of a long-suffering Swiss having to deal with another stupid foreigner. "Now if you will excuse me."

Chapter Twenty-Three

He put down the phone slowly. Something was terribly wrong. The colleague who had told him that Catherine had been transferred to a clinic, Les Mimosas, outside of Geneva, when the Germans occupied France was totally reliable. He always checked his sources. Then either the receptionist at the clinic was lying or Catherine had been admitted under a different name. His letters to her at the clinic had gone unanswered, not returned, just disappearing into a void.

More and more it looked to him as if Dr. Halevy was the key to the mystery. Alex had all along had a suspicion that Halevy was preventing him from getting in touch with Catherine, but he had assumed that was because he was considered a bad influence on her recovery. But now . . . He had also assumed that although Halevy had belonged to a secret student society at the University of Lausanne with Simatha and Essabi *pères,* he would have severed any ties he might have kept. Being Jewish, it was very unlikely that he would have any connection with a group that had offered its support to Hitler's Germany.

But now he saw more clearly, saw that the aim of the society was to oust the British from Egypt and elsewhere in the Middle East, and that only with the coming of the war did cooperation with the Germans become part of the equation. And, of course, Halevy had every reason to cover up his connection with an organization that was prepared to aid the

Nazis. And his patient Catherine Molyneux knew too much. Alex picked up the phone again.

"Peter, my masters want me to go to Switzerland *tout de suite*. Do you think Press Liaison could do the necessary? When? Tomorrow. Yes, I understand that's very short notice, but . . . Good. I won't forget."

The next morning he was on a flight to Switzerland by a roundabout route dictated by the war. The British embassy in Berne had assured British military Press Liaison that he would be waved through passport and customs controls in Geneva. The morning after that, he was in a taxi to the clinic Les Mimosas, or at least a street corner a few hundred feet away. He went into a café and began finding out about the routine of the clinic, in the oblique way that one learned in developing news stories.

The clinic was devoted to the care of people with mental or emotional problems, and every morning, in good weather, the ambulatory patients were given an hour of fresh air and exercise in the grounds of what had once been a luxurious villa, at ten o'clock, with Swiss exactitude. The café had a couple of rooms above for visitors and he took one for the night.

The third morning he was standing at a bus stop opposite the high iron fence around the clinic and its ancient cedars of Lebanon, appearing to read a newspaper. When the patients came out onto the lawn in identical hospital garb, he spotted Catherine right away. She did not look mentally disturbed at all, but the look of sadness and strain that she wore when he first met her had returned.

Finding her was that easy, but what came next would not be. Shaking with excitement he went back to the café and ordered a coffee and a double brandy. And then he went back to a vantage point and watched the comings and goings

253

through the massive front gate of the clinic for the rest of the day. Not just the clinic, he thought, as he looked around him, but all of Switzerland was like a hospital, antiseptic and cold. After the smells and sounds and colors of Cairo he found Geneva a bit repellent. And he was sure that the Swiss penchant for efficiency and attention to detail applied equally to security matters. As he observed the comings and goings at the gate, and the guards and identity checks, he could see no way that he could get into the clinic, let alone get Catherine out.

That evening he returned to his downtown Geneva hotel. He couldn't afford to be seen hanging around the clinic anymore. In his room he took Catherine's thick address book, that had been left in the houseboat, and went through it. There were two addresses in Switzerland. One was a firm that repaired and rebuilt cameras, the other was a Jack Barber with the Canadian consulate general in Geneva. He picked up the phone. He had nothing to lose.

"Jack Barber?"

"Speaking. Who's this?"

"My name is Alex Fraser. You don't know me, but I'm a close friend of Catherine Molyneux."

"Do you have news of her? Poor Catherine. I understand she went under psychiatric care again. Is she okay now?"

When Catherine was flown back to Paris, the word quickly got around that she had had another nervous breakdown. He had done nothing to correct this view. Apparently, no one knew that he and Catherine were at the Essabi farm when it was burned, and it was better that way.

"The answer to your first question is that she is still under psychiatric care, and to the second that she seems okay."

"Come again."

"I think she's okay and I think she should be released."

"Where is she?"

"Geneva."

"Not on my watch, she isn't. What did you say your name was again?"

"Alex Fraser."

"Well, Alex Fraser . . ."

"Would you care to invest a few minutes in finding out whether I'm worth talking to?"

"Where are you?"

"The Hotel Splendide."

"Okay then. The hotel bar in half an hour."

"I'll be there."

Jack Barber came into the hotel bar, tall and angular, looking a bit disheveled, looking as though he had had a hard day.

He sat down in a leather chair opposite Alex.

"A drink?"

"Canadian whiskey, they have it here. So, you're a close friend of Catherine's, are you."

"We live together, or did."

"Ah. What did her grandfather do?"

"He had paper mills."

The drinks came, and Jack Barber wrapped a cocktail napkin around his, stared into the whiskey.

"You won't blame me for being suspicious?"

"No."

"Well, tell your story. My main occupation here is listening to stories from and about expat Canadians and their woes, marital, alcoholic, financial. That's my job. But Catherine is a different matter. You had better be on the level with me."

"I am. She's being held at the Clinic Mimosa, just outside of town."

"Yes, I know where it is. What do you mean, 'held'?"

"They deny having a patient named Catherine Molyneux, but I saw her on the clinic lawn, through the fence."

"Why on earth would they be holding her?"

"For you to understand, I'll have to tell you the whole story."

"I'm listening."

"It's a long one, but I'll keep it as brief as possible."

Then he related everything that had happened up to the point that the Essabi farmhouse had been set on fire and he had had Catherine flown out to Paris and of his inability to get in touch with her.

"Now let me see if I've got this straight. Catherine is being held because she knows too much about a German spy ring in Egypt."

"I don't know that I would call it a spy ring, more a group of influential people who are trying to strike a deal with the Germans over the Suez Canal."

"It comes to the same thing."

"I suppose it does."

"That's a pretty fantastic story, you know."

"I know, but if you could talk to Catherine she will confirm everything."

"Well, I can talk to her if I can find her. They'll have a hard time keeping the Canadian consul from communicating with a Canadian citizen. And there are Swiss laws governing the treatment of people found incompetent, Swiss or foreign. I'll tell you what. I'll drive out there with you tomorrow morning. They know me. There've been Canadians there before, usually with the DTs. I'll go, but you'd better be telling the truth. You see, I'm from Montreal and I've known Catherine since we were children. I was once in love with her myself."

★ ★ ★ ★ ★

They drove through the gate of Les Mimosas with the Canadian flag flying. The guard in the guardhouse saluted. He must have phoned ahead, because the director, a flower in his lapel, was waiting for them in the entrance hall.

"Ah, Monsieur Barber, good to see you again. To what do we owe the pleasure this time?"

"Monsieur Gignilliat. This is Mr. Fraser, a new arrival at the consulate general. I'm taking him on my rounds with me. We're here in connection with a Canadian citizen who is a patient, a Catherine Molyneux."

The director looked perplexed. "I don't recall the name."

"Perhaps she is registered under another name."

"That would be most irregular."

"Perhaps, but I do need to make certain." Barber looked at his watch. "Do you mind if we look out the window as the patients come out for air?"

"I . . . well . . . of course not."

The three of them went to the window. Below, the patients were just filing out onto the lawn.

"I must tell you, Monsieur Gignilliat, that tall blond young woman is Catherine Molyneux."

"Perhaps a resemblance . . ."

"I've known her for years. There's no mistake. Now, may I see her passport?"

"Her passport?"

"Under Swiss law, you are required to keep in a safe place the passports of all foreign patients."

"Nothing under Swiss law requires me to show you her passport," Gignilliat replied in a less pleasant tone.

"I think that the Swiss authorities would hold that a Canadian diplomatic representative has the right to see a Canadian passport, issued by the Canadian government, of which it remains the property."

"I don't agree."

"Then shall I call the police and have them settle the matter?"

Without a word Gignilliat turned and walked away. When he came back he was holding a Canadian passport. Barber looked at it.

"I was sworn to secrecy," Gignilliat said.

"Well, now that the matter's resolved we'll be taking Miss Molyneux with us when we leave."

"You can't do that. I will be in violation of Swiss law, if I allow her to leave without a doctor's certificate of competency."

"You are already in violation of Swiss law for holding a patient under false pretenses. But I'll overlook that if we are not interfered with when we leave."

As they came down the steps of the clinic Catherine saw them and put her hands up to her mouth. Then she began running toward them, a nurse striding resolutely behind her. But Gignilliat had come down the steps behind them and waved the nurse away. The consulate general car pulled up at the foot of the steps. The guard at the gate looked puzzled at three people leaving when only two had come in, but saluted again.

His next entrance into the bar of the Hotel Splendide was in the greatest contrast to his last. He felt like a conqueror. Catherine still wore her clinic uniform but she too was transformed, glowing with happiness. They all ordered Canadian whiskey, Catherine a pack of Gaulois. A bellboy came to take Catherine's purchases of clothes and underwear and perfume up to *their* room. They toasted each other and Catherine lit a cigarette.

"Oh, bliss," she said. "It's been nearly a year since I've had a drink or a cigarette or . . . that other thing."

"Other thing . . . ?"

She laughed. Sex, of course, she meant.

"Don't turn red, Alex. Jack and I are old friends."

Jack laughed. "Well, what now, Catherine, now that you have a life again?"

"I want to go back to work. As much as I miss my chum here, I perhaps miss my cameras more. Sorry, Alex, but it's the truth."

"But there are some things that cameras can't do for you, as far as I know."

Now it was Catherine who blushed.

"How would you feel about becoming a Canadian photographic correspondent covering the war?" Jack said.

"Would they have me?"

"They would fall all over themselves to have the famous Catherine Molyneux as a correspondent."

"Would I have a uniform?"

"A spiffy one."

"Then it's a done deal."

They lay naked on the bed of his hotel room. She turned and lit another Gaulois.

"How was it, Alex?"

"Like a man dying from thirst being given cold, clear water." And then he told her about his vehicle hitting a land mine in the Western desert. "I know what that means, almost dying of thirst. And you even still do that thing with your . . ."

"Oh, that. In the sophisticated European circles in which I used to move it's called 'the grip.' There are advantages to having been naughty in your youth. Then when you find *the* man you can bring him a lot more than your average naïve girl."

The phone rang.

"Alex Fraser. Hi, Austin. What's up? ANC's looking for me? Tell them I'll be back tomorrow. Yes, I am interested. When? Any clues? No, I didn't expect there would be. Listen, Austin, you're going to have to find other quarters. Yes, that's the reason. You're a good sport."

"What was that all about?" Catherine said.

"That was the correspondent I've been sharing the office with. Listen, Catherine, what he told me was that Arthur Drummond has been assassinated, gunned down as he arrived at his Cairo residence late at night. The police haven't a clue."

"Do you?"

"Yes. The senior Narcissians had it done. Revenge. I had two conversations with Drummond, and it was very clear that murder was just another tool in protecting his masters in the Suez Canal Company. I have thought for a long time that he was probably the instigator of the attack on the Essabi farm, and I was wondering when his time would come."

"And so?"

"And so I'm going to have to settle matters with my 'uncle' before we leave Switzerland. I don't want this hanging over our heads with the war heating up."

"How settle?"

"I'm going over to the Society's headquarters in Montreux—it's only a few miles from Geneva—and tell him to leave us strictly alone."

"How are you going to do that? By the way, I think that's a very bad idea."

"Maybe, but something has to be done. How? The Swiss take a very dim view of scandals involving foreign intelligence agents in their country. Our friends don't dare go back to Egypt. They need their Swiss residency badly, and we can blow everything if they don't reach an understanding with us."

"I'm not convinced, Alex. And besides, we are leaving in the morning for Egypt."

"I'll do it this afternoon."

"Don't."

"There's no other way."

The villa that housed the Near East Philanthropic Society was even grander than that which housed Les Mimosas. It was on the side of the mountain above Montreux and Lake Geneva, and the cedars of Lebanon around it were equally old.

There was, of course, no getting past the gate. Two guards there, and their pistols were visible. He was connected by phone with a receptionist.

"I'm sorry, sir, but Monsieur Simatha is not available," was the canned answer he was given.

"He'll be available for me."

"I beg your pardon."

"Just tell him that Alexander Fraser is here on an urgent matter. I'll wait."

He was led past huge Chinese vases of exotic palms up a curving staircase, the air redolent with an incense-like odor. The long corridor on the second floor was hung with Oriental carpets of the highest quality. The door to Simatha's office was opened by a young woman who gave every indication of being Coptic. Simatha himself, who got up and came around his ornate desk, had a familiar look about him. And then he realized it was a family resemblance. He was tall, balding, with horn-rimmed glasses.

"Mr. Fraser, I was not expecting this."

"I imagine not."

"You resemble Simon."

"Yes."

"They killed my only child and both Essabi boys."

"I know."

"I had no other children."

"I know."

"Please, sit down."

Alex sat down in a chair beside the antique desk.

"I had hoped you would rejoin the family."

"Why should I?"

Simatha raised his palms, as if admitting the justice of the remark.

"I can understand that you might not wish it, after all that has happened, but listen to my point of view. The Simathas have survived for two thousand years, the Greeks, the Romans, the Arabs, the Europeans. But now our ancient line will end. There is no Simatha blood left on earth but yours. And you would be rich beyond anything you could possibly imagine."

"There are a couple of small obstacles, Monsieur Simatha. The first is that you imprisoned the woman I love. I cannot forgive that."

"That was Halevy's doing. I can see that she is released."

"She already has been."

"And your other obstacle?"

"You have turned the Society into an instrument of German policy."

"Mr. Fraser, try to see our point of view. Greeks, Romans, Arabs, the French, the British, next perhaps the Germans. But through it all our peoples, the Copts, the Jews, the Armenians, the other minorities, must try to free themselves from the foreign yoke, create homelands for themselves. If the Germans come to our part of the world, we will have to accommodate them just like the other conquerors, so that later we will be free to oppose them."

He could see a certain logic in what Simatha had said, but that was not what he had come for.

"That your line is coming to an end is regrettable, Monsieur Simatha, but I have my own life to live. I have told certain people about what I know. I want you and your organization out of my life, and if not, the Swiss authorities will be made aware, in a most embarrassing way, of what amounts to espionage on their territory."

"I think you have made an unwise choice, Mr. Fraser, but I accept the logic of your argument."

"Then we will be hearing no more from each other."

"If that is the way you wish it."

Alex rose to leave.

"By the way," Simatha said, "I knew Colonel Fraser quite well. It was his work in designing a lighthouse system for the Suez Canal that first brought my family into this business that began so well, and which has now ended so miserably. I am sorry."

The stars in layers and swirls, and the constellations, and the planet Venus, a huge bright pearl, began to fade as dawn came to the Sahara. He got up and stretched, brushed away the fine sand clinging to his body, lit the spirit lamp to make coffee. Catherine slept, curled up like a little child. Not all stories end badly, he thought, though this one was not yet over. One stray shell, Italian or British, and they would both be dead. But they would have lived. Before he met Catherine he had had no life. He spooned out the instant coffee, the powdered milk, and the sugar. They had lived.